WRITTEN IN STONE

A.D. WILDE

SWEETWATER SERIES BOOK 1

Book Cover by Dark Woods Publishing

Edited by Kylie Abel

Third edition 2025

Author website: www.authoradwilde.com

CONTENT WARNING

This story contains content that may be triggering to some readers. Please consider the following trigger warnings before reading.

YOUR MENTAL HEALTH MATTERS.

This is a dark military romance novel containing morally gray characters. There are scenes of graphic violence, gore, child sexual assault and abuse, child abandonment, death and suicide, torture, dismemberment, stalking, kidnapping, mentions of drug use and abuse, and a surprise pregnancy. The main male character also has a penchant for orgasm denial. If that's not your thing, please reconsider whether this book is right for you.

For all the good girls who want to be fucked like a bad girl.

One

Stella

I'M TEMPTED TO GET down on all fours and lick the pristine marble floors glistening beneath my worn-out sneakers just to see if they're as clean as they look. Or reach up and flick the precious stones dangling tauntingly low from the crystal chandelier the size of my Honda Civic looming directly above me. Or smear my sweaty, grimy fingers across the pretentious oil paintings lining the stark, white walls, just because I'm a bitter bitch like that.

Casa del Sol is beautiful—breathtaking really. But it's also completely devoid of character or charm. It's cold and empty, a mirror image of the woman who lived here. The grandiose mansion with the creaky wrought iron gates and gaudy statue in the roundabout driveway speaks volumes about the woman who dumped me at the front doors of a fire station when I was only a few days old.

Giulia Riva. My birth mother. A woman I've never met, and never will because the selfish bitch decided to die of cancer without so much as sending me a postcard before her grand departure.

"You must be Stella!" A short, plump woman in a maid's uniform approaches with her arms out, catching me off guard with a much too affectionate hug. I wheeze out the same sound a chew toy makes when put under pressure and bring my hands up to awkwardly pat the stranger's back.

For such a tiny woman, she sure is strong, because I can barely squeak out a *hello* before she finally releases me from her death grip and I can breathe again.

"You are just as lovely as Ms. Riva described," she exclaims, holding me at arm's length. I bite back a bitter groan and smile politely at the beaming woman in front of me. After all, it's not her fault Giulia didn't have the lady balls to face her orphan child and hired a private investigator to stalk her instead. "My name is Martina. Don't be fooled by my attire. I run this place. I hope Enzo was good to you today."

I glance over at the limo driver who's standing patiently at my side, his hands folded neatly in front of his perfectly creased slacks and his face puckered tight like he just sucked on a lemon. As much as I'd like to tell Martina that Enzo's been a giant grump since picking me up from my apartment early this morning, I decide to cut the guy a break.

"He was great. Not sure I would have survived the flight if it weren't for him." *Him and the sedative I slipped myself before boarding the plane.*

Martina claps her hands. "Wonderful. Well, let's not waste time, shall we? Would you like a tour? Or a bite to eat? What can I get you?"

"A tour would be great," I respond with fake enthusiasm. Something sarcastic about a gallon of wine and a sledgehammer sits on the tip of my tongue, but I remind myself that kindness is not weakness. Or whatever inspiring crap my best friend, Harper, is always droning on about. Life has not yet fucked her over, so she's still naively optimistic.

"Of course. Enzo, why don't you show Stella around, and I'll finish up in the kitchen?"

Enzo bows his head and gestures for me to follow him through the mansion. I count the bedrooms and bathrooms, but eventually run out of fingers and toes and give up. There's also a library, an indoor pool and gym, sauna and steam room. Sadly, I won't have time to enjoy any of it, because as soon as I have what I want, I'll be on the first flight back to my cozy little life in Detroit, flipping Giulia's lingering spirit the finger on the way out

We circle back to the kitchen where Martina dismisses Enzo, and now it's just the two of us. I take a seat on one of the bar stools lined up in front of the giant marble island and watch as Martina peels a carrot with a little too much enthusiasm. The poor vegetable never stood a chance.

"You have an appointment with Mr. Marchetti tomorrow. He's offered lunch at his office," she chirps from the other side of the marble slab.

"Oh. What for?" I ask, curious as to why I've been summoned by the lawyer handling Giulia's legal affairs.

"To finalize some details for the funeral."

Right. *That.*

Once I'm filled in on tomorrow's itinerary, Martina tells me there's a cluster of manicured trails behind the house that I'm free to explore. Deciding I need some time alone to process the last forty-eight hours of my fucked up life, I navigate my way out of the mansion and down a well-groomed path that leads to the wooded acreage at the back of the property. Finely crushed gravel crunches beneath my sneakers as I put the mansion behind me and squint up at the high noon sun. The thin straps of my top provide little protection against the harsh rays, but I don't care. I need to feel the heat. To embrace the scorch of the fiery ball kissing my skin.

The weight of the situation sits heavy like tar in my lungs. I take a few cleansing breaths of the warm California air, but it does nothing to clear the impending doom from my chest cavity.

Although Mr. Marchetti has so graciously informed me that Giulia has left her entire estate to me, I don't want a single dollar of it. It's all tainted, every last penny tarnished by the horrors I was forced to endure while Giulia Riva lived a lavish life of charity balls and caviar and expensive champagne. The bitch literally struck gold and built her empire from the ground up while I was bounced around from one shitty home to the next until I finally aged out of the foster system she left me to rot in.

So no, I'm not here for the money. I'm here because Giulia hired a private investigator to find me and I'd like to know exactly how much digging he had to do to hunt me down. Clearly, the precautions I've taken to remain hidden are no longer sufficient and I need to beef up my tactics.

The sound of a second set of feet rips me from my thoughts and the bony fingers of fear tap their way up my spine one vertebrae at a time, until they reach the base of my neck and scatter throughout the rest of my body.

A bead of sweat rolls down between my shoulder blades and absorbs into the thin cotton of my tank top. My heart takes off in my chest and I instinctively curl my fingers inward, preparing to defend myself against whoever's lurking behind me. But when I spin around and swing an arm, nobody's there.

Two

Stella

LUNCH IS SERVED IN an outdoor courtyard area at the back of the building that houses the law office. Ivy and flowers cover much of the stone walls surrounding the dining area. Pale yellow throw cushions decorate the outdoor lounge furniture off to the side. I wonder if this is where Mr. Marchetti eats lunch every day, because it's exactly where I'd want to spend my lunch breaks. Curled up on a comfy chair, reading a book, nibbling on delicious food that an attractive waiter drops in front of me.

I take a small sip of my wine, allowing the alcohol to warm my chest and settle my nerves.

The lawyer flashes me a bright white smile. "We have some minor details to iron out for Giulia's funeral. Nothing of huge importance to the average person, but to Giulia, it meant a lot to her that you had a say in them."

"Well, that's ironic," I snort, and it's completely unladylike. I put a lid on my crazy and slip back into the polite, well-mannered costume I've been sweating my ass off in ever since I was plucked from my apartment in Detroit and dropped into the ritzy world of Giulia Riva. Adjusting my posture, I try again. "I mean ... I never met her, so I'm not really sure why she'd care that I be a part of it."

Mr. Marchetti clears his throat and adjusts in his seat. He looks utterly uncomfortable, and I know he's about to defend Giulia. "Despite how it looks, Stella, Giulia cared very much about you."

Cynicism takes a back seat to the resentment that drives the emotional rollercoaster I've been riding. I stare down at the gold bracelet around my wrist. Mr. Marchetti gave it to me only moments ago, and it already feels like it's embedded itself into my flesh. I thumb the initials G.R. engraved into the charm dangling from the chain. For whatever reason, I feel compelled to wear it, as if somehow, it'll give me the answers I desire. But in this very moment, its delicate edge feels more like barbed wire burrowing into my skin.

I remember something Harper told me before I got on the plane to come here. *Bitterness is a thief of joy.* She has no idea how right she is. Because right now, I'm sulking at the proverbial bus stop while my bitterness rides off into the sunset with the little happiness I thought I had finally found.

"Mr. Marchetti, I—"

"Please, call me Carlo."

Softening, I repeat, "Carlo, I took a big risk coming here." I swallow around the lump in my throat and meet Carlo's empathetic eyes. Or maybe it's pity I see there. Either way, it does nothing for me. "To fulfill the final wishes of a woman who didn't give two shits about me my entire life."

"I understand it's difficult for you to make sense of, Stella, but I assure you, she loved you. She just ..." Carlo's mouth twists as he carefully selects his next words. "She tried to reach out many times over the years, but she was afraid of pushing you further away. At least from afar, she could admire you. Protect you."

"Protect me," I deadpan. "Perhaps if she wanted to protect me, she shouldn't have fed me to the wolves." My voice turns raspy, anger ripping at my throat.

Carlo leans back in his chair, his dove-gray eyes scanning my face. He's trying to decide whether it's worth beating this dead horse. We've been over it a few times already, and it always ends the same way. He tells me Giulia loved me, and I laugh in his face.

I remove the choice from him and push on. "How long did she have me followed for?"

Carlo clears his throat again. I think he's about to lie to me, but then he says, "As soon as she could afford to hire an investigator, she did. You would have been about ten years old, I believe."

An avalanche of emotions rolls through me, gobbling up any sense of security I thought I had. *Ten years old.* I was ten years old when Giulia hired a PI to follow me. How much did he see? What does he know? Was he there when ...

Oh god. My world tilts off its axis as dread seeps into my veins.

"Ten?" I screech, then rein it back in again. Lowering my voice, I repeat more calmly, "Ten. Giulia started watching me when I was ten and never bothered to reach out to me."

The lawyer inhales deeply, then says plainly, "Yes," as if this information harbors very little significance. To him, it may. But to me ...

Leaning forward, he reaches to set his hand over mine on the table, but I swiftly pull away and sink my hand into my lap. I can tell it offends him, but right now, I don't give a flying rat's ass how he feels.

"You're much like your mother, Stella," he says softly. I narrow my eyes at him. I know it's meant to be a compliment, but Giulia Riva was a weak, selfish woman, and I'm nothing like her. As if he can hear my thoughts, he adds, "She was a very strong, stubborn lady with a heart of pure gold."

Ice-cold irritation licks at my insides until they're raw. I stare at him and blink slowly, disbelievingly.

He's wrong about Giulia being strong. Strong women don't cower in the face of a challenge. And that's exactly what Giulia did. She cowered and ran when the going got tough.

Just like I did. Shit. Maybe we're alike after all.

"Let me ask you something, Stella. Do you often feel like you're ... lucky?"

I recoil, because what the hell is he getting at? Shaking my head, I state clearly and boldly, "Never."

Determined? Yes.

Inventive? Absolutely.

Lucky? Fuck no.

Leaning back in his chair again, Carlo narrows his gaze on me and angles his head. I maintain correct posture and meet his eyes with my own, refusing to show an ounce of concern for why he may be asking such an unusual question.

"You were accepted into a very respectable university program despite having mediocre grades and poor attendance in school."

Panic surmounts concern, and I'd like to know how he knows this about me. Feigning not giving a fuck, I ask, "Your point?"

Answering my question with another question, he responds, "And when you graduated, you were immediately offered a job at a prestigious investment firm doing exactly what you studied for. And part of your hiring contract was that your student loan, which you somehow were approved for despite having no credit history or co-signer, would be paid off in full provided you remained employed there for a minimum of one year. Is that correct?"

Shifting uncomfortably in my seat, I respond coolly, "That's correct."

"And when you broke your ankle while hiking when in college, and had no medical insurance to cover your medical care, somehow, miraculously, the hospital misplaced your file and forgave the debt. Do you remember that?"

Swallowing hard, I nod slowly.

Carlo leans forward and faces me dead on. "And yet you still don't feel lucky."

Silence stretches on as I consider Carlo's unnerving assessment of the last decade of my life, while my poor little heart rattles around in its cage, desperate to free itself and take off running. I don't blame it, because that's exactly what I'm considering doing too.

"Did it ever occur to you that perhaps you had a guardian angel you weren't aware of?"

Wetting my lips, I garble out the name of said angel. "Giulia."

I glance over my shoulder for the millionth time, but once again nobody's there. I set a fast pace and bolt down the sidewalk, dodging kids riding their bikes where people walk, young mothers pushing strollers, and a man selling knock-off designer bags at a folding table on the side of the street.

Despite successfully slipping past Enzo on my way out of the law office, I still feel like I'm being followed, a familiar fear nipping at my heels like the dogs of hell. It's like when you flip the lights off in the basement then race up the stairs, terrified that a flesh-eating monster will grab you by the ankles and pull you down into the darkness and rip you limb from limb.

Yeah. That's how I feel right now.

But I've felt this way since I was fourteen years old. The fear of being followed has woven itself through me over the years, and now takes up permanent residence inside me and I have no choice but to live with it.

But right now, my instincts are firing on all cylinders, and I know for certain I'm not wandering these streets alone. Gripping the strap of my cross-body bag, I skid to a stop, turn around, and begin walking in the same direction I came from. If someone's following me, they're in for a special surprise, because Stella Clarke refuses to cower.

Maybe this will flush them out.

But after marching back toward the law office for what feels like hours, I realize the courage I mustered was actually just plain old stupidity.

I pause again, just as an overwhelming presence behind me casts an ominous shadow, shielding me from the heat of the sun. I should turn around and face whatever predator's lurking behind me, but I'm frozen in place, and that's a new first for me.

Internal sirens wail at me to flee, to take cover from the storm brewing at my back. If whoever's behind me is as enormous as his shadow, then I shouldn't take any chances. I should run, hard and fast and far. I ignore the warning and spin around, coming face to face with nothing more than a silhouette outlined by the blinding sun.

But then he takes a step forward and a pair of piercing blue eyes come into view. Sweet, muscular Jesus this guy is intense looking. I swallow hard as I dare my gaze to wander over his tightly clenched jaw, shadowed by rugged dark stubble, and down a tanned throat, over the hard planes of his chest and shoulders covered by a black T-shirt stretched tight over his broad span. Then I search lower, down his muscular, heavily tattooed arms that could double as tree trunks. And then ... gulp ... to the bulge in the front of his jeans.

My eyes slam back up to his and a flush of heat creeps into my cheeks.

I've been caught red-handed, and now this mother-effer is smirking at me.

The deafening whoosh of blood in my head drowns out the hum of the nearby traffic and the obnoxious blare of car horns. A gentle breeze drifts by and gathers up the man's scent, wrapping it around me like a blanket. Pine and mint. Masculine and clean.

Dangerous and intoxicating.

But then I remember rule number one. The most important one of all: *trust no man.*

Popping a hip and crossing my arms, I swallow the pool of saliva gathering in my mouth and snap out, "Are you following me?"

Not only is this guy huge, but he's the epitome of tall, dark, and ruggedly handsome. He's terrifying in the sexiest kind of way. Everything about him screams *I'm in control and I like it rough.*

He folds his giant tattooed tree trunks in front of him and peers down at me. "I am," he answers dryly. At least he's honest.

As I suspected, his voice is big, just like the rest of him, and it sounds like he swallowed shards of glass because it's all gravelly and deep and, oh my god, why am I thinking about this guy's voice?

With as much snark as humanly possible, I respond, "May I ask why?"

He takes a step forward and I take one back, maintaining the distance between us. My chest tightens as my lungs struggle to take in oxygen. His gaze dips briefly down to my cleavage, then back up. A smug grin tugs at his lips, and I'm tempted to reach up and smack it off his stupid, beautiful face.

He quirks a dark brow and angles his head at me. "Nobody told you?" When I simply frown at him, he tells me, "I'm your security detail. One of three that will be shadowing you until the estate is settled and you move here permanently."

A familiar burning sensation flares beneath my ribs. It's the same burn I get every time I'm stopped by a police officer, or when a bank teller asks me for my ID. I stomp the flames out and feign indifference, refusing to show any signs of alarm.

Lifting my chin, I respond dryly, "And how do I know you're not just saying that so you can follow me home and murder me in private?"

A flicker of amusement crosses his face, then he reaches into his pocket and pulls out a black business card and hands it to me. I snatch it from him and eye the card suspiciously.

Sweetwater Security.

"You can call my boss or Martina, if you don't believe me."

I glance back up at him and narrow my eyes. So, he knows of the tiny terrorist that attempts to suffocate me with her deadly hugs.

"Uh huh. So basically, you'll be spying on me. Is that what you're saying, Mr. ..."

"Joel," he offers up his first name but not his last. "But don't worry, princess. I have much better things to do than sit behind a screen and watch you roam around your ivory tower."

My ivory tower. More like my temporary prison.

"Oh yeah? Like what? Eating small children for breakfast and crushing gravel with your teeth?"

"Exactly."

Sheesh. This guy has the personality of a canker sore.

"And I suppose I'll be seeing you around the mansion as well?"

"You will. But the property is surrounded by ten-foot-high fences and an impressive surveillance system. Nobody gets in and nobody gets out. So you won't see much of us."

"What, no fire-breathing dragons? How mediocre."

This time when he steps forward, I don't budge. And I'm wrapped up in that dangerous scent of his again.

Leaning in, Joel brings his mouth near my ear and says lowly, "I'm much more dangerous than any fire-breathing dragon, Stella. You'd be wise to get that through your head."

Three

Joel

I'M NOT SURE IF the little brat is brave or stupid, but she managed to work her way under my skin in a matter of seconds. I didn't have to meet her in person to know she's going to be a problem for me. I recognized that fiery little spark the second I laid eyes on her bright hazel eyes five weeks ago when Giulia Riva hired Sweetwater to follow her daughter around like lost puppies. But then yesterday, when the little spitfire spun around and started stalking back in the direction she came from, headed straight toward the danger I know she felt closing in behind her, I couldn't help but wonder what possessed her to do such a reckless thing. Average civilians typically steer clear of the threat of danger—not swerve full tilt towards it.

But Stella Clarke is far from average.

She may not know I've been hot on her tracks for over a month while she hums around and lives her simple little life, a life she manufactured out of nothing more than a few measly threads, but I can tell she's done well to hone in on her instincts.

She's smart. Intuitive. And brave to a fault.

I've stayed out of her way until recently. So have my teammates, Zak Shephard and Liam Davis. But I'd be lying if I said there isn't something about her that's captured my attention.

Naturally, I bitched and moaned to Mac, the head of Sweetwater Security, about the job. This isn't what we do. We're not personal babysitters or bodyguards who dress in Armani suits and speak into our sleeves. We're mercenaries, Navy fucking SEALs who operate outside the law. We lurk in the gray area between right and wrong. We take on jobs that the government can't be caught responsible for. But when I reminded my boss of these minor details, what was his excuse? That he owed Giulia a favor from when she backed him financially to get Sweetwater Security up and running more than a decade ago.

It turns out Giulia was a big supporter of our military, and when Mac was honorably discharged alongside a few of his mates, Giulia attended his retirement party and they hit it off, became friends, then ultimately business associates. When she got sick with cancer two months ago, she called in a favor. And now here we are.

And my curiosity is unusually piqued. Stella may have the rest of the world fooled, but I see right through that frigid, sarcastic veneer. She's not nearly as innocent as she leads society to believe.

Stella's a bad girl with a good girl image.

Hopping off the treadmill, I pluck my phone from my gym bag and pull up the live camera feed, flipping through each screen until I find what I'm looking for. Stella's curled up on one of the oversized chairs in the library, her nose stuffed in a book. I read her file when we took the job, but it was only a bird's eye view of what her life has been like. Enough information for us to do our job, but not enough to truly quench my thirst for the nitty-gritty details. Like why the only long-term relationship she's ever had is with her best friend, Harper Hilton. Or why she has seven different locks on her apartment door and uses every last one of them, double-checking them every time she comes or goes.

Or why she's pretending to be someone she's not.

Stuffing my phone away, I gather up my belongings and hit the shower, then head to the makeshift surveillance room we've set up in Giulia's office where Zak and Liam watch silently as I pace the floor like a caged animal.

"We'll stick to our deal, take shifts. I tagged along yesterday, so next time it's one of you fuckers." I stop and point a finger at my teammates.

Liam, the grumpy fucking caveman that he is, simply grunts. But Zak, always the one to do what's necessary to keep the job running smoothly, agrees to cover the next shift. I swipe a hand through my hair and nod a thanks to him.

"What about the funeral?" Zak asks, then turns back to the monitor and starts tapping through earlier footage. He won't find anything interesting on it, but I don't bother pointing out the obvious.

"We'll all go. Already worked the details out with Mac and Martina. We have a private flight on standby, so airport security won't be a problem. Sloane will take over surveillance remotely while we're traveling," I explain.

Dread injects itself directly into my veins and works its way through my body. After eight years of active duty as a Navy SEAL and four years of working for Mac at Sweetwater, the last place I ever thought I'd be is escorting a rich woman's offspring to Italy for a goddamn funeral.

Fuck my life.

I roll onto my side and check the time on my phone.

Four o'clock in the morning.

Right now, Zak's on live surveillance while Liam and I catch some rack time. But I'm doing more tossing and turning than sleeping.

I throw the comforter off my body and slip into a T-shirt and sweatpants and tuck my handgun into the back of the waistband. No sense stewing here when there's a perfectly good gym to take my frustrations out on. I leave the guestroom I'm stationed in and pad down the hallway toward the spiral staircase, pausing at the top of the steps to listen through the silence. The faintest sound of movement, although I'm not entirely sure what from, echoes down the hall. I glance down the dimly lit corridor toward a set of mahogany doors that I know Stella's behind.

When there's another sound of movement, I move swiftly and quietly down the hall and stop outside the room. Pressing a palm to the wall beside the door, I bow my head and listen, my eardrums straining against the deafening silence. Seconds tick by. Minutes, maybe. Just as I go to step away, the tiniest whimper comes from within the room. I grip my gun with one hand and the doorknob with the other, fully prepared to barge in, but freeze when I hear another whimper. This time, I know it's not one of pain or fear.

At first, I think perhaps she's dreaming. That is, until the soft sound is followed by a breathy moan. A wicked grin splits across my face and I back away from the door.

Oh, princess.

I can tell by the hollow darkness at the bottom of the doors that the lights in her room are all off. Closing my eyes, I welcome the sweet sounds of Stella pleasuring herself. My dick hardens painfully, but there's a time and a place for jerking off, and now's not it. Peering up at the tiny black globe on the ceiling, I release a ragged breath and reel in the urge to whip my dick out and fuck my fist.

Temptation bleeds through the door, testing the little restraint I have as Stella's sultry moans escalate into a seductive crescendo. I stand there and marinade in it as her orgasm peaks and her muffled cries pierce my blackened soul.

Curling my hands into fists, I glare at the door. The thought of what she was imagining, *who* she was imagining, does something to my insides. I've never been a jealous man. I'd have to keep a woman around long enough to develop those feelings and that's just something I don't do. Clenching my jaw so hard I'm sure my molars crack, I put as much distance as possible between me and that goddamn bedroom before I do something I'll surely regret.

"Good morning, Joel," Martina greets me the next morning in the kitchen, her tone far too chipper for my foul mood. "Oh, good morning, dear," she adds excitedly, her eyes darting to the doorway behind me.

I groan, knowing exactly who just graced us with her irritating presence. The *click-clack* of high heels confirm it. I turn around and fix my eyes on Stella standing demurely on the other side of the kitchen with nothing but a large slab of marble separating us.

I'm not a total barbarian—that's Liam's thing. But I'm not exactly a gentleman either. So, with zero delicacy, I let my gaze roam hungrily over Stella's body, snagging momentarily on her tanned, shapely legs accentuated by nude fuck-me heels. Her snug, black dress falls just above her knees and hugs every delicious curve of her body. Her tits are covered modestly, but the way the fabric cinches in at her waist emphasizes her full bust. Her long, dark hair falls in loose waves down her back.

She's fucking sex on heels.

My eyes finally settle on a pair of hazel laser beams burning a hole clean through my face. No doubt that if looks could kill, I'd be six feet under. She knows exactly what I'm thinking. I may have been hired to protect her, but there was nothing in the contract stating I can't also enjoy the view.

Peeling her scowl off me, she rolls her eyes and flips her hair over her shoulder.

Martina must pick up on my lack of discretion because the swift crack of a dish towel across my arm comes next. "Didn't your mother ever teach you manners, young man?" Martina chastises while frowning up at me.

I scoff. My mother taught me nothing. She was always too busy planning her next splashy dinner party to tend to the likes of her only child. It's my father who raised me, and he wasn't exactly what they call a *gentle parent*. He was rough around the edges, drank too much hard liquor, and could never get his anger under control. He was a product of the military—fucked up from too many missions gone wrong and overseas deployments.

Minus the drinking problem, him and I are the same.

I smirk down at the tiny, old woman who has all three of us Navy SEALs wrapped around her wrinkly little finger. Sighing, I murmur, "Sorry, Martina," then lean down and plant a kiss on her cheek and watch in amusement as a blush of pink creeps into her face.

Martina swats the air bashfully, then shifts her focus back to Stella. Crisis averted.

I lean against the counter and grin as Stella struggles to maintain composure. Careful, calculated movements. Deep, calming breaths. Intentional avoidance of eye contact.

I make her nervous.

Something about that sends a sick thrill straight to my dick. It's not my intention to cause her anxiety, but I have to admit that the depraved side of me enjoys it.

Martina chimes in. "Are you hungry, dear? I feed the boys every morning, so I make a spread." She waves her arm out, showcasing the vast selection of breakfast foods spread out across the island. It's always overkill with Martina, but we're men, and she's feeding us, so you won't catch us complaining.

"I don't eat breakfast. But if you'd like some help ..." Stella offers politely, and I narrow my eyes at her.

There's that veneer again. Polite, timid, fucking *sweet*. Ignoring Martina's protests to take a seat and relax, Stella picks up a whisk and begins stirring a bowl of pancake batter.

Martina tsks, then vanishes into the walk-in pantry. When Stella notices me assessing her, she grips the handle of the whisk a little too tight, and I know she's on edge. I set my coffee down and saunter toward her, delighted as her muscles tighten with each step I take, until I'm standing so close behind her that I can feel the heat radiating off her backside. Inhaling deeply, I fill my lungs with her scent. It's a blend of vanilla and something sharp, and it suits her perfectly. Sweet and spicy.

She flinches when I reach around, the inside of my arm brushing with hers, and take the whisk from her hand. She glares up at me. "I was using that."

Then she spins around and presses her back into the counter behind her, leaning away from me. This is the closest we've been, and it allows me a view of the light smattering of freckles over her nose and the flecks of bold emerald in her irises. I drop the whisk into the bowl, lean in and press my palms to the counter on either side of her.

She sucks in a sharp breath and holds it as her eyes flare with apprehension. There's a war waging inside of her. Like she knows she should fear me, but refuses to show any signs of weakness.

"Going somewhere special today, Stella?" I ask lowly, unsure what's on her agenda because it's Zak's day to tote around behind the hot little mess.

She lifts her chin and responds, "Lunch with Carlo."

"Hmm," I hum. Two lunches in two days. I'm beginning to wonder if the lawyer has further intentions than assisting with a bunch of mind-numbing paperwork. I stomp down the annoying twinge of jealousy nagging at my gut and lower my gaze to hers. The pulse in her neck jumps, and fuck if that doesn't make my dick twitch.

With every intention of making a point, I speak low and clear, leaving no room for doubt. "I stopped by your room early this morning." Stella's expression sobers as she picks up what I'm putting down. I ignore her discomfort and continue. "Such sweet sounds you make when you come."

I watch as all the blood drains from her face and her heartbeat takes off. I imagine that right now a million disturbing thoughts are flying through her mind as she recounts the symphony of moans and whimpers she performed while pleasuring herself in the wee hours of the morning.

"You ..." she stammers.

"That's right, princess. Keep it down next time, huh? Wouldn't want the other two to catch you doing that. I would hate for the guilt to fall on you when I remove their ears and eyeballs from their heads."

Then I dip my finger into the bowl of batter and slip it into my mouth, sucking the sweet, salty mixture off. Stella's eyes track my movement as I step back and shove my hands into my pockets. It's the only way I can stop myself from touching her.

Checkmate, princess.

Four

Stella

I storm back up the path toward the mansion, my body exhausted from my jog on the trails but a wicked blend of frustration, embarrassment and irritation preventing me from fully relaxing. How dare that giant, brooding jerk of a bodyguard listen in on one of my most intimate moments. And how dare he point blank tell me to keep it down.

Asshole.

But then I glimpse the guesthouse under construction off in the distance and my curiosity trumps my agitation. I pause and listen for the familiar sounds of hammers banging and saws zipping, but am met with only a light breeze rustling the trees around me.

Glancing around, I change course and head toward the partially complete building, stopping several times to listen for footfalls behind me. It's a terrible habit—one I haven't been able to kick.

I shove the feeling aside like I've learned to do and step up to what will someday be the front entrance of the building.

There are no doors or windows yet, but they've been framed in, so I can tell the interior is going to be bathed in natural light. I take a cautious step inside and peek around. Warmth envelops me, like a cozy blanket on a rainy day. The scent of freshly cut wood fills my lungs, reminding me of the time Harper and I rented a dusty, old cabin on a lake and nearly lit the place on fire when we stuffed too many logs in the woodstove.

Smiling at the memory, I saunter through the guesthouse.

"Hello?" I call out.

Silence.

The only sound is the patter of my sneakers on the plywood subfloor as I creep from room to room. I try to picture what Giulia had envisioned for the space, but it's impossible to do considering I never met the woman. I haven't a clue why she needed a guesthouse when I could fit my entire freaking condo building inside her dining room.

So instead, I let my imagination run wild. Rich hardwood would stretch throughout the entire house. There'd be a huge stone fireplace in the living room with a large wooden mantel, where traditional stockings would be hung during the holidays. The kitchen would be bright and spacious and airy, with an oversized gas stove and a chef-style fridge and freezer. Moving onto the master bedroom, the morning sun would flood through the floor-to-ceiling windows and cast warmth on the king-sized bed piled miles high with decorative pillows. Then there's the ensuite bathroom. A deep, claw-foot soaker tub large enough for two people would be the focal point. In the tub, you'd be surrounded by windows overlooking the vast forest and manicured gardens.

My lungs constrict, squeezed by the fists of hopes and dreams from my sad, empty childhood as I stand in the middle of the guesthouse with nothing but plywood and partially finished walls around me. Then something Carlo said earlier comes to mind.

Giulia wanted you to have a fresh start. She wanted you to create the life of your dreams from all the pieces she left behind. This is your clean slate, Stella. Run with it.

A lone tear slips down my face as I break rule number two: *no crying*. I swipe the droplet away with the back of my hand, angry that I allowed myself this moment of weakness, and stare up at the ceiling. "You knew where I was all along and you left me there. How am I supposed to accept all of this?" I sniffle, closing my eyes and imagining Giulia's voice, a voice I've never heard, drifting through the open space, reassuring me that I'm doing the right thing by being here.

A sudden, crashing bang startles me, violently ripping me from my imaginary conversation with my dead mother. My heart lurches into my throat, blocking my airways, and I bolt for the exit, only allowing myself to breathe once I'm safely outside.

I glance back at the guesthouse, relieved it's still standing and not piled into a heap of sawdust with me buried underneath. I press a palm to my racing heart and peek inside the building again, spotting a slab of lumber laying haphazardly on the floor.

I don't remember it being there when I went in. It must have been propped up against the wall and fell over.

What begins as innocently chuckling to myself for being absolutely ridiculous quickly escalates into maniacal laughter.

Good grief. I've clearly lost my ever-loving mind. Because this is what a sane person would do right?! Laugh at themselves after nearly shitting their pants when the ghost of their mother decides to play tricks on them by knocking over heavy objects.

Screw you, Giulia. Screw you.

———◆◇◆———

I close my eyes and suck in a deep breath, filling my lungs with oxygen to keep my body afloat as I lay on my back in the outdoor pool. My body sinks just below the glass-like surface as my fingers lazily skim back and forth at my sides and a million burning questions blow through my mind.

I've been here, at Casa del Sol, for only a few short days, and so far, the only information I've gained is that Giulia had me followed by a PI since I was an awkward, scrawny ten-year-old girl. But entirely controversial to that, I've also discovered she's pretty much the only reason why I had any hope at a normal life after I aged out of the system.

Even as a child, I knew I would never be able to afford to go to college or to rent, let alone buy a decent place to live when I turned eighteen. I always just assumed I'd end up on the streets like the rest of them. So I took up stealing from the shitty foster parents I was thrust into the arms of in hopes of scrounging up enough cash to get by for a few months when I turned eighteen. And when I was finally released from the grueling chains of the foster system, I ran as fast as I could with nothing more than a few dollars to my name and the hand-me-downs in my suitcase.

Then my so-called luck took a huge left turn, or so I thought, and things got easier from then on, and I settled into a comfortable little life. How naive I was to believe I accomplished all of that on my own.

But then all of this happened, and I'm right back to where I started: confused, disoriented, and bitter as fuck. I need answers, but I'm not entirely sure if I'm ready for them.

God must hear my inner monologue, because a deep rumble rolls through the thick, humid air like a warning. The thunderous vibration booms in my chest, rattling my insides. The incoming storm has been all over the news today. A potential hurricane is brewing. Why that sends a thrill through me is a topic I should probably bring up with my therapist, but I skipped out on my last appointment. Four years ago.

The crickets I heard singing their sweet lullabies earlier have all quieted down, hiding out until the storm passes. The flashing lights of planes flying overhead are now lost somewhere beyond a thick shroud of dark clouds. The steady thump of my heart whooshes in my ears. It sparks an unwelcome flashback.

"Where are you taking me?" My voice hitches when the vehicle hits a pothole and I bounce in the passenger seat of the rusty, old van.

Every time we hit a bump, there's this loud squeaking sound that comes from beneath my feet. It's worse than nails on a chalkboard.

"If you wouldn't have run off, maybe you wouldn't be asking that question," Roger snaps at me from the driver's seat. His knuckles are white from gripping the steering wheel tight. I know he's mad at me for calling Harriet in the middle of the night from a pay phone and ruining their date. He doesn't know I know about them though. And I won't tell anyone. I don't want Harriet to get in trouble for sleeping with a co-worker.

My eyes fill with tears. "I couldn't stay there any longer."

Roger sneers at me with mean snake eyes. "I'm beginning to think you like the attention," he accuses.

His gaze flits down my body then back up. I told my last foster mother I hated wearing dresses, and this is exactly why.

I shake my head, a warm tear sliding down my cheek and into my mouth. I lick the salty liquid from my lips.

"I'm sorry," I whine. I know I shouldn't have run away, but the boys at that house were awful.

"Not yet, you aren't," Roger mutters.

The change on the dash rolls from one side to the other as we take a corner too fast, turning onto a single lane dirt road with a dead-end sign. There's a weird nagging sensation in the pit of my stomach that's growing harder to ignore with each passing moment.

We're going the wrong way.

I'm fourteen—not stupid. I've been up and down that highway a hundred times in this exact van.

"*Where are we going?*" My question goes unanswered and suddenly I feel very sick. "*Roger, where are you taking me?*" I ask again, louder. I hold onto the edges of the seat as the van picks up speed down the bumpy road.

We pull over at the end of the road and I stare ahead at a thick treeline, the tall hardwoods naked, their dead leaves an orange and brown carpet over the forest floor.

"*Get out,*" Roger barks as he rolls out of the driver's seat. He's a big man. Taller than any I've met and much rounder.

"*No,*" I refuse, shoving the lock button down on my door so he can't open it.

He rounds the front of the vehicle and pulls on the door handle.

"*Unlock it. Now.*" His angry voice is muffled behind the glass. I shake my head. "*Guess we're doing this the hard way.*" He shoves a key into the lock and the door flies open.

"*I want to go home.*" I don't have a home, but anywhere would be better than here.

"*I have something to show you.*"

I don't like this. Whatever he wants to show me is out in that forest and I think I could survive never having seen it. I whip my head around in search of any sign of life but there's nothing but trees and dirt.

Roger leans over me and unbuckles my seatbelt, then grabs my arm and plucks me out of the van like I weigh nothing at all. I struggle against him, pulling free from his grasp, but land hard on my bottom on the gravel.

"Get up," he snarls, pulling me from the ground. Small, jagged rocks dig into my knees as I stumble forward. I get my feet under me and try to run, but his grip is too tight. My body slams back into his and he shoves me against the side of the van, knocking the wind out of me. I gasp for air like a fish out of water.

Then he hauls me away from the van and deep into the woods.

Five

Joel

LIAM'S ON LIVE SURVEILLANCE now, so I thought I'd hit the pool to burn some laps. But my plan came to a screeching halt when I realized I wouldn't be alone. Now, I'm lurking in the shadows like a fucking creep, watching Stella float on her back in a little black bikini that shows off every last one of her soft curves, and my dick is pitching a tent so large that boy scouts could camp under it.

Stella's eyes drift shut and every muscle in her body relaxes. Her arms drift lazily across the smooth surface of the water as she floats on her back. But then she slowly begins sinking below the surface, air escaping from her lips and bubbling to the surface. I consider jumping in but before I step forward, she comes back up in a panicked splash and gasps for oxygen.

She was daydreaming, and I can't help but wonder what could have possibly been important enough to rip her so far away from reality that she nearly drowned herself.

I still can't peel my eyes off her when she exits the pool and towel dries off. She glances over her shoulder more than once, and I know she senses that someone's watching her. Finally, I get the balls to step out of the dark and show my face.

She startles and sucks in a sharp breath of air, then begins chewing at me for scaring her.

I ignore her every word and state the obvious. "There's a storm rolling in. Shouldn't be in the pool right now."

She glances down at my swim trunks and quirks a brow. "Isn't that why you're out here?"

When I don't respond, she drops the towel from around her body and tosses it on a nearby lounge chair. My eyes follow a lone water droplet as it cascades down the slender length of her neck, into the canyon of her plump tits, and soaks into the thin string of her bikini top. There are a million reasons why I shouldn't want her, but right now, I can't think of a fucking single one.

Her expression galvanizes when she notices my wandering eyes, and she snatches her shirt from a chair and pulls it over her head in a hasty fashion. I grin when her bikini soaks through her top, leaving two round wet spots on her chest.

"Cold?" I ask suggestively.

She follows my line of sight to her nipples, and her eyes round with embarrassment. Her cheeks turn a rosy shade of pink as she crosses her arms in front of her chest, hiding her peaks from me.

Then she gives me the most dramatic eye roll I've ever seen in my life and I want nothing more than to fold her over my knee and spank her bare ass until my handprint is permanently branded on her.

But I'm feeling generous, so I offer her some reprieve from embarrassment and switch to scolding her instead. "I told you to check in with me before you went anywhere."

She scoffs. "I don't recall agreeing to that."

Stubborn little …

"Besides, I'm a big girl. I can take care of myself."

"Famous last words," I state, replaying the last time I heard that phrase from a woman who thought she could handle herself. Now she's sitting in rehab, clawing her way toward sobriety from the drug addiction her traffickers forced upon her. Those Russian pricks, the Petrovs, are still roaming free while Liam's baby sister, Rachel, suffers the aftermath of being held captive for more than nine months by one of the world's largest sex trafficking rings. But bodies have been hitting the floor ever since, and we're slowly wading our way toward the sick fucks responsible.

"Look. This is private property. I'm perfectly safe. Besides, I have you and your scary-looking minions following me every step of the way." She slides a pair of jean shorts up her legs, wiggling her hips as the denim stretches over her curves. "By the way, the next time you decide to loiter in the bush like a weirdo, maybe wear a little bell or something so I know you're there."

"We both know I don't need to do that, because you're fully aware when you're being watched, aren't you?"

Her posture adjusts, as if she's surprised by my observation. "I suppose so."

"And how does one go about acquiring instincts like that, Stella? Because I know you weren't born with them."

Her pretty pink lips part, her mask slipping free long enough for me to catch a glimpse of the unease plaguing her confidence. She swallows hard, then slips the mask back on with a shrug of her shoulders. "Just something I picked up along the way."

Something I picked up. There's a fine line between instincts and paranoia. The photos in Stella's file painted a vivid image of her internal struggle, and right now, she's staggering awfully close to the edge.

Closing the space between us, I suggest, "If there's something you need to tell me, then now's the time to do it."

She gazes back at me, her hazel orbs rounding and pulse hammering in her throat. Her eyes dart left for a millisecond before her head whips side to side.

Liar.

I snatch her hand in mine and tug her along behind me, my head on a swivel. I ignore her protests to slow down and drag her into the house, locking the patio doors securely behind us.

Goosebumps pepper her bare arms and legs as her teeth audibly chatter, and I'm certain it's from more than just the cold front rolling in.

"Tell me," I snap at her, and she flinches. Her vanilla scent clings to her despite her dip in the chlorinated pool, and I crowd her, not caring that I'm making her uneasy. Her comfort isn't my responsibility, but her safety sure as fuck is.

"I don't take orders from you," she snips out just as something registers on her face. "Actually, now that I think of it, *you* take orders from *me*."

A deep rumble vibrates in my chest. Pressing my thumbs to her hips, I back her against the patio doors. A halo of fog forms on the glass around her. She swats my hands away, so I press my palms flat on the door on either side of her head and lower my gaze to hers.

Everything about her is a walking contradiction. A soft, curvy body but a cold, resting bitch face and bad attitude. Bright hazel eyes, but something dark and disturbing lurking behind them. Fiery, confident words, but a cracked foundation of uncertainty.

It's a lethal cocktail—like smooth whiskey and arsenic. It's not difficult to see that she has her walls up high and strong, and I get the sense she doesn't let them down for anyone.

Her mouth opens and closes like she wants to say something, but she decides against it. Her tough exterior is breaking down, like ancient ruins over thousands of years. It's only a matter of time before it all crumbles into ash and dust, and the woman hiding behind it is stripped bare of her false sense of security.

I soften my tone, but only because I recognize that look on her face. It's the same artificial bravery so many women wear like armor when they've been hurt. "Finally, you have nothing smart to say."

Her hot breath fans across my chest, warming the cold, dark cavity where my heart used to be. But after years of being enslaved by the crippling grief of the lives I couldn't save, that warmth quickly evaporates, and I'm left with nothing but a block of ice there instead.

"We're wheels up tomorrow morning. Get some sleep." I step away from her, my lungs burning like someone just took a blow torch to them.

She scans my face for a moment too long, then she scurries off and I'm left standing there with a raging hard-on and a hollow ache in my gut that tells me this job is about to get interesting.

"How the hell am I supposed to get into that thing?" Stella stands awkwardly beside the passenger door of my truck wearing tight, black leggings and an oversized graphic tee. Apparently, her wardrobe is very eclectic, because since she's arrived, she's bounced from skimpy workout attire to a formal business dress with fuck-me heels to looking like she popped out of a *Rolling Stones* magazine.

"With your arms and legs, I presume."

She frowns at me, then returns her attention back to my truck, glaring at it like it might sprout horns and a tail.

I toss her hideous yellow suitcase into the back seat, then I open her door and reluctantly offer her a hand. She swats it away like a pesky fly and I shrug my shoulders and step back, gesturing for her to go ahead and struggle all on her own.

"Too bad you didn't wear one of those tiny dresses again," I say as I watch her awkwardly clamber into the passenger seat. "The view would be phenomenal from down here."

She tucks her arms and legs inside the vehicle and peers down at me over her nose. "Funny. But haven't you heard? Guys who drive jacked up trucks are compensating for something."

I lean a tattooed forearm on the frame of the door and grin at her. "Is that so?" She drives her nose high in the air with a confident nod. "Talk back again, princess, and I'll show you how wrong you are."

She snaps her mouth shut and I reach for her seatbelt but pause when she flinches away from me. Our eyes lock and I can see her rationalizing her thoughts. "Just buckling you in," I reassure before stretching the belt across her body and clipping it into place.

Then I slam her door, round the truck, and hop into the driver's seat. The engine roars to life, and I grip the wheel with both hands until my knuckles bleach white. I may be playing it cool on the outside, but fuck if my guts aren't all twisted up.

Uncomfortable silence fills the cab of my truck for all of five minutes before Stella starts asking questions.

"Martina said we're bypassing airport security."

"Yep."

"How long is the flight?"

"Does it matter?"

She twists her fingers into a knot and drops her gaze to her lap. She's nervous again. My spine tingles as the muscles in my back tense. Then she turns her gaze to her window and stares out into the distance, her thoughts consuming her.

"Are you always this anxious?" I ask cautiously, knowing she'll grow defensive if I'm too forward.

She hesitates, but finally nods. Stella's not exactly an open book, but she's not completely closed off right now either, so I'm going to run with it while I have a chance.

"That feeling of being followed never relents, does it?"

She shrugs her shoulders and intentionally avoids eye contact. Instincts are like a muscle group. You need to exercise them to keep them in shape, otherwise, you lose them.

"Listen. I know I asked last night, but if there's something you think I should know ..."

Her face whips my direction and there's a trace of fear etched across her pretty features. I hit a raw nerve again. "There's nothing for me to share." The guilt in her tone is more than just a little obvious, but she catches herself and backpedals. "Don't you think if there was, I would have told you by now?"

I check my mirrors. The only vehicle behind us is the town car stuffed with Martina, Liam, and Zak.

Bringing my attention back to the road in front of me, I respond, "No, I don't think you would. I think you're hiding something."

She laughs sardonically. "The only thing I'm hiding is the desire to shove you in front of a moving vehicle."

Her defenses will fizzle out soon enough. I work for an elite security company who employs the best of the best. The cream of the Navy SEAL crop. If the general public knew what kind of information Sweetwater Security could get their hands on, the whole system would come crashing down. There's nothing I can't dig up about Stella Clarke. And after reading her file, I think I might need to dust off my shovel and get to work.

"You're running from something," I accuse.

Her defensiveness amplifies, which only solidifies my theory. "Aren't we all?" she huffs and crosses her arms.

"You're a terrible liar, Stella. You may have everyone else fooled, but not me."

She scoffs. "Oh please, Mr. Security Guy," she says mockingly. "Enlighten me. What makes you think I'm running from something?"

I'd be lying if I said her reference to me as a security guy doesn't irk me, but I forge on. "Why would I tell you? So you can take notes of your giveaways and modify your behavior to do a better job of it?"

She narrows her eyes at me and responds dryly, "Precisely."

I grunt. "Sorry to disappoint you, princess, but you're shit out of luck."

I glimpse her in my peripherals and can't help the smirk tugging at my lips. Her mouth pinches tight as she concentrates all her energy into secretly plotting my death.

The jet waits in the middle of the tarmac, engine roaring and ready to go. The California sun beats down on the pavement, rippling heat waves blurring the air between the parking lot and plane. Two airport employees scramble over to us, unload our luggage, and haul it into the cabin. The pilot introduces himself as an old friend of Mac's from the Navy, and I know we're in good hands.

We board the plane and settle in. Stella chooses a seat as far away from me as physically possible. The plane makes it's ascent, and once the pilot turns the seatbelt lights back off, everyone begins to roam about.

Martina plops down beside me and the side of my face heats from her glare.

"What is it, Martina?" I ask without looking up from my phone.

She plucks the device from my hand and drops it into the cup holder, forcing my attention to her. "You can't keep your eyes off her." She tips her head in Stella's direction, who's sitting across from Liam and staring with wide eyes as he casually flips his switchblade through his tattooed knuckles. Scaring the living daylights out of innocent bystanders is what Liam does best, and right now, Stella looks like she's trying to decide what's worse—being carved up by Liam or jumping out of a plane thirty-five thousand feet from the ground.

I wipe my smirk away with the back of my hand and return my attention to Martina. "It's my job to keep eyes on her."

"Mhm."

Sighing, I remind Martina, "Your girl over there has walls higher than any sane man would attempt climbing. And fortunately, my mental faculties are completely intact. So, I'm sorry to burst your bubble, Martina, but me watching her has nothing to do with whatever you're thinking and everything to do with collecting my paycheck."

Stella's soft laugh cuts through the air. It comes fast, heavy, and completely unexpected, like a kill shot. And it hits me dead in the chest. I snap my attention to where the heavenly sound came from. My guts twist as I watch her giggle at Liam and Zak who are fighting over a bag of peanuts the size of a coin purse. Her eyes flash from the idiots, to me, then back again. It happens so fast that if I had blinked, I would have missed it. It's the first time I've heard her laugh. Hell, it's the first time I've seen her fucking smile.

Suddenly, I feel the need to smear my teammates from the face of the planet.

Martina chuckles, stands, and stares down at me with an all-knowing grin plastered on her weathered face.

Before she leaves, she says sweetly, "She may have some high walls, dear, but there's always a way to breach them. Just try not to leave a mess when you do."

Six

Stella

BLOOD SEEPS INTO THE *tiny crevices of the dead leaves that carpet the forest floor. The smell of damp soil, moss, and death permeate the air around me, filling my lungs with dread.*

Harriet. What am I going to tell Harriet? She's the only constant in my life. She's the only person who's always been there for me, no matter what. She's going to lose it when she finds out what I've done.

She's always told me I'm a strong girl. Strong girls can do hard things. I can do hard things! I may be only fourteen years old, but I'm smarter than the rest of the foster kids my age. I've been in the system since I was a baby. I've beared witness to the horrors of so many foster homes that I've lost count. And I've run from every single one of them. That's what they call me: a runner. This will be no different, except this time, I won't get caught.

I stand, pull my dress back down over my hips, and swipe away the last tears I will ever shed in front of another human being. But then I realize there's evidence everywhere. It's embedded beneath my fingernails, between my legs, and soaking into the ground in front of me.

Get rid of the evidence. I have to get rid of the evidence.

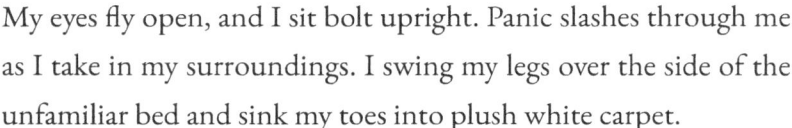

My eyes fly open, and I sit bolt upright. Panic slashes through me as I take in my surroundings. I swing my legs over the side of the unfamiliar bed and sink my toes into plush white carpet.

Where the hell are my shoes?

I release a breath when I remember I'm on a plane. To Italy. For my biological mother's funeral.

Right.

I stand on wobbly legs and check myself in the mirror hung on the back of the bedroom door. If the Crypt Keeper had a sister, this is what she'd look like. Dark bags hang heavy beneath my bloodshot eyes, my complexion is positively ghostly, and my breath is ... I lick the inside of my wrist and sniff it. Gross.

I pop into the ensuite and find a travel-sized tube of toothpaste and brush and make quick work of scrubbing my teeth. Just as I'm finishing up, there's a soft knock on the bedroom door. I recap the toothpaste then clamber toward the door, swinging it open with a whoosh, and come face to chest with a wall of black ink and muscles.

My life would be a boatload easier if he were covered in boils and smelled like an armpit. But instead, he's a freaking skyscraper, reeks of masculinity and something else that makes my mouth water, and looks like he just crawled out of a wet dream.

"Thought I'd come check on you," Joel says, all deep and gravelly like he also just woke up.

I smooth my oversized tee down my body and poise myself. "I'm fine." Really, I'm not fine at all. My nerves are completely shot, I'm exhausted, and planes make me supremely anxious. Plus, I'm not in the mood for small talk with a man I'd thoroughly enjoy poisoning with paint thinner.

He shoulders past me and steps into the room, pausing when his eyes snag on the rumpled bedding. Clearing his throat, he turns to face me and asks through clenched teeth, "Sleep well?"

"I slept fine. Now, do you mind?" I motion for him to leave.

Of course, he doesn't.

Instead, he closes the space between us and stares down at me with those icy blue eyes. I sway forward, as if some magnetic force is pulling me toward him, but manage to correct my posture before I topple over.

"We're landing shortly," he says, his warm, minty breath tickling the top of my head. "Come up front and buckle in. Pilot's orders. Not mine."

He snatches my sneakers off the floor, then ushers me out to the seating area where Martina, Zak, and Liam all turn their attention to me. I pad barefoot down the carpeted aisle, smiling politely at the guys, but both sets of eyes move to the brooding man behind me, then they look away.

The back of my head tingles with irritation when I put two and two together. Joel ordered them to stay away from me—to not socialize with "the job."

Controlling jerk.

I take a seat near the front of the plane. Joel plunks down across from me, his long, muscular legs stretched out, eating up most of the space between our seats.

When the plane begins its descent, I dig my fingers into the smooth leather armrests on either side of me and close my eyes, breathing in through my nose and out through my mouth.

"Not a fan of landing?"

I pop an eyelid and find Joel staring at me, his expression blank.

"Not even a little."

"Try grounding yourself," he tells me, as if I have any clue what that means.

I inhale another shaky breath and hold it. "We're hurdling toward earth in a giant tube. We'll be grounded shortly. One way or another." *Exhale.*

"You have five senses," he explains calmly, but my brain has decided to take a last-minute vacation and I can no longer think straight. "Open your eyes, Stella." I squeeze my eyes shut harder and hold my breath when the plane jostles. "It's just a little turbulence. Completely normal." Then I hear some rustling, the click of a seatbelt, and suddenly there's the warmth of a body beside me. I pry one eye open and peek over at Joel.

"Open your eyes." His voice is softer now, more compelling. I do as I'm told, sucking in a short gulp of air as my lungs gasp for oxygen. "Look around. Find five objects you can see."

I want to tell him to fuck off—that it's pointless. That the only way to get through this is to just suck it up and deal. But I can't get the words out. I give in and search my surroundings, locating five random objects and nodding when I've completed the first task. "Four objects you can touch." My eyes roam the cabin as he continues on. "Three you can hear. Two you can smell. And one you can taste."

Somehow, parts of Joel land in every single one of those categories. I can *see* his forearms flexing beside me. I could reach up and *touch* the hard planes of his chest. I can *hear* his deep, growly voice. I *smell* his fresh, woodsy scent. And I could *taste* his ...

Oh my god, stop it!

I mentally smack my screaming ovaries and my breathing returns to a somewhat normal rate. My fingers loosen their grip on the armrests at my sides, and my shoulders drop from my ears and relax against the buttery-soft leather.

Joel leans in toward me, his arm brushing with mine, and whispers, "You good?"

I close my eyes again and nod. "Where'd you learn that?" I hear him shift in his seat again, but I keep my eyes pinched shut for fear of going back to that place.

"The Navy."

His response catches me off guard. Peeking up at him, I say, "I didn't know you were in the Navy."

He tips his chin toward Liam and Zak. "All three of us were SEALs. Been together for years."

I glance over at his colleagues. Liam's deep in thought and fiddling with his knife again. He's big and burly and has a jagged scar slashed through one eyebrow that makes him completely unapproachable. But when nobody's looking, he seems ... I don't know. Haunted, perhaps. And then there's Zak. He's polite, well-mannered, but no less intimidating. There's something dark that hides behind his gentlemanly exterior. In fact, there's darkness in all of these guys. They just each have their own unique way of hiding it.

It makes sense now that they'd be SEALs. They're all well over six feet tall, Joel being the tallest by an inch or so. And they're in crazy good shape. I'd have better luck trying to shove a mountain out of my way than any of them.

"And now you do private security."

Joel shakes his head. "I wouldn't call it private security. This job is ... not our typical line of work."

Turning in my seat, I ask, "So, what kind of jobs does Sweetwater Security normally do?"

"Jobs the military can't," he responds vaguely, and now I'm even more curious.

"And what kind of jobs are those?"

My heart begins to hammer when Joel leans in, his lips so close to my ear I can almost imagine what it would feel like if he pressed them to my neck. "If I told you, I'd have to kill you," he whispers, inhaling through his nose then pressing back into his seat again.

My eyes widen at the dark undertone of his voice and a shiver rolls down my spine, but there's a smirk on his face, and I know he's screwing with me. But then a curtain of indifference closes over his expression again and I'm left with more questions than answers.

Challenging him, I ask, "So, you guys take down super villains or something?"

A muscle in his jaw slides and his eyes darken. I think he wants to tell me more, but instead, he states with zero emotion, "Or something."

Seven

Stella

W E LAND IN ITALY, and my nose is pressed to the passenger window the entire half-hour drive from the airport to the hotel. Joel remained deadly silent the whole time, weaving the rented SUV in and out of traffic, transporting us quickly and efficiently to our destination with Martina, Zak, and Liam following closely behind in another vehicle.

We roll up to the hotel, an old stone building with intricate Roman design and meticulously manicured flowerbeds surrounding the perimeter of the property. The walkway is clean enough to eat off. The hotel staff are polished to perfection.

I sling my hair up into a high ponytail and secure it with the elastic around my wrist, then peek down at my outfit, regretting choosing comfort over style for the trip here.

Joel hops out, grabs a cart and wheels it to the back of the SUV. I find a spot on the sidewalk and twiddle my thumbs as he tosses giant bags of luggage around like they weigh nothing at all. He pauses when he catches me ogling his arms, then winks playfully, and I wonder if maybe there's more to him than a bad attitude and bossy demeanor after all.

I roll my eyes and stare off into the distance at a young couple canoodling on a bench facing a lily pad-covered pond. There's a rock on the woman's left hand that could double as a paper weight.

A pang of jealousy hits me square in the gut, and I force myself to look away. I'll never have that. Not because I don't want it, but because men are unreliable, and I have some deeply rooted trust issues that stem far beyond the scope of what any therapist's fancy credentials could handle.

A clean-cut man in a snug burgundy suit greets us outside and offers to take our luggage up to our rooms. Joel slips a hefty tip into the man's hand and thanks him. The man ushers away with our belongings, a wide smile on his face and his pockets lined with Joel's money.

We check in at the front desk, the entire process going perfectly smooth, and take an ancient elevator all the way to the top of the building to a suite far too large for any one person.

I flop down on my back on the soft, pillow top mattress while Joel inspects the rest of the suite. I stare up at the popcorn-textured ceiling and roll the smooth fabric of the cotton duvet between my fingers. I'm so tired, pretty soon I'll need toothpicks to prop my eyelids open.

A few moments later, Joel storms in and drops my luggage onto the bed beside me. I steal a peek at the beat-up, canary-yellow suitcase. *Old Beatrice.* That's the name I gave her one evening when Harper and I had too much wine during one of our weekly girl's nights. All her edges are scratched and scraped, the paint of the hard exterior flaking off, exposing her dull gray shell. The *show me your boo-bies* sticker I picked up at a Halloween party is beginning to peel back. I've had Bea since I was a foster kid. She was a hand-me-down that I've never been able to part with because most kids get nothing more than plastic bags to tote their belongings around in, and she made me feel special.

And now, she's the only piece of my past I hold on to.

"The lawyer's landing shortly. He'll be coming by to brief you on the itinerary."

I prop myself up on my elbows and glance over at Joel. "Where are you staying?"

"Across the hall." Judging by the way his fists are balled, I'd say he's not too excited about that.

"And everyone else?"

"Zak's a few doors down. Martina's one floor below us. Liam's staying in a room across from her. You go nowhere without me. Do you understand?"

I roll my eyes. "Yes, master."

Joel's giant strides come fast and unexpected as he closes the space between us. Panic rips through me when he grips my upper arm with his huge hand and pulls me to my feet in front of him. I let out a yelp and lose my balance, toppling forward. My palms slam into his hard chest, then begin sweating profusely as a whole mess of sickening memories flood my system.

I struggle against his grip, but he doesn't release me.

Dipping his face to mine, he snarls, "Drop the attitude, princess, or I'll gladly crawl into that bed beside you for the next three nights. If you decide to challenge me on that, then be my guest. But I have a job to do, and although you may not like it, this is how it's going to be. Got it?" He gives my arm a firm squeeze before shoving me away.

I stumble backward, the backs of my knees bumping against the foot of the bed as wet heat pools in my panties. *Stupid, treacherous vagina.*

My mouth parts, then snaps shut as I stare up at him. I rub my arm where he had gripped me and scowl. He didn't actually hurt me, but there's a burning sensation where his rough hand made contact with my skin and I have no idea why I enjoy it.

The air around us crackles with tension. Joel rakes his eyes over my body, devouring every inch of me as he licks his lips. His heated gaze leaves a searing path of desire from head to toe. His threat to sleep in bed with me feels more like a menacing promise than anything else, but that would be asking for a disaster. Like playing on train tracks.

I nod frantically, agreeing to play by his rules. *Without attitude.*

He looks me over once more, gives me a curt nod, then turns to leave, pausing with his hand on the doorknob.

"Dinner's at seven. Be ready," he orders, not bothering to look back at me, then slams the door behind him.

As promised, Carlo stops by my room and briefs me on the itinerary for the next couple days, and, in a much more polite manner than Joel, instructs me to get ready for dinner.

I stand in front of the closet, scouring the vast selection of cocktail dresses, pantsuits, and casual attire that's been pre-purchased for me. I run a finger down an emerald-green, satin dress with a plunging neckline and high slit up one thigh. It's far too racy for a formal dinner with the group of Giulia's business associates that are handling Riva Jeweller's affairs now that she's no longer around to run the show. And it would no doubt attract undue attention, which is exactly the opposite of what I prefer to do.

I move onto the simple dress beside it: knee length, charcoal grey, high neckline. Much more appropriate.

But for reasons unknown, I reach in and pluck out the green dress, just because I'm feeling ballsy. I apply more makeup than usual, giving myself a dark, smoky eye, and slick on a crimson red lipstick. I tie my hair into a low, romantic bun at the nape of my neck, releasing a few loose tendrils to frame my face. Lastly, I finish the outfit with a pair of black, strappy heels and the gold bracelet Giulia left me.

I study myself in the mirror, not recognizing the woman I'm staring back at. I'm no longer a sad little girl trying to survive one day at a time. I made sure she disappeared, never to be found, never to be thought of again. But if she were here with me, I think she'd be proud of how far we've come.

I lift my chin and smooth my hands down my hips. Even though that girl is gone, her memory lives on. I'll never forget who I was, or where I came from.

A small *click* snatches me from my thoughts. I snap my head toward the door and watch in horror as the handle turns and the door cracks open. My heart lodges into my throat and I take a few steps back, nearly rolling an ankle in my skyscraper heels. My blood turns ice cold and I'm back in that place again, back to that awful, horrible day where I condemned myself to hell for all eternity. Once again, I'm a scared, little child with nobody to protect me.

"Stella." A familiar male voice floats through the room as Zak appears from behind the door. He angles his head at me, concern etched across his face. "Sorry if I startled you. Joel sent me." He waves a key card in front of him.

I blow out a held breath, relaxing only slightly, then hold a palm in the air. "Hang on. You guys have a key?" I screech. "To my room?"

Zak stuffs his hands into his pockets and shrugs. "Thought you knew that."

"No. I didn't," I respond dryly. It's only once my heartbeat returns to normal that my eyes roam over Zak. He's dressed smartly in a black suit and black dress shirt that's tailored perfectly to his giant body. He's exceptionally good looking and in incredible shape. But most importantly, he's not a giant asshole like Joel.

Surprisingly, I'm not at all attracted to him.

Zak stares at me with a puzzled look on his face.

Finally, he breaks the silence. "Are you ready?" His glances down at my dress then chuckles. "That's a stupid question. You look ..." he pauses, and I think he's going to compliment me, but he finishes with, "like trouble."

My shoulders slump and I peek down at the green satin that hugs my body. I admit, it's a little much, but when in Rome and all that crap ...

Zak scrubs the back of his head with his hand, and his eyebrows nearly reach his hairline. "You sure that's what you want to wear? I mean ..."

"Yes, I'm sure," I snap. "Why?"

He shakes his head. "No reason."

He offers me his arm, and I slip mine through his and let him guide me out of the room and toward the elevators. Somewhere along the way, he mutters, "Can't wait to see Stone's reaction."

I peek up at him and realize he's wearing a grin like he just won a high-stake bet.

At the mention of Joel, I say, "Joel said you guys are Navy SEALs."

Zak pushes the elevator call button and peers down at me with warm brown eyes. "He told you that, huh?" I nod. "Interesting."

"Why is that interesting?"

He thinks for a moment, and I begin to wonder if he's covering for Joel. Protecting him from something. "Joel's not much of a sharer."

"No kidding," I snort. "But he sure likes to dig around in other people's business."

Zak frowns. "It comes with the job."

"What else comes with the job?" I probe.

Zak considers this for a moment, and now I know for certain he's watching out for his friend. He ushers me into the elevator, then once the doors slide shut, he asks, "Ever hear of PTSD?"

My shoulders sag. Something in my chest cracks. I know first hand exactly what PTSD is and all the horrible side effects that come with it. The nightmares. The paranoia. The hallucinations. Some of them last for years, others a lifetime. Nodding, I wait anxiously for Zak to continue.

"We've all been through it, but Joel's was the worst. He's good now, I think, but he carries a lot of guilt around with him. Doesn't like talking about it, but he's changed. Soldiers often go in as one person and come out another."

I hold my breath and steel my spine, unsure how to react to this. Joel's solid, sturdy, and always in control. To hear that he struggled with PTSD, that he carries guilt around like a big, dark thundercloud, gives me pause.

"He won't admit it, but he's afraid of losing the people he cares about."

I speak around the lump in my throat. "So he pushes them away instead."

Zak nods. "It's not unusual. None of us keep women around long enough to fall in love, and kids are pretty much out of the question. We've seen too much of the world we live in. Hard to fathom bringing innocent life into it."

Although I don't truly know what Joel's been through, I share some of those values. So why does it feel like someone just plunged a steak knife into my heart?

"But that doesn't mean we don't yearn for those things," he adds suggestively, optimistically, as if to hint for me to read between the lines.

The doors slide open, effectively ending our conversation, and Zak and I are greeted by a bubbly hostess who looks like she should be on a catwalk and not seating people in a restaurant. Her smooth, olive skin glows under the dim lighting of the crystal chandeliers hanging high above us. Her ebony hair is pulled back in a sleek ponytail, not a single strand out of place. Her long, lean legs go on for days and days.

She ogles Zak, not caring that there's a whole-ass woman attached to his arm. Her ignorance would normally annoy me, but I have zero interest in Zak, so I'm otherwise unfazed. She turns on her heel and leads us through the restaurant and into a private dining room where Martina is fussing over the placement of the plates and utensils.

"Stella!" She claps her hands together and hastily makes her way toward me, ripping me away from Zak and wrapping me in her usual death hug. "You are beautiful."

"Thank you." I peek around the empty room. "Where is everybody?"

"They'll be along shortly." She turns to Zak and pats his chest. "You clean up well, Mr. Shephard."

Zak leans down and kisses Martina on the cheek. "You look gorgeous, Martina. As always."

Martina flushes and begins fanning her face. "Oh, these hot flashes," she chirps. Side-eyeing me, she whispers, "It's the change, dear. Just you wait."

Suuure, it is. Martina's well past the typical age of menopause, so I know her overheating has nothing to do with hormones and everything to do with the handsome SEAL who just complimented her and kissed her on the cheek.

Smirking, Zak straightens to his full height and steps away from us. An unexpected wave of heat engulfs me as all the oxygen in the room vanishes. A bead of sweat forms on my lower back as Martina's gaze falls over my shoulder. Every muscle in my body stiffens as an overwhelming presence approaches from behind, like a lion creeping up on his prey. It's the same feeling I got when Joel first approached me from behind on the street.

I steel my spine and turn to face the predator. My mouth fills with saliva. My heart leaps from my body and takes off running. I swallow hard and drink in the six-foot-whatever Navy SEAL walking confidently toward me, the hostess hot on his heels. Tailored black slacks, a brown leather belt, a crisp, white dress shirt with the sleeves casually rolled up his strong, tattooed forearms.

Our eyes clash, and wet heat pools between my legs. Those icy blues deepen in color with each step Joel takes toward me and I wither like a sad, little flower. His frigid gaze wanders over my body and his tongue flicks out, wetting his lips. It's such a small move, but it screams a thousand vicious words. He stops in front of me and his masculine scent invades my senses, hijacking what little confidence I had left, robbing my lungs of the last of the oxygen I managed to suck in.

Somewhere off in the distance I hear Martina babbling, but it's all muffled behind the sound of the blood rushing through my head. The pressure in my chest is so unforgiving, I feel like I'm pinned beneath a train car. My knees buckle and a million dirty thoughts fly through my mind at breakneck speeds. But the one that sticks ...

I want him, and I can't have him.

Eight

Joel

I HEAR THE HOSTESS behind me, her heels clacking on the floor as she takes quick strides to keep up with me, but I lose her somewhere along my journey through the restaurant. Everything around me blurs like tunnel vision the second I see Stella standing in that dining room. Thick, dark hair I want to wrap around my wrist. Blood-red lips I want to sink my teeth into. Smooth, dangerous curves wrapped up in emerald satin the same color as the flecks of green in her irises.

With every ounce of my pathetic being, I refrain from dragging her back to my room, tying her to my bed, ripping that dress to shreds, and fucking her brains out.

I want to tell her she looks beautiful, that she's the most incredible thing I've ever laid my eyes on. But the only words I can garble out are, "Nice choice, princess. Choose that dress for me?"

Her daring red lips part, and she responds hoarsely, "Haven't given you so much as a thought since you left my room."

I snatch her wrist, gentle this time, and tug her closer to me, her breath hitching as her body lurches forward. "Such a terrible liar," I growl, then release her.

Someone clears their throat and my attention whips to the man approaching us.

"Ah, Stella. You are gorgeous, as always." It's the lawyer, Carlo Marchetti. He steps in front of me and takes Stella into his arms, planting a kiss on either cheek. The lawyer turns to me and offers his hand. "Mr. Stone. So nice to see you again." I accept his handshake just as a thin brunette with fake tits suctions herself to Carlo's side. He introduces her as his wife, Andrea.

Liam strolls in a few moments later, ignoring everyone and stuffing himself into a seat at the dining table like the ray of fucking sunshine he is.

Other guests filter in and Martina and the lawyer introduce them to Stella. They're all Italian and oozing of wealth, much like Giulia did. Sweetwater performed background checks on all of them, so I know they're all clean citizens.

After the introductions, I pull out a chair for Stella. She eyes me suspiciously but accepts, and I settle in beside her. She only speaks when spoken to, keeping her responses short and concise, and I can see it smeared all over her face—she's completely out of her element. Her posture is stiff, her eyes are darting from one corner of the table to the next, and there's a pinkish hue to her cheeks that tells me her blood pump is working overtime.

But all I can think about is that fucking dress and those red lips. I know for a fact she wouldn't normally wear something so flashy. In all the photos in her file, she's wearing varying shades of gray, never one to seek out attention. But now ... Now she wants to play a dirty little game of temptation and I'll leave her no choice but to melt beneath the heat of the fire she's lighting inside me.

The entire table is encapsulated by something the lawyer is droning on about and I take the opportunity to peer down at Stella. Her dress has inched up her thighs, the high slit exposing tan, supple skin that's begging to be ravished.

I take a swig of whiskey and set my glass down on the clothed table, then drop my hand, brushing it along her silky-smooth thigh. She stiffens, swats my hand away, and tugs the hem of her dress down.

Her reaction causes a sick thrill to move through me. I skim the back of my knuckles over her leg again, and a flurry of goosebumps erupt beneath my touch.

Edging my hand higher, I pause at the top of the slit. I lean into her and whisper, "Tell me to stop."

The pulse in her neck jumps and her cheeks flush pink. She grabs her glass of wine and takes a greedy sip, then sets it back down without so much as a glance in my direction.

Somewhere in the background, the lawyer cracks a joke that I'm sure isn't funny and the table levitates into soft laughter. But not Stella. She sits stiffly beside me, her chest rising and falling in short, panicky breaths. She stares straight ahead, her eyes round and unblinking. I reach for an ice cube in the bucket next to me and slip it beneath the table. She sucks in a sharp breath when I press the ice to her bare thigh.

When she doesn't push my hand away, I draw a line upward, nudging her dress out of the way. A trickle of water beads over the curve of her thigh, then plops onto the carpet beneath.

I pause just before reaching her panty line, then sweep slowly back down toward her knee. She grips the edge of her seat beside her hips and parts her thighs. I quirk a brow at her, but she doesn't budge.

When I drag the cube between her thighs, I expect to find a thin layer of fabric separating my hand from her pussy. But I don't. My fingers meet nothing but smooth, hot flesh.

Bad girl.

I guide the ice between her pussy lips and press it directly onto her clit. A shiver wracks her body and her bottom lip trembles from the cold invasion.

She clutches my wrist, her fingernails biting into my skin, but she doesn't pull my hand away. I draw slow, rhythmic circles over her clit, and my dick is pressing painfully against the zipper of my slacks. I glance around the table, checking for any curious onlookers, and stop dead when I come to a set of wide, brown eyes darting between Stella's flushed face and mine.

Andrea.

Heat rises in her face as she stares back at me, and I know she's fully aware of what's going on beneath the table. I curl my lips into a cynical smile and wink at her. She clears her throat and fidgets awkwardly with her silverware, then forces her attention back to her husband, plastering on a fake smile as if she's been paying attention to him this entire time.

Focusing back on the task at hand, I study the hot little mess beside me as I push what's left of the ice cube inside of her. She sucks in a sharp breath and her muscles contract around my finger. I withdraw and smear her juices around her clit, massaging her most sensitive spot while cold water seeps from her.

Her entire body shudders and I lean toward her and growl, "Don't you dare come."

Her eyes flutter shut and she holds her breath, willing away the orgasm building inside her. She's fucking beautiful like this. Desperate and needy and completely at my mercy.

"Are you okay, dear?" Martina asks from down the length of the table, concern flashing behind her gray eyes.

I retreat and watch in amusement as Stella's lids fly open and she searches frantically around the table. All eyes are on her now, and she's barely keeping it together.

She clears her throat and shifts in her seat. "Yes ... uh, sorry. Just a little tired." She tugs her dress back down her thighs and pinches her knees together.

Martina scowls at me and I lift my glass to her in cheers.

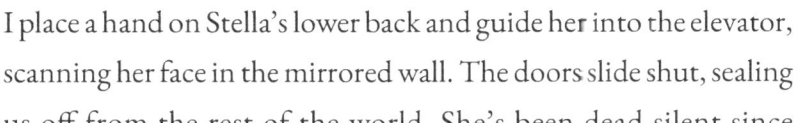

I place a hand on Stella's lower back and guide her into the elevator, scanning her face in the mirrored wall. The doors slide shut, sealing us off from the rest of the world. She's been dead silent since

Martina nearly caught us red-handed at the dining table, and her bottom lip has taken a brutal beating from her gnawing on it.

"You look beautiful," I offer, but she doesn't acknowledge it. "You can ignore me all you want, princess, but I'm not going anywhere."

She glares at the rolling number above the doors. "I'm not ignoring you. And eventually, yes, you will be going somewhere."

"Does that disappoint you?"

She turns toward me and narrows her eyes. "Not at all. In fact, it would be great if you'd go somewhere sooner rather than later. Hell, perhaps." She sweeps a tendril of hair away from her face. "I think you'd fit right in there."

I close the space between us and crowd her against the wall. She squeezes her eyes shut and presses her palms to my chest. Caging her in, I dip my face to hers, so close the tips of our noses brush.

"Joel." It's the faintest, cracked whisper, and fuck my name sounds good spilling from her lips.

I press my body against hers and let her warmth penetrate me. I've been sporting a hard-on all evening, and I want her to feel exactly what she does to me. Her soft, luscious body molds perfectly to my hard, rigid one, as if she were designed specifically for me.

"Open your eyes, Stella." Her lids pop open, her irises lit with flecks of gold and green in the dim lighting of the elevator. "Good girl." She winces when I reach down and pull her plump bottom lip from between her teeth with my thumb. "Are you afraid of me?"

She stares up at me with wide doe eyes, her fiery spirit doused with a cold bucket of unease.

"I ... I don't trust you," she responds honestly.

It's a punch to the gut. Something unfurls inside of me. Something dark and primitive and unfamiliar.

"Why?" I ask as my need to understand Stella takes root, creeping into the crevices of my blackened soul like a bad weed.

Her eyes drift shut again, her long lashes fanning out across her cheeks. I slide my hand gently down the slender column of her throat, stopping at her collarbone. Every muscle in her body tenses and a small whimper escapes her. Her core temperature rises with each second that ticks on as I hold her still in front of me.

"Why don't you trust me?" I repeat the question. I'm not a patient man, and I fucking hate repeating myself, but for Stella ...

"Because ..." she states, as if that's any sort of explanation.

When it comes to physical touch, there's usually a reason why a woman doesn't trust, why she flinches at the slightest contact. It would be a waste of breath to tell her that we're not all the same. She's likely heard that a thousand times in her life. Instead, I tell her, "You have no reason to fear me. I'll never hurt you."

She blinks up at me and slowly shakes her head. Time stands still as electricity charges the air between us, each painful zap a cruel reminder that I'm mere inches from something I want but can't have.

Our lips are so close, I can almost taste the sultry tannins of the wine she had at dinner. I could hike up her dress right now, wrap her shapely legs around my hips, and sink my dick into her. I could slam her against the wall and fuck her until she sees stars. Until she forgets all about whoever's to blame for her constant unease.

But *I fucking can't*. Because she's saying no.

I take a step back and catch a glimpse of myself in the mirror. My hair is disheveled, my dress shirt is rumpled, and my eyes are so dark, I barely recognize myself.

I've never looked so goddamn miserable in my entire life.

The elevator dings and the doors slide open behind me. Stella pushes off the wall and bolts past me. I stalk closely behind her as she paces down the hall, her heels sinking silently into the plush carpet.

I snatch her key card before she has a chance to unlock her door and force myself in front of her. She yelps when I grab her by the hand and tug her along behind me as I clear every room in her suite. Liam has already done this, and Zak has surveillance up and running, but I won't be satisfied that she's alone until I've seen it for myself.

When I'm done clearing the room, I release Stella's hand and she backs away from me like you would a snarling dog. But it feels like a giant rubber band is wrapped around my torso and is tugging me toward her. I pull against the restraint and storm past her, needing to get the hell out of here before I do something stupid. I reach for the doorknob and refrain from glancing back at her, because I think if I see the look on her face, that rubber band will tighten and I won't be able to resist any longer.

"You know the rules. My number is programmed into your phone. If you decide to leave your room, call me first."

Nine

Joel

WITH NOTHING BETTER TO do, I decide to review Stella's file again. She's a mysterious little thing. And some of her choices have been more than just a little ... *questionable*. In fact, her file is layer upon layer of red flags.

Besides, I need the distraction, even if it does revolve around the very woman who's responsible for my twitchy behavior and gut rot.

I lock myself in my room, pour myself a stiff drink, and dive into to the encrypted file Mac sent each of us in case we needed to reference it.

Unconventionally, I begin from the most recent intel and read backward, even though I know nothing would have changed since the last time I reviewed it.

Stella Clarke worked three jobs in college. She landed a decent job at a big Detroit firm after graduation and built a comfortable life for herself. Scrolling back further, I skim past some of the lackluster details and focus on the photos from the private investigator that Giulia hired.

The images depict somewhat of a story of her everyday life. Each picture a tiny fragment of a much larger one. A vivid collage of the constant anxiety lying like bedrock beneath her calm, albeit mouthy, surface. In nearly every photo, she's looking over her shoulder.

A shot from three years ago catches my attention. Stella sits at a table at an outdoor restaurant with Harper seated across from her. I zoom in on the screen, squinting my eyes to bring it into focus.

But it's not the girls I'm looking at. It's the man seated a few tables away.

I shake it off and move on to another photo from nearly a decade ago, but am stopped in my tracks when I spot a younger version of that same man across the street at a magazine stand. He's wearing sunglasses, so I can't see his eyes, but there's no doubt in my mind it's him. Stella's once again peering over her shoulder as she walks down the sidewalk.

It could be a coincidence, but it's highly unlikely. I send the photos to Zak and Liam in case the mystery man decides to make another appearance, and send an email to Sloane to get an ID on the guy. Then I grind my teeth and dial Mac.

"She has a stalker," I inform him immediately, now pacing the room.

"What the hell are you talking about, Stone?" Mac grumbles.

"I sent the details to Sloane for an ID, but he's in two separate photos seven years apart."

"You're certain."

"Yes. Without a doubt."

"How the hell did a hired PI miss that?" Mac asks gruffly, taking the words right out of my mouth.

We go back and forth, exchanging ideas, until finally coming to a decision. I snatch my laptop up, grab my bag off the bed, and storm out of my room.

No way in hell is Stella being left alone now that I know someone's been watching her. I knock twice, pull my spare key card from my pocket, and let myself into her room.

I drop my bags on the bench at the door and call out for her, but am met with only silence. I move through the suite, checking the bedroom last. I hear a shower running and glance at the cracked bathroom door of the ensuite, steam billowing out from around it.

Then I spot Stella's wallet laying open on the table beside her bed and saunter over to it, plucking out her driver's license.

Stella A. Clarke.

Her birthday indicates she's twenty-nine—four years younger than me. Nobody's passport or driver's license photos look good, but Stella's do. She's irritatingly beautiful all the time. I stuff her card back in her wallet and retrieve my laptop. I have to be missing something. There's a brief mention of her biological father, but we already know he's dead. It's been confirmed. And Giulia didn't have any other children, so it's not a brother.

I hear the shower turn off and I make quick work of closing down her file and tucking my laptop away. My eyes shoot to the door when Stella walks out, her body wrapped up in a plush, white hotel towel, barely concealing the parts of her I'm itching to get my hands on. She sees me sitting on the edge of her bed and nearly jumps out of her skin.

Clutching the towel at her chest, she screeches, "What the hell are you doing in here?"

I stand and stalk toward her. Without a trace of makeup on, she's even more gorgeous. She takes a giant step back in an attempt to keep some distance between us, but I'm not having it. I crowd her against the wall so she has nowhere to run. Staring down at her, I allow myself to suck in a lung full of her sweet scent, and gently twist a lock of her wet hair between my thumb and index finger, feeling the silky smoothness of it between my fingertips.

"It appears I'll be staying here after all," I tell her.

Batting my hand away, she shakes her head in refusal. "Absolutely not."

It's cute that she thinks she has a say. "Unfortunately for you, a few things have come up and plans have changed."

Part of me wonders if she already knows she has a stalker. She's always on edge, and constantly watching her six. And her file indicates she hightailed it out of Clapton when she turned eighteen. She ran, but from what?

"You've got to be kidding me," she half laughs. Her eyes dart to the single king-sized bed in the room then back to me. "There's no way you're sleeping in here."

Smirking, I promise, "I'll take the couch, princess. No need to get your panties in a wad." Her scowl only deepens and two little lines form between her pinched brows. "Not that you're wearing any."

She huffs and shoves past me, snatching my laptop bag off the bed and shoving it into my chest. "Get out."

I toss my bag back onto the bed and stand to my full height in front of her. "No."

Sour as a pickle, she accepts defeat and marches back into the bathroom, slamming the door and locking it.

Sighing, I decide to make myself comfortable on the sofa in her bedroom, not the living room, while Stella licks her wounds. When she finally reappears, she's dressed in skimpy cotton sleep shorts and a baggy T-shirt. She's not wearing a bra, and her nipples are poking through the thin fabric of her shirt. I bite back a groan and adjust myself in my jeans, thinking about how badly I want to suck those sweet little peaks into my mouth while she arches beneath me, begging for me to let her come.

Stella tucks herself under the blankets, shielding her body from my view, then reaches up and flips the bedside lamp off so the room is cast in total darkness with only the sounds of the air-conditioning and our breathing filling the empty silence.

I spend most of the night with my ears open and my brain reeling.

Ten

Stella

TODAY HAS FELT LIKE a long, endless drive down a desolate highway. The kind of drive where you zone out for a while, then when you finally snap back to reality, you're not sure how you got where you are, or if you blew through some red lights along the way.

I'm officially on autopilot, cruising mindlessly through hours of insincere condolences and *sorry for your losses*. And the day's not even half over.

I watch as onlookers' judgy eyes scan over me, silently appraising me like a piece of furniture. I hear the oohs and aahs when a stranger whispers to another that I'm Giulia Riva's daughter. I guess Giulia kept it quiet that she'd abandoned her child at birth—a scandalous secret like that would have no doubt made headlines.

I excuse myself from Carlo and Martina's sides and head to the ladies' room, wondering if anyone would even miss me if I were gone. I lock the bathroom door behind me and stand in front of the sink, staring emotionlessly back at the woman in the mirror.

I know Zak or Liam will be loitering outside the door like hawks circling roadkill, but they've been otherwise discrete since we stepped foot into the funeral home early this morning. I haven't seen Joel since this morning and I'm not sure if I'm grateful for that or not, because it's come to my attention that his overbearing presence has somehow morphed into a source of comfort. Frustrating comfort, but comfort nonetheless.

I press the heels of my palms into my eye sockets. I'm convinced if I don't get some normalcy soon, I'll fall off the cliff of insanity and be plunged into utter chaos for the rest of eternity. Swirling and swirling in a never-ending whirlpool of ...

Get it together, Clarke!

I need to get back to Detroit. To go back to a normal, boring life with normal, boring people and have normal, boring people problems, like what to make for dinner, or which shoes match my handbag.

But according to Carlo, all of that will be pretty much impossible. You see, it was Giulia's wishes that I not liquidate any of her properties. Yes, properties, *plural.* Giulia added a fun little clause in her will stipulating that I must remain the sole owner of said properties until the day I die, in which time they will be left to my children.

Ha! Joke's on her. There will be no children. I don't have a maternal bone in my body. And I don't want her stupid properties or useless possessions. I'll just refuse them. Simple as that. And if for some dumb reason I can't ... well, I've concocted a plan. Just because she requires me to hold on to the properties doesn't mean I need to *live* in any of them. I could rent them out. Or just let them sit and rot like she left me. After all, karma's a bitch.

A knock on the door jostles me from my train of thought.

"Just a minute," I call out as the doorknob jiggles.

I quickly wash my hands, then pounce for the door as the person on the other side continues to test the handle. When I swing the door open with a *whoosh*, my heart lodges itself into my throat. On the other side stands a stone-cold Navy SEAL looking just as grumpy as he always does. His eyes rake over me, and I feel that familiar tug low in my belly that indicates my uterus is running the show now.

"There's someone here to see you," Joel says with a similar amount of emotion as a sheet of drywall, then turns to walk away.

There's a slight flutter in my chest as I step out of the restroom and trail closely behind him as he navigates a clear path through the crowd of people. It's like watching Moses part the freaking Red Sea. And the women ... dear Lord, ladies, get it together. Pretty soon I'll be able to swim in the puddles of drool and other bodily fluids accumulating on the floor as every woman takes notice of the sexy, brooding man at my side.

He must be used to the attention, because I don't see him so much as glance in another woman's direction. Joel stops abruptly and nods toward the main entrance. My eyes follow his line of sight to a leggy blonde in a deep purple dress that looks like it was sewn directly onto her body.

"Harper!" I squeal in excitement and rush over to my best friend and wrap my arms around her. Her pretty floral perfume fills my nose and I'm overcome with a sudden wave of homesickness. God, I've missed her. "I can't believe you're here." I fight to enforce rule number two, but my emotions are a slippery slope these days.

"Of course, I am. I couldn't let you do this alone," she chirps, her giant blue eyes welling with tears.

Harper pulls back and holds me at arm's length, assessing me for any damage. But then her gaze shifts over my shoulder, and I know exactly what she's about to say before she even opens her mouth.

"Who's the hottie?" I peek over my shoulder and find Joel standing beside Martina, his hands stuffed casually in his pockets, his heated gaze scorching my backside.

Sighing, I respond regretfully, "Security."

Harper smiles all sweet and innocent and waggles her fingers at Joel. "He's staring at you like he wants to gobble you up."

"It's his job to watch me, Harper."

She quirks a perfectly groomed brow at me. "Uh huh."

Moving on. "Come on. I want you to meet some people." I grab her by the hand and drag her through the crowd and stop in front of Martina and Carlo. I introduce her to each of them, and watch in awe as both fall in love with her the second she opens her mouth.

"And you ..." She spins to face Joel and points a painted fingernail at him. "You better be taking good care of my best friend."

Harper lifts her chin and glares at him. Even in six-inch heels, she's no match for the man.

But Harper's a beautiful, feisty, long-legged freight train. Once she gets rolling, there's no stopping her.

Joel smiles down at her with perfect teeth and sprinkles on all the charm. "Of course," he says politely.

It's the first time I've seen him genuinely smile like that and, holy shit, it's lethal. I avert my eyes, because if I keep staring at him, I think my panties might go up in flames.

"Good," Harper chirps, then one of her ridiculous ideas springs to life. "Because tonight, we're going out."

My attention slams to Joel again and his dazzling smile evaporates before my eyes. "Absolutely not," he counters gruffly, all his prior charm completely gone.

Harper pops a hip, crosses her arms, and angles her head up at him with a smug grin plastered on her pretty face. "We'll see about that."

The gathering after the funeral takes place in a fancy hotel, where a spread of Italian appetizers and drinks are served. Harper sticks by my side for most of the day, but whenever I'm consumed with something dead-mother-related, she disappears into the pool of wealthy, flirtatious Italian men that gravitate toward her like moths to a flame.

Suckers.

I take a seat at the bar and order a glass of wine. The bartender, an attractive young man with warm, brown eyes and dark, wavy hair, sets the glass in front of me.

He flashes me a crooked smile. "You're very beautiful," he says with a thick, sultry Italian accent.

"You're very young," I respond, watching his forearms flex as he uses a dish towel to polish a glass.

"Not *too* young." He waggles his brows and grins.

I can't help but laugh, welcoming the pleasant distraction. He's just a baby, probably barely pushing twenty, but that doesn't mean I can't enjoy the attention. I smile over the top of my glass, then take a sip.

He narrows his eyes at me in observation. "You're Ms. Riva's daughter."

"Biological daughter," I elaborate, then backpedal. "I mean ... I just recently found out that she's ..."

He raises a palm. "You don't need to explain."

I spin my glass on the marble bar top. "How did you know?"

"You're a spitting image." He nods in the direction of the giant, blown-up photo of my dead mother.

My stomach turns sour as resentment spills into my system. "I'm nothing like Giulia."

His expression sobers and he murmurs an apology, then busies himself with another patron. I turn in my seat and search the room for Harper, spotting her hanging off the arm of some poor sap she's suckered into inviting her away for a weekend on his yacht.

I shake my head at my friend's theatrics, then let my eyes roam freely, stalling when they land on Joel. Our eyes lock for a brief second before I spin back around, peeling myself free of his magnetic force.

I clear my throat, recapturing the bartender's attention. "Do you do this full time?"

Don't look back. Don't look back. Don't look back.

"Part time. Putting myself through university." He plants his palms on the bar top and leans toward me.

I reach across the slab of wood between us and offer my hand. "I'm Stella."

He accepts my handshake, placing a gentle kiss just below my wrist. "I'm Stavros. But my friends call me Stavi."

Before I have a chance to respond, Stavi's gaze falls over my shoulder. His eyes round at the corners and he spins away, cutting the conversation off without any explanation. All the tiny hairs on my body rise, screaming at me to run. But something makes me stay. Stupidity, probably. It feels like lately I haven't had two brain cells to rub together.

I turn and glare at the brooding SEAL marching toward me. Within a heartbeat, his long strides have closed the space between us, his presence overwhelming, irritating, and completely unnecessary.

"We were just talking."

"No such thing," he responds, his eyes sliding accusingly to the bartender then back to me.

I slam back the last of my wine and wince when the alcohol burns my throat as it slips down into my stomach. I wipe the excess from my mouth and drop off the barstool, wobbling in my heels. Joel wraps his giant hand around my wrist and keeps me upright. I'm not entirely sure how much I've had to drink today, but I do know I've had very little sleep, and even less food. So I'm feeling the buzz.

I jerk away, my skin tingling where he touched. "I'm fine," I hiss.

"You're not fine. You're being reckless."

An insane person's laugh bubbles from my chest. "Reckless?! Why? Because I was having pleasant conversation with the friendly bartender?"

Joel's lips curl. "Don't play this game with me, princess."

"This isn't a game. This is my life. And *stop calling me 'princess.'*"

"Then stop behaving like one."

I blow out a frustrated breath and straighten my spine. "I need some air." I bolt straight for the nearest exit, nearly rolling an ankle on the way out.

I burst through a set of French doors onto a balcony overlooking a sea of historic buildings and brace myself against the railing and close my eyes.

Inhale. Exhale. Inhale. Exhale.

Gah! It never freaking works!

Eleven

Stella

I GLANCE AROUND AND spot a large rock about the size of a lunch box at the edge of the clearing. I run over to it and drop to my knees, prying my fingertips underneath it and lifting it from its hole. The rough surface burns the pads of my fingers as I struggle to upheave it. Earth worms wriggle in the damp soil beneath it. "Sorry guys," I mutter, and lay the shredded, pink cotton down over them, dropping the rock back in place with a plunk.

I take another look around, spotting the trail of kicked up leaves from where we walked into the forest and I decide it's best to head back toward the highway.

The sound of flowing water breaks through the rustling leaves. I stare down at my filthy, bloody hands. I have to clean myself up first.

I circle the perimeter and spot a tiny creek off in the distance, then race toward it. First, I wash the blood from my hands, then I remove *my shoes and step carefully into the frigid, flowing water. The cold numbs the pain between my legs as I rinse my trembling body.*

I know Harriet will blame herself for this. I know she'll be heartbroken when she finds out the man she loved was evil. A man she's worked alongside for years and years. A man who was supposed to help me. Not hurt me.

So I concoct a story. One that will protect not just myself, but Harriet too.

It has to work. I have to make sure it works.

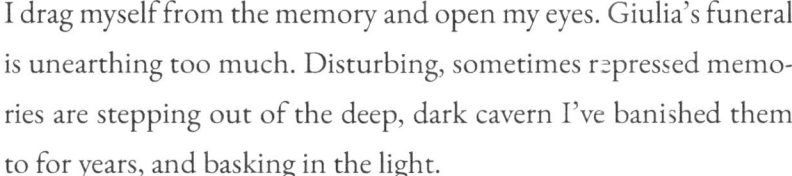

I drag myself from the memory and open my eyes. Giulia's funeral is unearthing too much. Disturbing, sometimes repressed memories are stepping out of the deep, dark cavern I've banished them to for years, and basking in the light.

I'm not sure how long I've been out here, but it's long enough that I've calmed down and reined in my crazy.

Gripping the metal handrail, I stare out at the view beyond the balcony. Between the old, stone buildings, the sun casts shadows into dark alleyways. Vibrant gardens dot the scene, adding just a splash of color to the otherwise gray cityscape. The warm, hazy sky is layered in pink-and-orange hues as the sun settles in for the evening.

Someone clears their throat and I turn to find Joel hovering around the doorway, his lips pressed into a firm line. We stand there, staring at each other, challenging the other to speak first.

When he realizes I'm not going to be the one to break the silence, he says, "Let's go for a walk."

"The only walk I want to do is away from the cliff I push you over." Okay. So maybe I haven't fully reined it in. Joel takes a step forward and I hold a palm in the air. "No, Joel. I really need some space right now."

"What you need is something to eat," he counters.

On cue, my stomach growls. "What I need is for you to vanish from the face of the planet."

A muscle in his jaw ticks. "I'm enjoying this as much as you are, Stella." He takes another step forward.

"Great. So why don't you and your minions pack up and leave. I'll survive without you."

Another step. "Sorry, but I have orders."

He's not going to take a simple no for an answer, so I make an excuse. "Harper's inside. I can't vanish on her."

"I think your friend is just fine."

I glance past Joel and find Harper with her head tipped back laughing. Then I spot Zak in a nearby corner, his eyes dark and hands flexing as he watches over my friend.

Returning my attention to Joel, I ask, "Promise we won't be gone long?"

"If you promise not to stick a fork in my eye at the restaurant."

I snort. "No guarantees."

Joel's lip twitches, then he snatches my hand in his and leads me down a set of stairs at the side of the balcony.

When we hit the cobble sidewalk, I ask, "Where are we going?"

"I know a spot."

Of course he does.

Joel tucks me into his side and guides me down the sidewalk without releasing my hand. We walk in silence, not a single word exchanged the entire ten minutes it takes us to arrive at a cute downtown bistro hidden behind a cascading waterfall of hanging greenery. We're seated at an outdoor patio under the shade of a sun-bleached umbrella. The waiter drops off freshly baked bread and ice water. I stare at the ice cubes floating in my glass, and feel the heat creep into my cheeks as I recall what it felt like when Joel used an ice cube to ...

"You're thinking too hard," Joel says from across the table, his eyes fixed on me over the top of his menu.

I shove the memory away with the rest of my dirty thoughts. "I'm not thinking," I respond, then backpedal, because that sounded dumb. "I mean, too hard." I flush at the word *hard*.

Oh my god, Stella. You might as well just crawl into his lap and lick his face, you horndog!

Joel sets his menu down and pulls his phone from his pocket and frowns at it, then tucks it away again. He searches around us as if expecting to see someone he knows.

"Is something wrong?" I ask, unease suddenly creeping into my bones.

"No," he responds tersely.

How lovely. Another mood swing. "Why'd you bring me here, Joel?"

His eyes cut to mine. "You looked like you needed a break."

"How considerate of you," I say plainly. "But I don't peg you as the type of guy to do things out of the goodness of your heart. So, what's in it for you?"

He leans forward, props his elbows on the table, then responds lowly, "I'm still trying to figure that out myself."

I angle my head and stare at him, surprised by that response. I lick my lips, and his gaze darts to my mouth. His eyes linger there a few seconds too long before he leans back and stretches his long legs out under the table, folding his arms in front of his wide chest. His foot bumps my foot and I jerk it away.

"I've been doing some light reading," he says out of nowhere.

"Am I supposed to be impressed?"

He smirks, then asks thoughtfully, as if to himself, "What are you hiding, Stella Clarke?"

I square my shoulders and face him dead on. Then I lie through my freaking teeth. "Nothing. I'm an open book. If you have questions, just ask. Otherwise, I'll gladly put this conversation to rest. For good."

His eyes narrow into slits as he picks me apart, piece by piece.

"Where'd you grow up?"

I shrug. "All over."

"Ever meet your father?"

Shaking my head, I answer honestly, "No. Apparently he liked to beat on Giulia. When she got pregnant, he began threatening her life and mine. She fled Italy, immigrated to the US, then dumped me at a fire station a few days after I was born. My father died in prison several years later when another inmate stabbed him in the jugular. That's all I know about him, and all I really care to."

A flicker of something lights behind Joel's eyes, but it's quickly snuffed out. He seems satisfied with that response, so he continues on. "Did you know Giulia hired a PI?"

I release a long, drawn-out sigh. "Not until recently. But I know she had me followed for quite some time."

Joel's mouth presses into a firm line. He leans in toward me, crooks a finger. I lean forward, matching his position. There's something lingering on the tip of his tongue. He wants to tell me something, and for a brief second, I think maybe he knows too much.

"Does the name Wyatt Danvers ring a bell?" he asks lowly.

Recoiling and completely stunned, I respond truthfully, "No. Should it?"

Joel leans back again and studies me, obviously trying to dictate whether I'm being honest or not. I am. That name means nothing to me. I can see Joel's decision register on his face. He believes me.

"You're worrying me," I tell him softly.

His brows draw together. "You have every right to be worried. You're being followed."

My heart takes off in my chest. My stomach contents sour. My ears start ringing. It feels like I've been placed in a pressure cooker on high heat. I panic and stand abruptly. My water glass spills over on the table as my chair topples onto the patio stones behind me with a loud clatter. Joel stands and grabs me by the wrist before I have a chance to bolt for the exit.

Correcting my chair, he orders, "Sit." His tone is demanding, harsh. "You and I are going to have a conversation." I stare up at him through blurred vision. My heart's beating so hard, I can feel my pulse in my eyeballs. "Sit down, Stella," he repeats, this time gentler.

I obey, despite every nerve in my body screaming at me to run. Joel leans back in his chair as the waiter comes by and drops our meals off and refills our water. When he disappears, Joel starts talking.

"I read your file," he says carefully, probably expecting me to freak out. I don't. I figured he would have done some research considering he's been probing at me to tell him what I'm running from, what I'm hiding, so this is no surprise to me. I also know he was only asking those questions to gauge whether I'm going to be honest with him or not. He already knew the answers. "The PI Giulia hired happened to capture a few photos of a man named Wyatt Danvers. He popped up in more than one, so we have reason to believe he's been stalking you."

Shaking my head, I desperately try to rack my brain, to comprehend what Joel's telling me right now. "I don't know a Wyatt Danvers."

Joel pulls his phone out and sets it on the table in front of me. I stare down at the screen. It's a picture of a man with sandy-blond hair and striking green eyes. Familiarity nags at my insides. I've seen him somewhere before, but I can't place him.

"I ... He looks familiar, but I don't know him."

Joel flips to another photo. Same man but he's aged a few years, now in his late twenties or early thirties. And I still can't put my finger on where I've seen him before.

When we've established that I'm going to be of no use solving this little mystery, Joel urges me to eat the meal in front of me, but my appetite has waned and I've sobered up entirely.

I've felt like I'm being followed since ... *that day*. Since that awful, horrible day when I was forced to do something that no human being should ever have to do.

And now? I think maybe my demons are coming for me. And something tells me that Wyatt Danvers is one of them.

Twelve

Joel

THE GOOD NEWS IS that Mac has agreed to reach out to the PI Giulia hired. The bad news is Sloane can't locate Danvers. He popped up on a street camera four days ago, but has been off the grid ever since. Which means for now, I'm keeping Stella securely at my side.

She barely ate a bite at the restaurant after I informed her she's being stalked, and for some fucked up reason, that bothers me more than the idea of some creep following her around. It's almost as if I give a shit about her well-being beyond the extent of what's required of me while playing babysitter.

Snatching Stella's hand in mine, I lead her off the patio and onto the street. Every step we take toward the hotel causes my hackles to rise as the instinctive desire to stall overwhelms me. To salvage every stolen moment I have alone with her.

I make a last minute decision to stop and tug her toward me, our bodies colliding as she spins into me. She lets cut a yip as all the air is forced from her lungs on impact. She still instinctively flinches when I touch her, but I've also noticed in the matter of a few short days, she's grown accustom to my abrasive and abrupt physical contact. In fact, I think she enjoys relinquishing control and allowing me to make my advances. I've never been subtle about my desires. And I won't start now. She claims she doesn't trust me, but deep down, I can see she does, and she just doesn't want to admit it. Because admitting it would mean allowing herself to be vulnerable. And that would just be the worst thing in the entire goddamn world for a woman like her.

In her mind, vulnerability equals weakness. And well, that's just not fucking true.

Just one more minute. That's all I need.

I brush a few strands of loose hair off her shoulder, dragging my knuckles across her collarbone and over the swell of her breast. Her body responds instantly as goosebumps pepper her bare arms. Her hazel eyes flare, her irises sparkling with that sinful shade of green I've decided is my new favorite color.

She didn't expect this. Fuck, neither did I. But I can't keep my hands off her. I've never wanted a woman so bad in my entire life. The rest have all been quick fucks—in and out. But with Stella ... it's a mystery. *She's* a mystery. There's something different about her. Something that makes that dark cavern in my chest come to life. And damn if I don't love the feeling.

But I have questions that need answers. And persistence is one of my finest qualities.

"I don't want to let you go back in there," I admit, sliding the pad of my thumb over her cheek.

She stares up at me through long, dark lashes. "I have to."

"Promise you'll stay close by."

"Why? It's not like he'd—"

I snake my arm around her waist and drag her up into me, cutting her off. Nuzzling my nose into her hair, I whisper in her ear, "Just do as your told, woman."

She gasps when I gently bite her earlobe, her body sagging against mine. I drag my nose down the sensitive side of her neck, inhaling her sweet, spicy scent that I'm addicted to.

"Joel," she breathes out. And fuck, I want to hear her say my name like that when my cock is buried deep inside her.

I walk her backward into a nearby alleyway and cage her against the wall. In here, we can pretend the outside world doesn't exist. Just her and I and the shadowy darkness.

She lets out a whimper when I lower my lips to within an inch of hers, pausing just before they touch. She's right there, so close our breaths mingle as we inhale each other's diffused air. I want to taste her. I need to. But I won't kiss her first, not when I know she's been hurt before.

Her eyes flit to my mouth, then back up. The ball's in her court.

We stand there, panting, exchanging looks that speak a thousand words. Then she rises on her toes and presses her lips to mine. It's soft and sweet and so goddamn good. I let out a deep growl when she hums against my mouth, the sound traveling straight down to my dick.

I clamp an arm around her waist and drag her body up against mine, desperate to consume her in the same way she consumes me—with blistering intensity. Our mouths and bodies and hands grow frantic. I'm a crazed man and simply can't help myself. Stella's made me into a glutton, greedy for more. For all of it. For all of *her*.

But it's not enough. With Stella, it'll never be enough. She grinds her hips into mine, and I know she can feel my throbbing cock. I sweep my tongue along her bottom lip, savoring the taste of her. The deep-seated desire to own her on every level is sickening. Primal. I've already decided she's mine. She just doesn't know it yet.

I give her ass a firm squeeze and rock into her, eliciting a small mewl from deep in her throat. She bucks against me approvingly and bites down on my bottom lip. Hard.

I pull back and swipe a drop of blood from my lip.

"That's going to cost you, princess," I sneer.

Her hazel eyes blow wide. She shakes her head and attempts an apology, but her jaw snaps shut the second I bring my thumb to her mouth and smear the blood across her bottom lip.

"Lick it clean," I demand harshly.

And she does, her pink tongue darting out and licking the blood from my finger and her lips, her eyes never leaving mine. What a sweet little vampire she'd make. Then my mouth is on hers again, this time rough and demanding. She opens up for me like a rose in bloom and I want to reach down inside of her and suck the soul right out of her. Her hands glide over my chest and shoulders, snaking around my neck. When I peel my lips from hers and drag them down her neck, she tilts her head back, allowing me easier access.

She's pliable. Submissive. Her fiery, sharp edges have rounded, softened with desire.

I suck and kiss my way up her neck and behind her ear, cherishing every last drop like my last.

"Joel," she whispers, her eyes closed, and mouth parted.

"Don't say it," I snarl into her throat and continue my escapade.

I slip the strap of her dress over her shoulder and bite into the swell of newly exposed flesh.

"Ah," she cries out and digs her fingers into my back. I didn't draw blood, but it'll leave a mark. I plant a gentle kiss over the indents from my teeth, soothing away the pain, then tug the fabric over her other shoulder and pull it down so it pools loosely around her rib cage. My eyes flash to her black strapless bra, her full breasts heaving over the top.

Oh, the things I'm going to do to you.

She hooks a finger into my belt and pulls me back in close. Her tongue sweeps over my bottom lip, lapping at the fresh drop of blood bubbling from where she bit. She hums in approval. I kick her feet apart and force a knee between her legs, pressing upward into her core. The hem of her dress rolls up, exposing those beautiful, thick thighs.

I reach down the front of her panties and slide my middle finger up her slit.

Withdrawing my hand, I suck her juices off my finger and growl, "Fucking nirvana." My fingers slip back into her panties and I find her clit and strum it. She lets out a soft moan as her body arches into mine.

"So wet. Did I do this to you?"

She nods and rushes out, "Yes."

I smear her juices around, then carefully slide a finger inside of her. Her pussy clenches around me, tight and hot and wet. Her fingers find purchase in my shoulders, and she whimpers.

"You going to leave proof of your arousal on my thigh, baby?"

Embarrassment blossoms on her pretty face. Her mouth opens and closes as if she wants to say something. But when I crook my finger into her sweet spot, she chokes out a raspy, "Oh god, yes."

I slip my free hand around her throat, but I don't squeeze. Her pupils dilate with fear and her breath quickens, but she doesn't fight me on it.

"I won't hurt you," I remind her. "I'll never hurt you, Stella. Not in any way you don't want me to."

I feel her swallow against my palm, then she releases a puff of air and nods. She thrives under pressure, like a diamond crystalizing from the weight of the world she carries on her shoulders. But right now, she's battling to keep her panic at bay. She needs to move on from whatever shit is haunting her from her past. And in order for her to do that, she needs to step outside of her comfort zone.

Or be pushed out of it.

Pumping my finger in and out of her, I add a second and shudder at the way she stretches around me.

Seizing the opportunity while I have her vulnerable and at my mercy, I drag my mouth to her ear and whisper, "Emma's such a pretty name."

Her body goes tense, her heartbeat reaches a crescendo. Her hands fly to my forearm as she grips it tight in an attempt to peel it away from her. Her reaction is to be expected. She knew I read her file, but she has no idea how deep that information runs.

"What ... How ..." she stammers, unable to form words.

Chuckling at her obvious shock, I tell her, "I know you changed your name. But what I can't figure out is *why*."

Her eyes flare with horror. "No. How ... I thought ..."

Tightening my grip around her throat ever so slightly, I press on. "There's nothing you can hide from me, princess."

She shakes her head violently. "No. I can't ..."

"Yes you can." I emphasize my statement with another thrust of my fingers. She whimpers and rocks into it.

"Joel. Please don't ..."

The sound of someone clearing their throat douses our heated moment. I peer down the alleyway to the sidewalk. A woman in her sixties stands there, her arms crossed and her foot tapping steadily on the cobble stone beneath her worn-out leather shoe.

I glare at the old, uptight prude and slip my finger out of Stella's pussy, bringing it to my mouth and sucking her juices off. Her tangy sweetness is like crack, and I'm a fucking junkie. The stranger scoffs, a disgusted look on her weathered face, and stomps off down the street.

Stella panics, shoving me away and tugging her dress back into place. "Fuck, fuck, fuck."

"Relax," I tell her.

"What were we thinking? No. Never mind." She waves a dismissive hand in the air. "I already know what *you* were thinking. But what the hell was *I* thinking?"

I grab her by the elbow and drag her into me. "You have no clue what I was thinking."

She stares up at me and blinks. Her lips are swollen from our kiss, her cheeks rosy from arousal, her eyes are wild. She's so beautiful, it hurts.

"You may think you know, princess, but you have no goddamn idea what's going on in my head. There's something between us, and I have every intention of exploring it further. You'll have to get used to that, because I'm not going to stop until I have what I want."

Her eyes drift shut as she regulates her breathing. "And what is it that you want, Joel?"

I study her face for a moment too long. Her eyes pop back open, and I see the worry clouding them. I've just dropped a huge bomb on her, and she's already rebuilding those walls with expert skill. I can practically hear the bricks clinking into place.

I don't bother responding. Because she already knows the answer.

———◆◐◆———

"Still no trace of Danvers. But we've located the PI and he's cooperating," Mac informs me.

I pace Stella's room like a caged animal, listening to my boss on the other end of the phone, while Stella rifles through her suitcase.

I can still taste her arousal on my tongue, still feel her lush curves pressed into me. When she asked me what I wanted and I didn't respond, she just stared at me like none of what's happening makes any sense. She's not wrong. But it's as simple as this ... we met less than a week ago. Well, she met me. I've known her for more than six weeks. But I'm already right and purely fucked because I know without a doubt in my mind that she's what I want.

Every last bit of her.

But instead of laying it all out there for her, I simply released her, then followed her back to Giulia's celebration of life, where she said an impromptu goodbye to all the guests, then headed straight up to her room to hide from reality.

"What does he know?" I ask Mac.

Mac blows out a ragged breath. "He wouldn't divulge details over the phone, but he witnessed some shady shit. When you're back, we'll set up a meeting."

"Alright. Keep me posted on Danvers." I end the call more frustrated than when I answered it.

Stella must sense my agitation, because she pauses and stares at me expectantly, waiting anxiously for me to explain.

I shove a hand through my hair and pin her with an empathetic look. "The PI your mother hired knows something. He refused to detail it over the phone, so my guess is whatever he knows is important."

There's a strangled look on her face, like she's worried about what the PI might know.

She strolls to the minibar and pulls out a bottle of something clear, then fiddles with the cap. I take it from her and twist it open, then hand it back to her. She drains the bottle in a single shot, then sets it down on the counter.

"We're meeting with him when we get back," I tell her.

That must trigger something, because her posture stiffens.

"No," she responds too fast.

I close the space between us, reach up and drag my thumb across her pouty bottom lip, smoothing away the puckered lines from her obvious distress. "He might be able to help."

She shakes her head and looks at everything but me. Those gears are turning again, and I think she wants to tell me something. Perhaps answer some of the lingering questions I have about the holes in her file.

"Stella." I hook her chin and tilt her face to mine. "You can run from your past, but not from me. I know you hate that I can see right through you, but you're going to have to face it at some point."

Her eyes spark with fury. "I'm not running."

"No? You changed your name the second you turned eighteen then bolted. And now you're reluctant to meet with a man who may be able to help us figure out why Wyatt Danvers is following you."

She shakes her head frantically, and I release her chin with a sigh. So be it. I'll get to the bottom of it with or without her cooperation. I check my Rolex, noting the time.

"Harper will be here shortly. I'll give you some privacy, but I'm not leaving. Be ready in an hour."

"Wait," she stops me. "Where are we going?"

"Out," I tell her, then leave the bedroom and plop down on the sofa in the living room.

Harper somehow finessed her way into getting us to agree to take her and Stella out for the evening for some fun. Initially, I refused, but then the memory of Stella's smile, the sweet sound of her laugh on the plane ride here, sprang to mind and I crumpled like tissue paper.

Besides, I'm an opportunist. Tonight won't be a complete waste. I admire Stella's determination to keep her past a secret, but like every other job I've done, I'll come out on top.

And I have every intention of doing so tonight.

Thirteen

Stella

"OH MY GOD, STELLA!" Harper swats my arm playfully. "You naughty girl."

I should have kept my mouth shut, but I'm on my third mini bottle of vodka and it's been a long day. The cat's out of the bag. And by *cat*, I mean my racy encounters with Joel.

"I thought you swore off men." She crosses her arms accusingly at me, but her shit-eating grin betrays her. Harper's a sucker for drama, and I'm a walking, talking dumpster fire of it.

"Shh. He's in the next room. It's not like this can become anything serious. You know I don't do ..." I wave a dismissive hand in the air, "*that*."

"Girl, you need to let your guard down a little. Just go with the flow for once and don't think about things so much. Besides, the man is H-O-T." She swoons, then continues. "If a man like that looked at me the way Joel looks at you, I'd rip my panties off, climb him like a tree, then Tarzan straight onto his dick."

"What a lovely visual. Thanks for that. And might I remind you that you prefer guys in suits who drink fancy liqueurs and cheat on their wives? Not brooding, tattooed alpha males who have bad tempers and even worse manners."

Harper frowns, then whines, "I only slept with one married man. And I didn't know he was married until his wife came home early and caught us doing it on the kitchen table."

I cock a brow. "The tan line on his ring finger didn't give it away?"

She shrugs her shoulders and looks away. "He told me they were recently separated. I believed him. It was a lesson, okay? I'm changing my ways."

"Uh huh. And by that you mean ..."

She swats the air, tsks, then begins rifling through her suitcase, tossing pieces of brightly colored clothing in every direction until the room resembles the aftermath of a Harper-shaped tornado.

"Still traveling light, I see."

"Better to have what you don't need than need what you don't have." She holds up a tiny red dress. "What do you think?"

I eye the flimsy scrap of fabric. "I'm pretty sure the tag on my thong is made of more material than that." Harper spins to face the mirror, holding the dress in front of herself and angling her head. "It'll look great on you," I add.

I walk to the closet and begin perusing. Nearly every article is black, which is exactly how I like it. Black is simple, easy, and a great option for people who prefer to stay out of the lime light.

Harper spins around and tosses the tiny red dress at me. I don't bother catching it. "You're wearing it," she chirps.

Pursing my lips, I say, "I don't think so." Then I turn back to the closet and select a pair of dark jeans and a simple, black halter top from the closet. I could pair it with a black, strappy heel. Or maybe some cute ankle boots.

Harper appears behind me in a flash, yanks the clothing out of my hands and discards it on the bed. "Get your ass in that dress," she demands, her pink-painted fingernail pointed at the floor as she stomps her foot like a petulant child pulling a temper tantrum.

Going up against Harper is like facing off with a great white shark. She's majestic and beautiful and will rip you to shreds with her teeth. We argue for a few more minutes about why I shouldn't wear something that barely covers my nipples and Harper threatens to cut holes in all my favorite T-shirts.

I eventually accept defeat with a long, dramatic sigh, and stuff myself into the stupid dress.

When we're finished getting ready, Harper calls shotgun and hops into the passenger seat of the SUV. Joel's eyes rake over my barely concealed body, his expression just as hard as the bulge in the front of his jeans. I arch a brow at him and flash an all-knowing smirk, then climb into the back seat behind Harper.

Harper interrogates Joel while he drives, firing off questions about where he grew up, what he does for fun, if he prefers dogs or cats.

And because it's Harper, if he has any hot, single brothers. Evidently, he does not. But he does have a couple of crazy insanely hot Navy SEAL teammates. One of which was growing awfully twitchy as Harper flirted with some of the guests at Giulia's celebration.

I catch Joel peeking at me in the rearview every so often, as if he's checking for my reaction to his very vague responses. He doesn't like talking about himself, and I respect that about him, but it doesn't mean I'm not curious. I know very little about the man who's been working tirelessly to unravel everything I've aimed to keep neatly packed away.

The twenty-minute drive that felt like a million years finally ends, and Joel helps Harper and I out of the vehicle and ushers us toward the front doors. A buff security guy with slicked back hair and a black suit lets us in without question. I peek up at Joel in silent wonder, knowing damn well there's a handgun tucked into the back of his waistband that he's smuggling into a nightclub without even an ounce of hesitation.

His giant hand settles possessively on my lower back, my bare skin burning from his sizzling touch. Harper flanks my other side, gripping my hand and squeezing every time she spots a cute new prospective boy toy as we make our way through the club.

I search around the crowded space, skimming over the cluster of sweaty, writhing bodies on the dance floor. Italians sure know how to party, because the clubs in Detroit don't have nearly as much vibe as this one. Strobe lights dart from corner to corner, sweeping streaks of neon light over the open concept bar. The base of the techno music thumps deep inside my chest like a second heartbeat.

Joel leads us to a table at the back of the club. Zak and Liam are both there, clad in jeans and tees, their rippling muscles and tattoos on display for all the salivating women. Joel introduces the guys to Harper. Liam looks her up and down and grunts like a caveman. Zak smiles politely but it's forced, and averts his eyes as if she's the sun and will blind him if he stares directly at her.

Harper doesn't seem bothered by their reactions. Instead, she informs us she needs a drink then bustles toward the bar. Zak follows closely behind her. It's then that I spot him steal a peek at her backside.

Busted.

Liam mutters something murderous under his breath and tags along behind Zak, then Joel and I tow along at a slower pace.

Harper orders a gin martini, extra dirty, extra olives. Based on that information alone, I know exactly how tonight's going to go. The last time she ordered a martini like that, I woke up in my bathtub, fully clothed with a headache so bad it felt like someone had drilled my brain with a jackhammer. And Harper was passed out on the floor beside me, hugging the toilet.

"Let's dance!" Harper bumps into my side and struts onto the dance floor as if she owns the place.

"Are you coming?" I ask Joel. He just frowns so I shrug my shoulders. "Suit yourself." I grab my drink from the bartender and work my way through the crowd of people, ignoring the heat of Joel's gaze on my backside.

It isn't until I'm on the dance floor that I realize it's not men dancing with women. It's men dancing with men, and women dancing with women.

Joel brought us to a gay bar.

One of my gay colleagues brought me to a gay bar in the city once. I had the time of my freaking life. But this? Now? With Joel? The math isn't *mathing*.

"That man wants to fuck you so bad," Harper shouts over the loud thrum of music.

Not this again. I roll my eyes and spin around, grinding my backside into Harper while I search for Joel at the bar. He's leaning against the counter with a dangerously hungry look in his eyes. His gaze is so searing, I swear I can feel my skin curling from my body.

"Why do you think he chose this bar, girl?"

I turn back to Harper. "Probably the closest one to the hotel."

"Sweet baby Jesus, you're blind as a bat. There were four other clubs between the hotel and here. He brought you to this one because he doesn't want another man sticking his hand in your cookie jar."

A woman about our age in leopard print pants and a purple tube top flashes Harper a smile. Harper smiles back, but then makes a highly inappropriate gesture with her hands indicating she prefers penises. The woman smirks, flips her hair over her shoulder, then moves on.

I flick Harper's arm. "You're nasty, you know that?"

She beams at me, then shouts, "Not as nasty as you are."

I push Harper's accusation aside and find the beat. My eyes drift shut, and I let my body sway and rock as the tension from the day drains from my limbs. A sticky heat cloaks me, the air hot and humid from all the writhing bodies. I feel a trickle of sweat cascade down my chest and dip between my breasts. I drag my hand into my hair, then down the length of my body, feeling the smooth silk of my dress beneath my fingertips.

Every one of my senses are heightened. I can feel every puff of air, every skim of a stranger's clothing or flesh against mine as we bump and grind in the middle of the dance floor.

I drop my head to the side and imagine what it would be like if Joel were behind me right now, his hard cock pressed against my backside as we move in unison to the rhythm of the music. His hot breath tickling my neck as he growls against the sensitive spot beneath my ear, telling me all the filthy things he wants to do to me.

I slide my hand over my hip, my fingers teasing the hem of my dress, lifting it just an inch as if it were Joel's hand instead of my own.

But then a solid wall of heat presses against my backside and a large, rough hand wraps around my wrist, gently guiding it away from my bare thigh and tucking it into my side. A familiar mint and pine scent laced with something distinctly masculine overpowers the smell of sex and alcohol.

My eyes pop open. Harper dances a few feet in front of me, a smug smirk plastered on her face as she watches me gasp for air.

"Were you thinking about someone in particular, princess?" God, his voice is so thick and husky.

I take a step forward, needing to distance myself from Joel, before reluctantly turning around and meeting his eyes.

My heart flies out of my chest as his dark gaze roams over my body and he wets his lips. I press a hand to my throbbing heart and stare back at him.

Joel's eyes shift back and forth between my mouth and cleavage. Suddenly, I'm sent crashing forward into him. My drink goes flying and lemon-flavored alcohol sloshes onto my dress. Joel catches me in his arms, props me upright, and before I can even blink, fists a man's collar and drags him off the dance floor like a rag doll. He tosses the flaccid body toward Liam, who makes quick work of hauling the guy to the exit.

It all happens so fast, so efficiently, that my head is spinning.

Joel stalks toward me with clenched fists and a murderous look marring his face. I panic, because I recognize that look anywhere. I'm about to be scolded. So I do what any reasonable person would do in my situation and I bolt toward the front door, needing to get the hell out of the crowded bar. I feel Joel hot on my heels, but I don't stop until I'm bursting through the steel door and into the cool, crisp evening air.

Inhale. Exhale. Inhale. Exhale.

Joel powers through the door behind me. "What the hell are you doing? You can't just run off like that."

"What am *I* doing?" I spin and scream at him. "What are *you* doing? You can't just throw people around like that."

Inhale. Exhale.

I face away from him, wrapping my arms around my shivering body. There's a line of people waiting to get inside who seem to be interested in how this conversation might play out. I glare at each and every one of them. *Would you like some popcorn for the show, assholes?*

Joel ignores our audience. "I'm here to do a job, Stella. Nobody touches you."

I bring my tone down a notch. "It was just a drunk guy who lost his balance. Not someone who deserved to be flung like dog shit over the neighbor's fence."

Joel's eyebrows shoot to his hairline as he stares back at me with amusement. He drops his hands to his hips and takes a step forward. I match it and step backward. "I don't give a flying fuck who it was. *Nobody touches you.*"

I focus on the space between Joel's eyes, imagining how satisfying it would be to plunge a screwdriver through it. "You're ridiculous."

He drags a hand through his hair, messing it up in all the right ways. "And you're a giant pain in the ass."

I laugh manically, unable to calm the chaos in my mind. But when I speak, my voice cracks from the weight of my frustration. "I'm going back inside to find Harper. Then I want to leave." I turn to head back into the club, but Joel snatches my wrist and drags me into him.

I stumble in my heels, but Joel reacts quickly, bending down to scoop me up and throw me over his shoulder like a ten-pound sack of potatoes.

"I'm not done with you yet," he mumbles.

I pound my fists against his backside and scream, "Put me down."

He splays one giant hand across the backs of my thighs and swats my ass with the other, then takes off across the parking lot.

I lift my head and search the line of people outside the club. Some look concerned, others look entertained. When a scrawny man who Joel would no doubt squash like a bug steps forward, I roll my eyes and flick my wrist, dismissing him. The man hesitates, but steps back in line, and I consider saving his life my good deed for the day.

A few more strides and we're at the SUV. Joel sets me on my feet and my survival instincts kick in and I turn to run, but he snakes an arm around my waist and pulls me backward, slamming my back into his chest.

Then he says lowly, "We're going to have a little chat, princess."

Fourteen

Stella

"I can't leave Harper in there alone," I pant, winded from my struggle. It's the same excuse I used earlier, so I know it's not going to fly.

"She's not alone. Zak and Liam will take care of her."

Joel opens the door, forces me inside the vehicle, then rounds the hood and hops in beside me, pressing the lock button so we're trapped inside together. Suddenly, the large interior of the SUV feels entirely too small, like the walls are closing in around us and all the oxygen is being vacuumed out.

I cross my arms and pin him with a look I hope makes his skin sizzle. "What do you want from me, Joel?"

He pinches the bridge of his nose and squeezes his eyes shut. When he opens them again and looks over at me, I can see his internal struggle. "I can't keep my hands off you."

I scoff. "No shit, Sherlock."

His eyes rake over my body. "You're trying to kill me, aren't you?"

I glance down at the red silk that clings to my body and realize the hem has inched up, my black lace panties playing peek-a-boo between my thighs. I anxiously tug the flimsy fabric back down, a tidal wave of embarrassment crashing over me.

The green dress. Joel's fingers exploring my body beneath the dinner table surrounded with Giulia's business associates. The ice cube.

A muscle in his jaw slides as his eyes darken to a stormy shade of blue. "I need to know what you're hiding. Why you changed your name and ran. It could help us."

Back to this, I see. "I'm not hiding anything, Joel. I grew up in foster homes and when I aged out, I wanted a fresh start and to put the past behind me." He opens his mouth to speak but I cut him off by raising a palm in the air. "Please. Just stop pushing."

"You're not leaving this vehicle until I have answers." He grips his jean-clad thighs with his enormous hands, refraining from touching me again. Then he grits my name out in anguish, like it's physically painful for him to speak it.

I'm so frustrated, so angry, that I can feel the steam billowing out of my nostrils. He knows I'm lying, and I can't help but feel a twinge of shame for trying anyway. So, I say, "You wouldn't understand."

"Try me," he responds coolly.

His expression has softened, but his fingertips have bleached white. It's all very tempting, but once I reopen this wound, it'll gape wide for the world to see. There will be no closing it up and stitching it shut. I'll be completely exposed and raw, and something tells me Joel would enjoy that.

Joel reaches over and sets his hand on top of mine. It's a sweet gesture, completely uncharacteristic of him, but I flinch anyway. His body goes rigid, his face hardens into sharp lines. Even in the dark, he's ruggedly handsome in an intimidating sort of way. And he's burrowing himself beneath my skin, settling in like a tick on a dog. What if he goes digging? What if he finds out what I did and I don't get a chance to explain myself? How much does he already know? He read my file, so I know he knows some things, but I haven't seen what's in there. Truthfully, I've been avoiding asking for the simple fact that I'm terrified of what he might tell me.

But now I'm being backed into a corner. Given an ultimatum. Tell him and risk everything. Or keep it quiet and risk everything.

Either way, *I'm risking everything*.

Maybe he'll understand. Maybe he'll tell me it's all okay and that he'll take my secret to the grave.

But *maybe* is for hopeful idiots. And I'm not one of them.

Refusing to accept defeat, I garble out, "I can't."

"Fuck, woman. You have to trust me. We've all done things we're not proud of."

It's like there's a strap wrapped around my torso, squeezing until my ribs are turning inward and puncturing my lungs. And here come the tears ...

Rule number two. Rule number two. Rule number two!

"We have all night, Stella. You're not leaving here until you tell me."

The whooshing of blood in my ears is so loud, I can't hear my own thoughts. I fight for oxygen, but my lungs are filling with lead. I suck in short, sharp breaths, unable to stop the panic attack that's ripping at my throat. My entire world feels like it's imploding, and pretty soon, I'll be sucked into oblivion. Incinerated by the secrets I've harbored for so many years.

I can't do this. I'm a disaster waiting to happen, and if I continue on like this, I'm going to drag everyone around me into the pits of hell, where they too will burn for all eternity.

"Ah, fuck, princess." Joel lunges at me and his mouth crashes over mine in a bruising kiss. It's not sweet or gentle or tender. *It's rough.* Animalistic. My breath hitches and I think my heart stops beating as my dirty, filthy soul lifts from my body and Joel's kiss breathes new life into me.

One strong arm coils around me, dragging me into the safety of his embrace. His other hand grips the back of my head, fisting my hair. I skim my palms up the hard planes of his chest and hold on for dear life as his mouth plunders mine, taking everything he needs from me and then some. Stars flicker behind my eyes and I'm plucked from reality and dropped into a euphoric state of bliss.

It's overwhelming and frightening and amazing and freeing, and I never want it to stop.

I sweep my tongue into his mouth, deepening the kiss. He lets out a deep groan that vibrates all the way down to my clit.

Joel's kiss consumes me like a violent tornado consumes everything in its path. He's dark and powerful and dangerous, but then he softens and I'm reminded that every storm eventually comes to an end.

This will be no different. Eventually, this chaotic cyclone of desire and emotions will come to a crashing halt and I'll be left to reconstruct. Alone.

Joel grips my ass with both hands and squeezes. His rough embrace is a stark contrast to the tenderness of his mouth and I let out a soft moan of approval.

I feel safe here with him, like he's bulletproof armor and nothing can penetrate me as long as I'm wrapped up in his Kevlar cocoon.

He lifts me onto his lap, guiding my legs to either side of his hips so I'm straddling him. His hard cock strains against his jeans and rubs against my throbbing clit. I grind my hips against him uncontrollably, desperate for more friction. Desperate for release. But I know release will never come. I'm a broken shell of a human being, drained of the ability to be vulnerable like *that* with a man.

Joel's skilled fingers knead the aching muscles in my back, working away the tension that always lingers. He drags them down to my ass, then over my thighs, massaging me tenderly. My body sags as I melt to putty in his hands.

He sucks my bottom lip between his teeth and gives it a gentle nip as he slips his hand under my bottom, the tips of his fingers tracing the lace edge of my panties. Then he tilts his hips upward, giving me the friction I crave.

"Joel," I pant. This is too much. It feels too good. Too right.

"Tell me what you want," he whispers hotly, then sinks his teeth into the sensitive flesh beneath my ear.

"Ah god. That. I want that."

"Pain? Is that what you want, baby? Is that what you *need*?"

Arching against him, I nod frantically. "Yes. Pain."

Shaking his head slowly, he lets out a soft chuckle and tells me, "Satan did a good job when he designed you for me."

His deft fingers skim beneath my dress and up my body to my heavy, aching breasts. He brushes his thumbs over my pebbled nipples, and I let out a porn star whimper.

Surely that's not me making those sounds.

He slides his hands back down, slowly, softly, as if memorizing each hill and valley of my ribs. Then he grips my ass and grinds me down on top of him, giving me just the right amount of friction.

He nuzzles the thin straps of my dress with the tip of his nose. They slip off my shoulders and the fabric pools around my waist, exposing my bare breasts to him. His eyes darken and he licks his lips. Then his mouth comes down on my nipple, sucking and nibbling and scraping his teeth over the sensitive bud.

I grow dizzy and set my hands on his shoulders to keep my balance as he takes his time torturing me like that, alternating sides until my hands are in his hair and my body is rocking in sync with my heartbeat.

You could plug me in and power the entire universe with how much electricity is buzzing through me right now.

"Tell me you want me, Stella. Fuck, I need to hear you say it. I won't take what I want until you do."

I rock into him, but his hands grip my hips, his thumbs digging into my flesh. He holds me there, still and steady, his eyes boring into mine as he waits for my approval.

It stops me dead in my tracks. This man is .. *respectful*. He requires consent. It's unexpected and comforting and confusing all at the same time.

In all the one-night stands I've talked myself into, I've never had a man ask me what I want. I didn't think it was physically possible for the male species to give two shits about what a woman needs—what she's comfortable with.

"You, Joel. I want you." It comes out breathy and desperate. And it's the god's honest truth. I want this man so much, it hurts.

A wicked grin splits across his face and I get the sense he's plotting something evil. Guiding me back and forth, he rocks me slowly, deliberately over the bulge in his jeans. "Then tell me what you're hiding."

I shake my head. Absolutely not. Then fumble with his belt buckle and unzip his pants. With trembling hands, I slide my palm into his boxers and wrap my hand around his hard length. My fingertips don't meet.

Oh my god.

There's no way that thing is going to fit inside of me.

Joel smirks at my obvious hesitation. "Something wrong, princess?"

I shake my head and he chuckles. The big jerk knows exactly what I'm thinking.

I abandon his cock and my fingers fly over the buttons of his shirt, splaying it open to expose his sculpted chest and stomach.

Jesus, Mary and Joseph. The muscles. The tattoos. I glide my hands over his chest and abs and swallow the saliva pooling in my mouth. I've never seen anything so incredible. Sheer masculinity encased in black ink. His skin is warm and soft, his entire body like velvet-wrapped steel.

With a groan, he tugs my panties to the side and skims his fingers up my slit. "Always so wet for me."

I collapse forward onto him when he pushes one large finger inside of me, stroking that sensitive spot deep inside that only he knows how to find. He presses his thumb against my clit, and I nearly explode into a million tiny pieces.

"Yes," I moan.

More, more, more!

He fists the back of my hair, angling my head and bringing his mouth to my ear. "So perfect and tight. I can feel your greedy pussy sucking me in deeper. Fuck, baby, I can't wait to feel you clench like this around my cock. I can't wait for the first time I get the privilege of fucking you so hard, so fucking rough, that you can't sit right for a week. And when you're too sore to take my dick, I'll use your pretty little mouth instead. But only if you're a good girl and tell me what I want to know."

He slides another finger in, stretching me. I cry out and dig my fingers into his shoulders. It hurts. God, it hurts so much. But when he starts rubbing my clit again, I relax around him, melting into him, and the sharp pain dulls into a delicious ache mixed with pleasure. Every muscle in my core contracts with each slow, agonizing thrust of his fingers.

But then he pauses, his hand perfectly still between my legs.

"Joel, please. Don't stop." I buck against him, praying he'll pick back up where he left off, but he tugs on my hair and my back arches uncomfortably.

"You want to come, baby?"

"Yes." *And I want to smack the smug look right off your face and force you to finish what you started.*

Joel plunges his fingers back inside and circles my clit with his thumb, but only once, before retreating again. "Then tell me what I want to know."

Motherfucker!

"I ... I can't." Is death-by-lack-of-orgasm a thing?

His hot breath fans my bare chest. "Tell me, and I'll give you everything you want." He presents his unfair offer with another perfectly timed thrust of his skilled fingers.

I shake my head. If I open my mouth to speak, it'll just come out a garbled mess of vowels that make zero sense.

His eyes flare like hot coals and his lips curl into a snarl, baring his teeth. "Tell me while I fuck this sweet little cunt with my fingers, or I'll bring you right to the edge, so close to coming, that you'll be begging me for release. Begging me to take pity on your needy, weeping pussy. And just when you're about to tip over the edge, I'll rip it all away from you without an ounce of remorse. I will destroy you and I won't even bat a fucking eyelash. Is that what you want, baby? To be destroyed by the man who was sent to protect you?"

He curls his fingers inside of me to send his point home, and I feel my traitorous pussy weeping, just like he said.

"No, please," I pant. How dare he hold my orgasm hostage. How dare he use sex as a weapon against me.

I swallow the lump in my throat and steel myself. I can't break now. Not after holding this secret in for so many years. But it's been slowly poisoning me, wrecking me from the inside out.

"Tell me," he snarls, gripping my hair tighter.

I cry out in agony, my scalp tingling from his grip, but god it feels so good. My juices coat the insides of my thighs and Joel's hand. My pussy throbs, begging for release. The ache in my core builds to a painful level.

Joel sinks his teeth into my shoulder, sending shock waves of pain through my arm and up my neck.

"Ah. Please, Joel. Don't make me do it."

Our bodies are fused together, welded by a feverish sweat. I couldn't leave if I wanted to. I'm consumed, swallowed whole by the alternating pleasure and pain as Joel works me over. I climb higher and higher, teetering on ecstasy. A cry lodges in my throat as I hover a million miles away from my fucked-up reality. It would take less than a light breeze to send me flying over the edge.

"Say it. *Now.*"

My eyes squeeze shut as I'm drawn into a state of undeniable vulnerability, like a comet being sucked into a black hole. I'll never be the same again. I'll never recover from this. It isn't until the coil inside me snaps that I shatter.

"He took it," I cry out as my orgasm tears through me. "He took it."

Joel's hand stills briefly, his fingers still buried inside of me. Violent sobs wrack my body, wave after wave, as I bust through rule number two with the subtlety of a sledgehammer.

"Took what?" Every ounce of pain, every hauntingly dark thought weighs me down until I'm crushed beneath the unforgiving terror of the truth I've been harboring. "Fuck, baby. Talk to me."

"He ..." I sniffle. "He ..." I can't get the words out. It's all too much. The power Joel has over me is too fucking much.

"He what?" he bellows, and I flinch again.

A fierce shiver rolls through me. Tears stream down my face as I fall apart in Joel's arms. An avalanche of tremors and emotion come barreling through me. The dam walls break, releasing everything I've been holding back.

"I can't say it." I've never said it. I've just lived in this perpetual state of denial, convinced that if I didn't speak my truth, I could pretend it never happened. That I'm not shackled by the chains of that day.

I collapse onto Joel's chest and he tenses beneath me, his breathing growing ragged. The heat of his rage permeates me, setting my insides alight.

"Who?" His tone softens. He plants a gentle kiss on my temple, then buries his face in my hair. "I need a name, baby."

I cry for what feels like hours while Joel holds me, stroking my hair, trailing his fingers lightly up and down my spine while he warms my insides with sweet words of encouragement. Not only did he just give me my first orgasm with a man, he's the first one to ever care for me like this.

I drain myself of every tear I've ever held back. Then, I step beyond the ruins, out of the prison I've created for myself, and finally forfeit.

But freedom always comes at a cost. One I'm not sure I can afford.

Fifteen

Joel

I'M BLINDED BY RAGE, a haze of crimson blurring my vision.

He took it.

Stella's heartbreaking words play over and over in my head. I knew she was hiding something. I fucking knew it. And now I'm ready to hunt down the motherfucker who did this to her and rip him to pieces with my bare hands.

I grip her by the shoulders and force her back so I can search her face and repeat myself for the third time. "A name, princess. Now."

When her eyes finally meet mine, that's when I see it—*the pain.* Cruel, relentless, toxic pain that's been buried for far too long. I swipe the tears from her cheeks with the pads of my thumbs and cup her jaw in my hands.

She closes her eyes, her long, dark lashes glistening with tears against her cheeks, and I resist the urge to put my fist through the dash.

"Stella." Her lip trembles and she sucks it between her teeth.

She hiccups and it's the cutest little sound. I place a soft kiss on her lips, and she gives in. Her shoulders sag and she stares down at my chest as if the answer is etched there in ink.

"Roger Donovan," she rasps.

Roger Donovan. I catalogue the name for later when I hunt him down and gut him with a very dull, very rusty fillet knife.

"When?"

She blows out a ragged breath, whispers my name, shakes her head, and completely freezes me out.

"Tell me when, and I won't ask any more questions." *For now.*

She lifts her lids and searches my face, then says, "I was fourteen, and he was a social worker."

A rolodex of unanswered questions flips through my head. Before I have a chance to ask any of them, there's a knock on the window. Stella flinches. Fuck, I hate when she does that. I pull her chest to mine to hide her exposed body from view as I lower the window down a few inches to find Liam on the other side, his eyes darting between me and Stella.

"What?" I snap at him.

"Mac called. You might want to, uh ... you know." He nods suggestively before turning and disappearing across the dark parking lot.

I raise the window back up and galvanize my arms around Stella when she tries to lift off me.

"What are you doing?" she sniffles, her tears already drying and the pained expression on her face fading.

"When I promise you that nobody will ever touch you again, I mean it. Do you understand me?"

She wraps her arms around herself, the heat of the moment long gone. Then she nods.

"Good girl." I pull my phone from my back pocket and call Mac as Stella pulls the flimsy straps of her dress back over her shoulders. I bite back a groan as I watch her fingers skim over her smooth, tanned skin right in front of my eyes. She's pure torture. "Talk," I snarl into the phone when Mac answers after one ring.

"It's the PI. Some kid found him passed out on a park bench with a needle in his arm. He's alive, but in rough shape."

The PI has a drug problem?

"Anything on Danvers?" I ask, my eyes trained on Stella. I know she can hear Mac through the phone, and judging by the beating her bottom lip is taking from her teeth, I know she's nervous.

"Nothing. But uh, Stone. We might want to consider putting her in a safe house for now."

I don't even think before I speak. "She's not going to a safe house. She'll stay with me." Stella's spine straightens and she stares at me with an amusing bewilderment on her face.

There's a silent pause on the line, then, "Fine. Check in later." Mac ends the call.

Stella's face pales. "Absolutely not," she argues and hoists herself off my lap and into the passenger seat.

"You don't have a choice."

"Like hell I don't."

"It's my place or a safe house. You choose." I make quick work of buttoning my shirt back up, doing up my jeans and buckling my belt.

She huffs and crosses her arms, an adorable pout on her pretty face.

That's what I thought.

I drive Stella back to the hotel while Harper hitches a ride with Zak and Liam. Apparently, the three of them did some bonding at the club and the guys insisted on escorting the boisterous blonde while I take care of Stella.

Fourteen. She was just a kid.

I fire off a message to Sloane, asking her to look into Roger Donovan, the social worker. Once I know Stella's safe, I'll pay him a visit.

Stella roams quietly around the hotel suite, her eyes darting from the large expanse of windows showcasing a pitch-black sky lit by a million twinkling stars, to the dark corners of the room.

"Still feeling uneasy, I see."

She shoots me an apologetic look then plops down on the edge of the bed and knots her fingers in her lap.

"I shouldn't have told you." Her voice cracks, and it nearly shreds me to pieces.

I close the space between us and tilt her chin with my finger. "Your secret's safe with me. My job is to protect you. Not ruin your life."

My phone buzzes in my pocket. I pull it out and answer it. "What?" I bark into the device.

"Jeez, Stone. It's just me." *Sloane.*

I grunt out an insincere apology, gesture to Stella that this will only take a minute, and head out on the balcony, sliding the patio door shut behind me.

"What did you find?"

"Roger Donovan, deceased, immigrated to the US with his parents when he was four years old. Graduated college in California and snagged a job as a social worker. Got married, had a couple kids, then moved to Michigan. His wife, Maria, died in a car crash a few years ago. His daughter, Trinity, lives in Arizona with her husband and two young children. Donovan's son, Lucas, went—"

"Woah. Hold on," I cut Sloane off. "Donovan's *dead*?"

"Affirmative." When I don't say anything, Sloane clears her throat then continues. "Roger Donovan was pronounced dead fifteen years ago after a hitchhiker attacked him and a teenage girl that was in his care. Donovan's body was never found. Hitchhiker was never identified or located. The girl escaped the attack with nothing but a few bumps and bruises. Police picked her up walking down the highway. Report says she was in shock when they found her, but otherwise fine."

My gut sinks like a rock in a lake. "Who was the girl?"

Sloane pops her gum then sighs and says, "I think you already know." *Emma Romano.*

My hackles rise as I stare through the patio doors at Stella. She's pacing, wearing a hole in the floor, and gnawing on her thumbnail.

Anger rolls through my veins like hot lava as more and more information comes to light.

"Anything else I should know?" As if she can feel my eyes boring through her, Stella pauses at the foot of the bed and stares at me like a deer in headlights.

"Nothing of importance. But if I come across something, you'll be the first to know."

"Thanks, Sloane." I end the call and turn to stare out at the sky, fighting to rein in my temper. Roger Donovan is dead. Emma Romano was with him when he was allegedly attacked by a hitch-hiker, then he went missing.

The patio door slides open behind me. Stella stops beside me and stares out at the midnight sky. I glance down at her profile. Fuck, she's beautiful. And smart. And manipulative.

"So, that was Sloane," I tell her, my tone laced with accusation.

Her face snaps to mine, her eyes rounded at the edges. "And?"

Turning to face her, I wet my lips and say, "You left a few minor details out earlier. Care to elaborate? Or would you like to hear my theory on what really happened that day?"

Her face goes slack and she turns to bolt, but I grab her by the arms and spin her around, so her back is pinned against the railing.

I grip the iron banister at either side of her waist until my knuckles feel like they'll bust through my skin.

"Always running," I sneer, shaking my head, then bringing my face to within an inch of hers. "I promised I'd keep your secret, Stella. That promise still stands. But, the way I see it is you have two options. You can make this easy, fill in the blanks for me. Or you can waste my time and make me go digging again. Which one will it be, princess?"

A gust of wind blows by. Crickets chirp. A plane engine roars over us. I press my body into hers so she can feel the heat of my threat.

"You have three seconds to speak, or I'm going to assume you've chosen the hard route."

Tears flood her eyes as her mouth opens and closes. Finally, she chokes out, "Roger went missing."

"That's a good start, baby, but there's more to that story and I need to hear it."

She sniffles and sets her hands beside mine. Her pinky reaches for my thumb, as if she's seeking comfort in the contact. Just that tiny gesture makes my blood simmer to a steady boil.

Narrowing my eyes at her, I ask, "You were attacked by a hitch-hiker?" Her eyes shift to the left and she nods. The sadist inside me roars, beats his chest, then the sick fucker smiles. "Liar."

Sixteen

Joel

STELLA LETS OUT A yelp of protest when I spin her around and fist her hair, folding her over the edge of the balcony. She grips the railing tight, her heartbeat pounding and all the blood rushing from her face. I bury my nose in her hair and inhale deeply. I can practically smell her fright, and it's mixing deliciously with her sweet vanilla scent.

"Oh, princess. When will you learn?"

"No, Joel. Please, I—"

"Shut up," I snap. "And listen to me."

Her breaths come hard and fast as she stares down at the concrete ground more than ten stories beneath us. The loose strands of her long, dark hair are swept up by the cool night breeze, drifting lazily in the evening air. I skim my free hand down her waist, slowly and intentionally, memorizing every sensual curve of her body. When I reach her satin-covered ass, I splay my palm across it.

"You're lying to me, Stella. I know it, and you know it."

"No. I'm not lying. He disappeared ..."

"That part's true. Roger went missing." I tug her dress up over her ass and peer down at her trembling bottom. "But you know exactly where he is, don't you?"

She lets out a whimper, her body shivering as goosebumps scatter across her smooth flesh. "N-no. I swear."

Skimming my fingertips beneath the edge of her black lace panties, I whisper, "Such a terrible liar," then snap the lace against her ass. "I bet if I slipped these to the side, I'd find you soaking wet."

Her head whips from side to side.

Grinning, I push a finger through the flimsy fabric and rip the side of her panties in one quick movement. The scrap of lace slips down her legs and pools at her bare feet.

Now she's completely exposed. *For me.*

"If I'm right, what do I get?"

She tilts her head and peeks over her shoulder at me. The air in front of her lips dissipates in tiny puffs of white as she pants in fear.

"What do you want?" she breathes out.

I smooth a palm over one ass cheek, her skin cool to the touch. "I want the truth."

She blinks a few times, then asks, "And if you're wrong?"

I chuckle. "We both know I'm right, princess." Bending her forward, I slip my finger between her legs from behind. Shaking my head, I relish this win like the arrogant motherfucker that I am.

"Soaked." When I slide my hand around the front of her, push my finger between her pussy lips and circle her clit, she lets out a soft moan, her knees buckling. Her grip on the railing tightens.

"Joel, please. Someone might see ..."

"Let them watch, baby. Because even though they'll get to hear your sweet, sultry sounds as I make you come ... get to watch as you tremble beneath my touch ... they'll never have you. They'll never feel you. Taste you. *Fuck you*."

She gasps when I push one finger inside her tight pussy.

"I'm going to fucking destroy this sweet cunt of yours, Stella." She bucks against my hand, her back arched and her ass pressing against my hard dick.

I slip my finger out, raise my palm, then bring it down on her ass with a sharp *thwack*.

"Ah," she cries out, her body jerking forward.

I glance down at the blooming handprint on her cheek, then smooth the pain over with my palm.

"I'm going to ask you questions, and you're going to answer every single one of them with a simple yes or no. If you lie, I spank you. And Stella ..." I bring my lips to her ear. "I will always know when you're lying."

She shudders and begins begging. "Joel, please. Fuck," she pleads. "I can't ..."

Angling her head, I take her mouth, kissing her deeply until her body relaxes and she's moaning. She breaks out in a cold sweat when another breeze sweeps in, slapping against her bare skin damp with sweat.

Breaking the kiss, I tell her, "You can, and you will." She takes a calming breath. "Use your words, baby."

"Okay. Yes, I'll do it."

"Good girl. First question … was there a hitchhiker?" I already know there wasn't, but a sick part of me wants her to lie again, just so I have the pleasure of doling out her punishment.

"Yes."

"Wrong answer, baby." *Smack!* She jerks and yelps but I smooth my palm over the welt to massage away the sting. "Let's try that again. Was there a hitchhiker?"

She whimpers, then lies again. "Y-yes."

Excitement licks at my insides. This time, I punish her with two hard smacks, one right after the other.

"Ah," she cries out and jolts, her feet nearly lifting off the ground.

"Lie one more time, and I won't let you come " Raising my voice, I ask her for the final time.

She shakes her head. "No. No. There wasn't."

"Mm. Good girl." Slipping my fingers between her glistening folds, I reward her truth with a few strums of her clit. "You're fucking dripping wet, baby. My sweet little liar. You like this, don't you?"

She sucks her bottom lip between her teeth and moans. Her lids flutter shut as I massage her bundle of nerves until her hips are swaying back and forth. "This one's going to be hard for you to talk about. But I need you to be honest with me."

"O-okay."

"You said Roger Donovan took it." She squeezes her eyes shut and a lone tear slips free. I lick the droplet from her cheek, tasting her salty sadness on the tip of my tongue. Dragging my mouth back to her ear, I whisper so only she can hear me. "Did you kill Roger Donovan, princess?"

Her entire body hardens to granite as she stands before me trembling with need. Her breathing pauses briefly, then she breaks into a sob. "No," she garbles out, one wild hazel eye staring at me over her shoulder.

My palm tingles. Every cell in my body lights with a dangerous level of intoxication. I've jumped out of planes into shark-infested waters. I've scoured the jungle for days without food or water. I've even climbed Mount Everest. But none of it compares to the high I get from this.

With a wicked grin, I growl, "If you wanted more pain, all you had to do was ask." I withdraw my finger from her pussy, raise my hand, and come down on her ass with five more harsh cracks, all in quick succession and with only a single word separating each blow.

"Stop ... fucking ... lying ... to ... me."

She bucks and cries out. Her head drops between her shoulders and I swiftly reach around and give her what she needs to break free of the pain.

This time, I slip two fingers inside and she lets out a sultry moan and sways her hips, her swollen pussy lips on display for me from behind. Fuck, she's so tight and hot. So goddamn perfect.

I release her hair and slide my hand around her throat, pressing my thumb to her erratic pulse. She swallows, hard. Her back arches, her tits pressed against the railing, her hands gripping it tight.

"Tell me the truth, Stella."

"I ..." she pants as her pussy contracts around my fingers. I increase the pressure of my thumb rolling over her clit and tighten my hand around her throat.

"Tell me you killed Roger Donovan." I can see her emotions seeping like honey from the cracks of her unstable foundation. "Tell me that sick fuck put his filthy hands on you when you were fourteen years old. That he assaulted you. Raped you. And you fucking killed him for it."

Fresh tears stream down her face, and I know she's close to breaking again. But I'll be here to pick up her pieces and glue her back together, whether she believes it or not.

Massaging her clit and pressing my hard cock against her, I snarl, "Tell me you killed him, Stella. I want to hear you say it."

"I did it. I killed Roger Donovan."

With a satisfied grunt, I spin her around, push her back against the railing, and drop to my knees before her. Then I devour her, sucking her clit and greedily lapping at her juices. She slides her hands into my hair and claws at my scalp with short fingernails as her body is overcome with violent tremors and she breaks out into a full-blown sob.

I slide two fingers inside her and curl them, massaging her sweet spot as I suck and nibble on her clit. Her knees buckle and her pussy clamps around my fingers.

She cries out, "Ah, fuck. Joel."

I eat her straight through her orgasm, until she's slumped against the railing and completely spent. Then I stand, smear my wet fingers across her lips, and kiss her. Her fingers find purchase in my shirt and she moans into my mouth. But now my cock is painfully hard, straining against the zipper of my jeans, and there's no way I'm going to take advantage of her vulnerability right now.

Breaking the kiss, I tug her dress down over her bottom and pull her into my arms. She covers her face with her hands and burrows into my chest and cries.

Pressing my lips to the top of her head, I close my eyes and rein in the urge to crack skulls. "Shh. It's okay."

"I—" She hiccups. "He—" Another hiccup.

She lifts her lids and peeks up at me through wet lashes. I cup her jaw in my hands and stare into her big, watery eyes, stroking her cheeks with my thumbs.

"They never found his body," she grates out.

"I know, baby." With a proud smirk, I say, "You must have done a damn good job hiding it." Her brows furrow and she shakes her head. Her lips part like she wants to say something but doesn't. I lean down and plant a gentle kiss on her mouth.

I snatch her shredded panties off the ground and stuff them into my pocket, then scoop Stella into my arms. I carry her back into the hotel, shut the patio door behind us and lock it, then set her on her feet at the side of the bed, draw the curtains, and flip off all the lights except for a single lamp.

"What are you doing?" she asks as I stand in front of her and thumb the pulse in her wrists.

"Thinking," I respond.

"Oh." She's doing much of the same. With a sniffle, she asks quietly, "Are we still meeting with the PI?"

"He overdosed. He's in a medically induced coma and will stay that way until the doctors say so."

We stand in silence, staring at each other for what feels like eternity. Fuck, her eyes are unique.

Stella twists her mouth in thought. "I want to tell you everything."

"When you're ready."

She lets out a soft, humorless laugh. "I don't think I'll ever really be ready. And I have a sneaking suspicion you're not going to let me keep it to myself."

"And you're only realizing this now?"

She pulls away and begins pacing, so I take a seat on the edge of the bed and rest my elbows on my knees. When she opens her mouth and begins to speak, I regret ever pushing her beyond her limits.

Every word is like a punch to the gut, but I absorb everything she says, memorize every insignificant detail. I commit her to my goddamn memory. Stella Clarke carves herself into me like an ancient hieroglyph written in stone. I notice every time her posture changes, when her breathing becomes erratic, how her pitch heightens when she's trying not to cry. She's so fucking strong, and she doesn't even realize it.

By the end of it, my body thrums with the violent need to rip throats. Stella killed Roger Donovan, got rid of the evidence of his assault, then made up a bogus story so Harriet, another social worker who was sleeping with Roger, wouldn't blame herself. Stella, at the age of fucking fourteen, felt the need to protect a grown-ass woman from that pain.

Then she wandered for hours, lost in the forest, until she found her way to the highway where she walked some more. By the time a cop picked her up, she was in shock and completely turned around. She had pointed them in the direction of where she thought Roger was, where his van should have been, but when the cops scoured the forest, they found nothing. Not a trace of blood or otherwise.

He just ... *poof.* Vanished.

And now I'm not entirely sure if she changed her name and made herself difficult to find because she was worried about the cops happening upon some evidence and coming for her, or if she thinks perhaps Roger's still roaming about.

There's so much more to Stella than meets the eye. There's so much darkness and depravity, I could fall into her abyss and spend an eternity trying to navigate my way out.

But then there's the light. Her cute, nervous laughter. Her warm hazel eyes that light up when she talks about something she loves. Like Harper. Or the moon. Or how she wishes she could go back and study something other than finance.

By time she's finished, she's drained. And I have no idea what the fuck to say. I've never been an emotional man. I'm not great at the romantic shit or showing people I care. The only thing running through my head right now is how the hell I can locate Roger, dead or alive, and give Stella the closure she needs. The peace I know she's been seeking for fifteen years.

Until he's found, I don't think she'll be able to move on from this.

Seventeen

Stella

I DAMNED MYSELF TO hell for all eternity at the tender age of fourteen. The only evidence of my corruption is a rotting corpse laying somewhere in the woods just outside of Detroit. It's been there for fifteen years, likely ripped apart by hungry scavengers, picked at by vultures, and polished clean by maggots, just as my blackened soul ever since that day.

Roger's death wasn't an accident, nor do I carry any sort of remorse for what I've done. But I'd be lying if I said I wasn't fucked up well before that day. Sure, it was the straw that broke the proverbial camel's back, but the blood on my hands is merely a by-product of years of abuse and neglect. Years of running from shitty foster homes, only to land right back in the hands of the system and tossed into a new home with a new temporary family.

It doesn't matter how strong you are. How capable or smart or resourceful. That shit will chew you up and spit you out, and you'll never even have a glimmer of hope at building a normal life for yourself. Sure, you can tape and glue those cracks. You can patch the holes with putty. But in the end, all you'll be left with is an ugly, weakened vessel of your being.

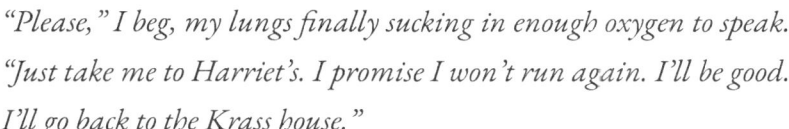

"Please," I beg, my lungs finally sucking in enough oxygen to speak. "Just take me to Harriet's. I promise I won't run again. I'll be good. I'll go back to the Krass house."

Long, dirty fingernails dig into my bare arms. I whimper and protest as he drags me farther and farther away from the vehicle and into the forest. Dead leaves crunch beneath my shoes. A cold breeze kicks up dust and dirt and whips my hair into my face.

Eventually, I stop struggling. I stop fighting. And I just follow. The less I struggle, the less he squeezes.

We stop at a clearing in the bush and I begin trembling all over.

"Wha-what are we doing?"

Roger ignores my question. Bile burns my stomach and throat as it rises to my mouth. Since I stopped struggling, Roger's grip has loosened enough that I think I can get away. He's bigger than me, but I'm younger and faster.

I rip my arm free and bolt, heading back in the direction of the van. If I can make it to the highway, I can flag someone down. I pump my legs as hard as I can, the wind screaming in my ears to go faster. Faster!

I glance back without slowing down. Roger's right behind me. I scream as he reaches forward and grabs a fistful of my hair. I slam backward and fall to the ground, Roger's huge body landing on top of me, once again knocking the wind out of me.

"No! Stop! Help! Help!" I scream and kick and yell until my voice breaks and all that comes out is air.

"You little bitch!" Roger pins my thighs under his knees, crushing my legs with his weight. I struggle against him, clawing at his chest and face, scratching at anything I can get my hands on. But he grabs my wrists and pins them over my head, squeezing them in one of his giant hands as he puts all his weight on me, crushing my lungs with his stomach. I can't breathe. I can't move.

"I've waited so long for this. Every chance I thought I had, someone always fucked it up. That stupid bitch you're so fond of … she likes to fuck my plans up."

I cry out when he grinds his hips into me, and that's when I feel his erection against my leg.

No. Please, God, no. I don't want my first time to be like this. It can't be like this.

I turn my face away from him, the stench of his breath an acidic cocktail of booze, cigarettes and the fish tacos he devoured in the van after picking me up. It mixes with the smell of dead leaves and damp fall air. I try to swallow my vomit but begin choking on it, sputtering as Roger reaches between us and pulls my dress over my hips. He rips my underwear roughly from my body.

It hurts. It all hurts. His hands are rough and abrasive. I cry out when he grinds into me again and a sharp rock digs into my spine.

I squeeze my eyes shut and force myself to imagine I'm somewhere else. None of this is real. It can't be real.

But then I hear the clanking of a belt buckle and the zipper of his pants, and I'm dragged violently back to reality. Roger shifts his weight, digging his knees further into my thighs as he positions his hips between mine and lines his penis up with my virgin hole.

"No. Please," I beg, but it's pointless.

He leans forward and runs his tongue from the corner of my mouth to my ear, licking my tears from my face. His tongue feels like a razor blade and his saliva burns like acid.

He snarls in my ear, "Beg some more. I like it when you beg."

I shake my head and struggle against him, focusing on getting one hand free.

But it's too late. He takes from me what I can never offer to someone again. And I wasn't ready for it.

But then he loosens his grip on my wrists enough for me to rip one hand free. I smack and scratch at his face, dragging my fingernails down his cheek, but he presses his belly down onto me, crushing me further with his weight.

I dig my free hand into the dirt at my side, crunching a handful of soil and dead leaves in my fist. But then my knuckle brushes something cold and hard and I reach for it, clasp my hand around it, and swing it upward toward Roger's head. He jerks, his eyes wide with shock as a trickle of blood rolls down his face and he struggles to remain upright. I swing my arm back down, then up, and smash it into his skull again.

This time, he topples forward onto me. But I don't stop. I hit him again.

And again.

And again.

Until there's so much blood on my hand that the rock slips free from my grip.

I wiggle out from beneath him, clawing my way away from his still body laying face down in the dirt. I hug my knees tight to my body and rock back and forth as a pool of blood gathers around his head, staining the soil and leaves a dark red.

Something warm touches my arm and I sit bolt upright, my chest heaving and my body slick with sweat. I frantically search around the dark room, my eyes struggling to adjust.

"Stella. Baby." Joel's soothing baritone voice floats through the deafening silence. "Just a dream. You're alright." He pulls me into him—my back to his bare chest—and sinks an arm beneath my head, wrapping the other around my body, holding me tight. Then he pins my legs beneath one of his, so I'm cocooned in his warmth.

It's been so long since I've had that nightmare.

"It's normal to have them after revisiting something traumatic," Joel whispers.

Did I speak out loud?

"Want to talk about it?" His voice is thick with sleep and I hope I didn't wake him.

"Not really. Hang on." I spring to my knees and stare down at him in the pitch black. "You're supposed to be sleeping on the couch." I don't need to see his face to know there's a smug grin plastered on it. I can *feel* it.

"I was. But I woke up to you thrashing and mumbling something about dead leaves. Crawled in beside you in case you decided to go nuclear and throw something across the room at me."

"Oh." I flop down on my pillow, then feel over my body to make sure I'm fully clothed. I am. After I told Joel everything, he insisted I get some sleep, then sauntered off to the couch without so much as a goodnight. I knew he'd think differently of me once he knew the truth. It's fucked up, really, so I don't blame him for pulling away.

Joel goes to roll out of bed. "Alright then. Well, I guess I'll ..."

I reach for his arm. "Wait ... I mean ... you can stay. If you want. Just promise me you won't try anything."

There's an uncomfortable silence where we sit there staring at each other in the dark, then the blankets rustle, and the bed moves. And I'm left laying alone again.

<hr/>

"Stella. Earth to Stella," Harper snaps her fingers in front of my face, and I'm yanked from my thoughts. Autopilot has become my default setting lately. "We're landing," she tells me with an empathetic smile. She knows how much I hate this part of flying.

The plane dips lower, and I drop my head back against the headrest and close my eyes as my stomach does that icky swoopy thing it does when landing. I need a distraction. Any distraction. Just not ...

I crack my lids and find Joel's frigid gaze pinned on me, his jaw clenched tight and his lips pressed into a firm line.

Hot and cold. Hot and cold. I can't keep up with this guy.

The plane jostles, and I replay the flight to Italy when Joel coached me through a grounding technique. But just like the first time, every sense revolves around him. Only now, those things I think of are no longer hypothetical. All of my senses have been invaded by Joel. *Every last one.*

I exhale roughly and force myself to stare out the tiny window as the ground comes nearer. We land successfully, panic attack averted. But now my panties are soaked, and my heart is fluttering. It's been doing that a lot lately, and I should probably see a doctor about it. My heart ... not my wet panties. I already know the cure to that ... but unfortunately for me, I'm being forced to play house with the very man responsible for my ailment.

Once my feet are firmly planted on the ground, I pull Harper in for a hug. I hate that she has to leave, but her grandmother is a gazillion years old and Harper's all she's got. So she's headed back to Michigan to take care of her.

"Awe, Stell. Stop it. You're going to make me cry, bitch." She fluffs my hair off my shoulders and delivers me a nauseating dose of pity. "I'll see you in a few weeks, m'kay?"

I nod, choking back tears, then hug her again.

Eighteen

Joel

"THIS IS ... WOW." Stella looks at me, blinks, then stares back at my house. "You're just full of surprises."

I pull into the four-car garage at the side of my home and the door slides shut behind the tailgate. I hop out and round the hood, then lift Stella out and set her on her feet. I grab her luggage, punch the security code into the keypad, and lead her into the mudroom. Once we're behind closed doors, I rearm the system and listen for the beep.

Nobody gets in. Nobody gets out.

I show Stella around the house. It's not nearly as grand as Casa del Sol, but I've done well for myself. I've had an extensive military career, made a few smart investments, and Sweetwater pays us what we're worth.

Stella rounds the kitchen island, dragging one lazy finger across the black granite countertop and my dick twitches in my jeans. Seeing her here, in my house, barefooted and sexy as fuck in ripped jeans and a tee, all I can think about is throwing her over my shoulder and hauling her away to my bed.

"Did you design this place yourself?" she asks sweetly.

"Mostly."

"Think you could give me some pointers?"

I angle my head at her in question. "For what?"

She stops in front of me, so close I can smell her perfume. Something passes over her and she straightens her spine.

"Giulia's guesthouse," she drawls, peeking around at the open concept kitchen and living area, then back at me. "I'm not sure why she decided to go ahead with construction when she knew she was going to die."

I take a step toward her, closing the space between us as she presses her back into the counter and wraps her fingers around the edge of the granite.

Caging her in with my palms to the countertop, I ask, "Do you plan on moving into it?"

She shakes her head. "No. I can't live there. It feels ... weird."

Leaning in, I respond, "That's fair. And if I help you, what do I get in return?"

She grins up at me and my entire world rights itself.

But then my phone vibrates in my pocket and I grumble. Reluctantly, I pull it out and read Liam's text to call him immediately.

"There's an envelope here for Stella. No return address. Martina picked it up when we stopped to grab the mail."

Stella mouths, "What is it?"

I point a finger in the air indicating to give me a minute. "Open it."

There's some rustling, then a string of muffled curse words. Messages start filtering through on my phone as I glare at the screen.

Pictures. One after the other. Photos of Stella at the grocery store as she peruses the produce section. Of her leaving her apartment. One of her at the beach with Harper. I grind my jaw at the zoomed in shot of her in a bikini.

Stella approaches cautiously and peeks at my phone.

"Oh my god," she rushes out, her hand flying to her mouth.

I flip through the next few photos, stopping on one that makes my stomach roil. Stella's sitting on a patio with Harper, her head thrown back laughing. It's the same patio as the one in the photo Giulia's PI captured of Wyatt Danvers. Adrenaline rushes my system as pieces click into place.

The only difference between the PI's photo and this one, is that this one was taken from the table Danvers sat at. It's he who took these pictures and now he's waving them around in front of us, flaunting his obsession and making himself known.

Stella stares up at me, her face tight with anxiety.

I put the phone back to my ear. "There's a note," Liam says next, and my heart bangs against my rib cage as I read the message.

Dearest Stella,

I stopped in to offer you my condolences, but you disappeared before I had the chance to. You're getting good at that, by the way ... disappearing. Anyway, I'm so very sorry for your loss. The death of a parent is never easy.

But what I really wanted to tell you is that although it's been fun, I'm growing tired of the chase. For years, I enjoyed watching you peer over your shoulder. Watching the blood drain from your face every time something went bump in the night. But when you disappeared this time, I was certain I'd never find you. But here you are, in sunny California. It's ironic, really. California is where I was born. I spent the first few years of my life there, until my parents decided to move across the country and settle down in Michigan. Perhaps it was meant to be, because years later, I bumped into you, and you changed my entire life. You made me the man I am today. Or monster ... depending on whose side you're on.

Nonetheless, I've decided your time has come to an end. You'll run out of places to hide, eventually. So for now, I encourage you to enjoy what little life you have left. Because this time, I have every intention of keeping you for myself.

I'll be seeing you soon, little piggy.

Anger licks at my insides with a forked tongue. That motherfucker was right under our noses, right here in California.

"Run everything for prints."

"Already on it," Liam responds.

I track Stella's movements as she takes a seat at the island and drops her head into her hands.

"Put Martina in a hotel with good security. Nobody gets in or out without us knowing about it. I want Shephard sent to watch over Harper until this is all dealt with. And you post up at the mansion in case this fucker decides to pop by again. Whoever he is, I want his head on a goddamn stake."

I end the call and dial Sloane, who tells me she still hasn't located Wyatt Danvers. But there's footage of a kid dropping that envelope off at the mailbox, which means Danvers is smart enough to have hired him to deliver the package instead of showing his face. Sloane agrees to track down the kid and question him. Then I call Mac, who informs me that the PI is now conscious and able to speak.

I sink the heels of my palms into my eye sockets to relieve the pressure building behind them, then pad over to Stella, spinning her chair and lifting her chin with my finger. She looks fucking exhausted.

"He's getting bolder, leaving evidence of his obsession."

I watch the gears turn over in her head but I can't get a read on her beyond the despair in her eyes.

Lowering my gaze, I tell her, "Nothing is going to happen to you. Do you hear me?"

Her bottom lip trembles and there's doubt in her eyes, but my brave girl nods anyway.

Sensing her preparing to run and hide again, I slide my hand around the nape of her neck, tilting her head back so she can't pull away.

"Wyatt Danvers isn't going to be around much longer. You have my word that nothing will happen to you. Nobody will touch you

as long as I'm by your side. They'll have to go through me first."
I brush my lips over hers, and her shoulders finally relax. "Tell me
you trust me, Stella. Tell me you believe me when I say I will burn
this fucking world down if it means keeping you safe."

Her eyes drift shut as she inhales deeply, then whispers, "I believe
you."

I crush my mouth to hers, drinking from her like a thirsty man
who's been wandering the barren desert for days. She whimpers
then sets her palms on my chest and pushes away.

Running. Always fucking running.

"Show me the pictures of him again," she rasps, her tone sharp
with determination.

Her request surprises me.

The words *fuck no* sit right on the tip of my tongue. I want to
refuse, for her to never lay eyes on his fucking face again, but log-
ically, it makes sense to revisit the pictures. She's been unearthing
a lot the last few days, and that may be what it takes to spark some
sort of memory that leads us to Wyatt Danvers.

I grab my phone from the island and pull up the picture of her
and Harper on the patio. Stella's brows furrow as she studies the
screen.

Shaking her head, she murmurs, "I can't place him." I scroll to
the next photo and she shakes her head again. I show her a few of
the photos Sloane dug up. But once again, nothing.

Stuffing my phone back into my pocket, I tell her, "We'll pay the
PI a visit tomorrow. See what he knows."

"We?"

Smirking, I angle my head and ask, "Didn't think I'd be leaving you here alone, did you?"

She hums thoughtfully. "You sent Zak to stay with Harper."

I cross my arms and widen my stance, preparing for the storm I feel brewing. "I did."

"She's not going to like that."

"Zak's polite and well-mannered. Has the patience of a saint." *Far more than Liam and I.* "Your friend will be just fine."

The next couple hours are a blur of phone calls and emails—all the background noise of the job that none of us care for.

Stella's curled up on my couch, watching a true crime documentary, her shoulders wrapped in a thick, fuzzy blanket that I hadn't even realized I own. Must have been my maid that tucked it away in a closet somewhere. She's always harping on me about making my cave more lady friendly. Whatever the hell that means. I make a mental note to give her a raise immediately.

I take a seat on the sofa next to Stella and glance over at her staring numbly at the stone fireplace. "Stella. Talk to me." I touch her thigh and she flinches.

Fuck, I hate that!

She slowly turns her face to mine. The dark circles under her eyes are deeper than usual. Her expression is cold and blank, the color of her irises dull, cloudy, lifeless. I hand her a glass of red wine and she accepts it with a trembling hand.

"What's going on in that head of yours, princess?"

Staring down at her glass, she mutters, "Everything."

Scooting closer to her, I set my hand on her leg again. She tenses, and it nearly sends me flying into a fit of rage, but quickly relaxes. Fuck Roger Donovan and his rotting corpse, wherever it may be. Fuck Wyatt Danvers and his sick obsession with my girl. Fuck Giulia Riva for ever putting Stella into this position in the first place, regardless of whether or not any of this is her fault.

"Everything's going to be fine. You have my word." I'm torn between soothing her and hunting down every person who's ever wronged her and dismantling their bodies one limb at a time.

"I'm beginning to think it won't be. This whole thing is so fucked up, Joel. I thought I had my life under control. I really did. I had a decent job, a cozy apartment. I was ... normal, for once in my life. Then wham! It all comes crashing down." She laughs humorlessly to herself, then reels her sanity back in. "I feel like everything I thought I knew about myself was all wrong. Like I'm some fictitious character in one of the universe's sick plays. My whole life has been a lie. And now this."

I swipe a tear from her cheek with the pad of my thumb. "Tell me another secret."

She scoffs. "Don't you think I've shared enough?"

"No. You shared the biggest one, but I want to know more." *Need to know more.*

She shakes her head, but I know she's considering it. It's only taken a few days, but slowly, her walls are coming down. She's opening up to me, and I'd be a fool to think that's not a special fucking phenomenon.

Remembering some of the shit my military therapist told me years ago, I tell her, "I think deep down inside, you like that I know, because it means you have someone to bear the burden with. You have someone to share your dirty little secrets with. After all, misery loves company. But you own your life, Stella. You own your experiences, your memories, your traumas. It's up to you to decide how to handle them, how they'll affect you. You hold the power. Not me. Not Roger Donovan or Wyatt Danvers. No one but you."

There's a clarity in her eyes now, like she's finally accepting her fate.

"I know you have plenty more tucked away, Stella. Tell me something I don't know."

Her resolve weakens as she considers whether this is a smart game for us to be playing. I already know it's not, but I don't give a fuck.

She opens her mouth, then snaps it shut again.

"Say it, baby. I want to hear every dirty, sick, fucked up thing about you. Give me all your faults and darkness. I'll eat that shit up like candy."

She swallows hard and closes her eyes. With reddening cheeks and a deep, calming breath, she admits, "I've never had an orgasm with a man ... not until ... you know."

Well, fuck me sideways. My ego inflates to the size of Texas. I did that for her. It's then that I decide giving Stella a first of something feels fucking incredible and I want to do it more often. But I don't express any of that, because this is about her. Not me.

Stella peeks up at me innocently, as if what she just told me shouldn't affect me. "That's how fucked up I am. I couldn't ... I thought Roger ruined me forever. But then I met you and ..."

"And what, princess?"

Her eyes drop to my chest. "I realized what it truly meant to be ruined by a man."

My chest tightens and my blood pressure shoots through the roof. The truth can either set you free or rip you to fucking shreds. Somehow, this one does a little of both.

"Look at me," I demand. She shakes her head. "I said fucking look at me." Her gaze tracks up the column of my throat to my eyes. I cup her face in my hands and carefully consider my next words. Stella spooks easily, understandably, and I refuse to be the reason she forfeits the progress she's made.

"Joel." The way my name rolls off her tongue—so goddamn sexy. "I don't know what to do," she admits, and it fucking pains me to watch her, as strong and capable as she is, struggle with this.

"You don't need to do anything right now."

I pull her into my lap and wrap my arms around her, granting her the permission she thinks she needs to bury her face in my chest and sob. It's more than just her tears I'm desperate to absorb. I want every ounce of pain she feels. Every crippling fear. Every horrific nightmare that haunts her. I'd take it all from her if I could.

I kiss the top of her head, inhaling the scent of her shampoo as she grips my back, her fingernails biting into my skin through my shirt. Eventually, her sobs fade to nothing more than sniffles and hiccups.

"I've cried more in the last week than I have in fifteen years," she mumbles into my shirt. "You must think I'm nuts."

I chuckle but don't respond, because .... well. If it walks like a duck and talks like a duck ...

She lifts her head and stares up at me through wet lashes. "This is where you reassure me that I'm not actually nuts. That I'm just going through it."

A smirk tugs at my lips. "Decided it's better to keep my mouth shut than to lie to you."

I coil her hair around my fist and angle her head back, brushing my mouth over hers. Her lips are a sweet, salty cocktail of red wine, tears, and a distinct flavor that's purely, authentically Stella.

"You're walking on thin ice," She warns. "But thank you."

I nip at her bottom lip. "For what, baby?"

"Breaking me."

I kiss her forehead, swallow the inappropriate comment I want to make, then settle her back onto the sofa. "Wait here."

She blinks up at me, a puzzled look on her face, and I disappear down the hall. Minutes later, I return to the living room to find Stella perched anxiously on the edge of her seat, empty wine glass in hand. I take the glass from her, top it up, then lead her down the hallway to the guest ensuite. I'd prefer to have her sleeping in my bed with me, but I know she's not ready for that. And after she emptied herself of her past and told me every fine detail of Roger's assault, I'm having a hard time beating my guilt into submission for ever pushing her out of her comfort zone. Even though I know that's what needed to happen.

"You ran me a bath?" she asks, surprised that I'd make such a gesture.

I set her glass on the tub ledge and turn to her. "Is it so hard to believe I want you to be comfortable while you're staying in my home?"

She clamps down on her bottom lip, a playful glint in her eyes. "I just didn't peg you as a guy who cared much about that."

I cross my arms and smirk down at her. "That's awfully presumptuous of you."

She glances at the frothing bubbles rising in the tub, then back to me. "Awfully presumptuous of you to think I'm just going to undress in front of you."

"I didn't ask you to."

That playful glint vanishes into thin air. "Oh."

I walk to the door, pausing before I leave Stella alone to relax. "Take as long as you'd like. There's more wine in the kitchen if you want it. I don't keep much food around because I'm not home very often, but if you're hungry, we can order in. Otherwise, make yourself at home."

Then I leave the bathroom, closing the door carefully behind me and adjusting my hard-on in my pants.

Jesus Christ. I'm so fucking fucked.

Nineteen

Stella

I slip out of my clothes, folding everything neatly beside the sink and unclasping the gold bracelet from Giulia and gingerly placing it on the top of the pile. Then I ease down into the warmth of the bubble bath Joel drew for me. The temperature is perfect, and my body is blanketed by a frothy layer of bubbles that smell of lavender.

A pang of jealousy radiates throughout me and I eye the feminine bottle of bubble bath suspiciously. I shove the thought aside and sink into a state of relaxation, dropping my head back on the bath pillow and closing my eyes.

There's a soft knock on the door a moment later and I perk up, rearranging a few bubbles to strategically cover my lady bits. "Come in."

Joel appears at the foot of the tub, his hair messed and face pinched into a tight scowl.

I quirk a brow and stare at him expectantly. "Forget something?" I ask, curious why he returned so soon.

It's then I spot the fluffy gray towel in his hand. He clears his throat, averts his eyes, and drops the towel on the ledge beside the tub. When he turns to leave, I open my big, fat, stupid, horny mouth. "Stay."

He pauses, his back to me, and glances over his shoulder. "Stella."

Disappointment floods my system. Why does he always have to say my name like it tastes funny?

"I don't mean ... I just meant sit with me. I don't want to be alone."

He's still facing away from me, and now his chin is dropped to his chest as he struggles to maintain composure. He's battling something internally, I think.

"You can shut the lights out, if that helps," I add.

He groans, then marches to the vanity and starts rummaging around beneath the sink. A moment later I hear the crisp flick of a match as he lights a candle and sets it beside my glass of wine. I eye that suspiciously too, because no way would Joel Stone ever be caught purchasing candles. Then he flips the lights off, and we're shrouded in darkness with just the soft glow of a single dancing flame.

He takes a seat on the tile ledge of the tub by my feet, props his elbows on his knees, and cranes his neck to stare down at me. In this light, I can't see the color of his eyes, but I can feel them on me as the heat of his gaze burns a hole straight through me.

We sit in total silence, the only sounds the subtle fizzing of the bubbles as they slowly dissipate, the steady drip of the faucet, and the occasional hiss of the candle flickering.

I lay my head back and watch him down the length of my nose. His body is rigid, growing more tense as the layer of white clouds concealing my body slowly disappear before his eyes. When there's nothing but a few translucent patches floating on the now tepid surface of the water, my heart begins to hammer against my rib cage. I'm completely naked, exposed to Joel, while he's sitting fully clothed at my feet.

With my eyes on his, I drag my hand between my breasts and over my stomach. When his gaze tracks my movement, he stands abruptly and takes a step back as if I've burned him.

"You're playing with fire, princess," he says with warning, his hands flexing at his sides.

"I like the heat," I breathe out.

There's a deep growl that comes from his side of the room as he watches my trembling hand trace a lazy line from one hip to the other.

"Mm," he hums, and the sound vibrates all the way to my throbbing clit. "Touch yourself for me."

My heart is beating so wildly, I'm positive it's creating waves of its own, but I do as I'm told. Spreading my knees wide, I slip my hand between my thighs and circle my clit, eliciting a satisfying reaction from him. His gaze darkens and he glances over at my neatly folded clothing. He storms over to it, snatches my panties, unbuckles his belt and parts his jeans, then slaps one palm to the wall as his other hand frees his hard cock from his black boxers.

He's thick and long and hard and my mouth is pooling with saliva. I swallow, and watch as Joel's head dips, his eyes roaming freely over my body as he wraps my panties around his cock and begins fucking them with his fist wrapped tightly around his length.

Jesus Christ, why is watching him jerk off into my panties so hot?

"Is this what you wanted?" he asks, his voice husky and rough with desire.

"Yes," I croak out, arousal coiling itself around my throat and squeezing.

Joel wets his lips, and oh god, I want his mouth on me. As if hearing my thoughts, he asks, "What else do you want?"

Instead of telling him with words, I show him. Arching my back, I massage my clit and use my free hand to pinch my hardened nipple, releasing a soft moan as my orgasm begins to build. Joel pumps his fist harder and his breathing grows ragged.

"Slide a couple of those pretty fingers inside, baby," he instructs, and I obey, gasping as I begin to finger fuck myself while Joel's hand picks up the pace. "Mm. Such a good girl. Fuck you're gorgeous, Stella."

I pump my fingers faster, riding my own hand and applying pressure to my clit with the heel of my palm. Tension builds low in my belly and I don't take my eyes off Joel as he tells me things that make my head spin and my pussy ache with need.

"You're doing such a good job. Fuck, I want to be buried deep inside you right now. God, Stella, you're fucking perfect. Eyes on me when you come, baby."

I come hard around my fingers, my limbs thrumming with energy and my pussy convulsing while my thrashing body splashes about in the now cool bath water. My name spills from Joel's lips as well as a string of colorful words as he grunts out his release into my panties and bangs his fist on the wall beside him, his dark eyes never leaving mine.

It's then that I realize nothing will compare to having Joel's hands on me, rough and demanding and safe. I wasn't lying when I said he's ruined me, and we haven't even had sex. It's been less than a week since I met this man, and he's already carved himself into my soul. I'll never be the same again. I sink down into the water, exhausted and completely unfulfilled.

Joel stands to his full height, stuffs my panties into his pocket and his cock back into his jeans, rakes his eyes over me once more, then disappears out of the bathroom, slamming the door on his way.

Bright morning light streams through the bay windows on the other side of the room. Rays of sun cast warmth across the king bed I'm sprawled out on. I stretch like a cat beneath the satin sheets and glance over at the clock on the nightstand, groaning when I realize it's nearly noon.

I crawl out of bed and pad over to the ensuite, locking the bathroom door behind me. My toiletries are neatly situated on the vanity. My bath items have taken their place on shelves inside the walk-in shower. Embarrassment unfurls inside me when I spot my travel-sized bag of tampons perched on the back of the toilet.

Joel must have unpacked for me while I was sleeping. Which is mildly confusing considering after I clambered out of the tub last night and went in search of him, he had locked himself in his bedroom and I haven't seen him since.

When I finish checking to make sure everything I need is here, I get dressed, brush my teeth, comb my hair, and apply a light dusting of makeup. Then I make my way down the hall.

I find Joel sitting at the kitchen island, scowling at his phone.

I approach him the same way you would a wild animal—with extreme caution. "Good morning."

His eyes shoot to mine and his scowl softens, but only a fraction. "Morning," he grunts out. "Sleep well?"

"Like the dead." I smile gently at him, hoping my grim sense of humor will lighten the mood. It doesn't. I take a seat in the chair on the opposite end of the island from him in case he decides to rip my head off. "What's the plan today?"

"Hospital," he deadpans, his eyes fixed on his cell phone again.

"Do you think the PI will have anything useful?"

"Yes. One way or another, he'll give us something."

One way or another. My imagination runs wild with ways to make someone talk. "When do we leave?"

"After you eat something."

Food's the last thing on my mind and I don't normally bother with breakfast. Besides, what I'm really thinking about is whether I can somehow snag a neck brace from the hospital to deal with all the emotional whiplash Joel's inflicting on me.

"I'm not hungry," I inform him blandly.

"You'll eat."

There's no winning with this guy. He's impossibly stubborn. Joel rises from his seat and pops two slices of bread in the toaster. I roll my eyes and watch as he slathers peanut butter across the toast and pours me a coffee. He slides the plate and cup across the island at me, then leans against the counter and watches me eat. His icy, blue eyes flare as I make a show of swiping a dribble of warm peanut butter from my chin and pop my finger in my mouth, sucking it clean.

His gaze tracks the movement and he licks his lips. "Keep it up and we won't be leaving this house," he threatens. His deep baritone voice echoes through the kitchen and straight to my throbbing clit. And now the peanut butter isn't the only warm, sticky thing I'll have to clean up.

I take another bite and mutter through a mouthful of ooey, gooey goodness, "Prove it."

A flicker of amusement flashes in his eyes as he stalks toward me, spinning my chair around so my back is to the island. I swallow the food in my mouth and stare up at him, unsure what to do with my hands. He leans forward, pressing his weight into his palms on the island on either side of me. His masculine scent mixes with the smell of the peanut butter, and all I want to do is slather him in it and lick him clean.

"Your mouth is writing checks your body can't cash, princess."

My tongue darts out, sweeping a lone crumb off my chin. Joel's lips curl into a snarl, baring his teeth, and now I'm not sure what the hell I was thinking.

"What ever are you talking about?" I ask coyly, my confidence waning beneath the intensity of Joel's gaze.

He glances down at the aching spot between my thighs. "I think I'd rip that perfect little pussy of yours to shreds." My eyes widen. Jeez, this guy has a filthy mouth. But he's right. I've now not only felt, but seen first hand that monstrosity he calls a dick. "You're wet right now, aren't you?"

"No." *I'm soaked.*

Joel's hand slips around my throat, his thumb pressing beneath my jaw to track my pulse the way he likes to do. My spine lengthens as he tips my face up to meet his and brings his lips to mine. Panic rises in my chest, as it always does, a flood of heat and desire and fear filling my lungs and panties. I wouldn't stand a chance against him. All he'd have to do is squeeze, and he could snuff the life out of me like a harsh blow to a candle. Why the thought of relinquishing power to Joel appeals to me is something I'm not fully prepared to explore yet.

Our eyes lock and something darkens behind his.

"Breathe, Stella. I'm not choking you."

I suck in a gulp of air like I was just held underwater, when really, I've been drowning in something much deadlier.

His hand slips free from my throat and he disappears as quickly as he had come. I press a palm to my chest to calm my racing heart.

Note to self: do not poke the bear unless I want to be eaten alive.

Twenty

Stella

JOEL SPEAKS IN HUSHED tones to the security guard hanging around at the front entrance of the hospital. The guard nods and shakes his hand dutifully, then directs us to the PI's room. Joel clasps my hand in his and leads me down a long corridor of stark, white walls and dingey, gray floors. It smells like death—like sterilizer and decay.

I slam the brakes on in the waiting room, sudden panic ripping at my insides. Four hallways branch off this room, all lined with heavy, steel doors with flaking paint and sick people laying in tiny beds behind them.

Joel turns toward me. "What's wrong?"

I slide into one of the blue leather chairs and drop my head into my hands. "I just need a minute."

Joel squats in front of me and wraps his hands around my thighs. His touch is warm, heavy, and safe, but it does nothing to melt the ice clogging up my arteries right now.

"Stella." He pinches my chin between two fingers and lifts my face to his. "Eyes on me, baby. It's just a hospital."

I stare forward at him, but his handsome face twists and contorts. I grow lightheaded as the room around me begins to spin, faster and faster until everything's just a streaky blur of chaos. Then it all stops, and I'm staring back at a set of snake eyes, the stagnant hospital air now pungent with the stench of dead leaves and damp soil. Gasping for oxygen, I struggle to get my panic attack under control as unease sinks its teeth into my throat and blocks my airways.

Something is off. I can feel it.

Joel takes a seat beside me and pulls me into his lap, cradling me like a newborn baby. I hear him tell me it's all okay, to just breathe, to try grounding myself. But it feels impossible. The world is ending and there's nothing I can do but sit here and watch it all implode around me.

"Tell me what's going on in that head of yours, baby. Describe it to me."

"It's … it's …" I tremble in his arms. "Something's off."

The obnoxious squelch of sneakers on tile causes my panic to heighten. I glance down one of the hallways and watch a nurse disappear into a room. All the hairs on my body stand on end when another hospital employee bristles past, disappearing into that same room like its some sort of black hole sucking medical professionals in until there's nobody left but Joel and I.

I stand abruptly and stare down the hall. Joel follows my line of sight just as a third person runs past, and I just know.

"That's his room," I garble out, that nagging feeling in my gut now a violent heave of terror and instinct.

We both stand staring, waiting for someone to exit the room and carry on as if everything is fine. But that doesn't happen.

Joel grabs my hand and pulls me down the hall toward the black hole. My feet weigh me down each step of the way and a foreboding sense of dread overwhelms me.

We're not getting the answers we came here for.

We stop outside the door and I squeeze my eyes shut, already knowing what we'll find on the other side. I can feel it in my bones. I can feel the death. I can smell the metallic tang of it. It's the same feeling I felt when I stared down at Roger's lifeless body.

"Fuck," Joel snaps, pulling me into his chest and gripping the back of my head with his big hand, shielding my eyes from the sight before us.

What used to be a constant beeping sounding from a machine stalls.

Beeeeeeeeep.

And I whimper as a woman's passive voice rhymes off a date and time.

"Let's go." Joel tries to usher me away, but I resist. "You don't need to see this," he tells me when I turn my face toward the room.

My heart plummets into my stomach and I clasp my hand over my mouth to stifle the scream ripping at my throat.

Sticky, crimson red pools on the floor beside the bed. Bloody footprints are smeared from the hospital staff slipping through it in their rushed efforts to save a life. A man's still body is sprawled out on the tiny cot, his left arm hanging limply from the side of it. My eyes dart to the large gash that runs from his wrist to his elbow. His face is pale gray, his mouth agape and eyes lifeless and glassy as they stare into nothingness.

A nurse unplugs the machines and drapes a white blanket over the body. It all feels so final. A whole human life ... *gone*.

It's not the PI's lifeless eyes that are haunting me. It's not the open gash on his arm from where he sliced himself to bleed out.

It's the smell that lingers in my nose. The sharp, coppery stench that you instinctively know is blood before you even see it.

"I have an address for you," Joel's colleague, Sloane, says through the Bluetooth in Joel's truck. "It's an old, abandoned house. I think maybe that's where Danvers has been crashing while in Cali. I can send Liam to scope it out instead if you don't want to take ..."

"No," I snap before Joel has a chance to respond. "I want to go. Please. I need to be a part of this."

Joel's eyes cut to mine. He's all sharp lines and hard features. He doesn't seem at all affected by the gory scene at the hospital, and

I wonder how many dead bodies he's been around. Surely, that's not something people can get used to without years of relentless exposure.

Sloane sighs dramatically through the speaker. "Stone. You want the address or not?"

Joel returns his attention to the road. "Yeah, we'll go check it out now."

Thank god.

Joel's phone dings with an incoming location and he hits the *go* button, pulling the map up on the fancy GPS on the dash. It's large, black, and blocky, like something the military would have in their vehicles. I'm not sure why I'd expect any less.

"Good luck," Sloane says before ending the call

"You're waiting in the truck," Joel grates out through clenched teeth.

"But I could help. Maybe we could lure him—"

Joel shuts that idea down immediately. "No fucking way. The whole point is to keep you safe. Not throw you into the arms of danger."

"Clearly, he's after something I have. So ... put me to use."

"Absolutely not."

"So I'm just supposed to sit in this truck while you have all the fun?"

"Yes. That's exactly what you're going to do. The windows are bulletproof." Again ... not surprised. "You'll be safe in here for a few minutes while I scope it out."

I cross my arms and pout. I know it's childish, but at this point, I don't give a flying monkey's ass what Joel thinks of me. Our only hope for answers just ended his own life, and I'm sick of the world throwing this kind of crap at me.

The GPS alerts us that we've arrived at the address Sloane provided and I stare anxiously ahead as we inch down a long, pothole-riddled lane. A shiver rolls up my spine as we approach a run-down house. Dead vines crawl up the gray stone building, shielding more than half of it from the California sun. All the windows and doors have been boarded over. Gardens that would have once been beautiful are now unkempt and wilted from being strangled by weeds.

It looks like a house from a horror movie—uninhabitable and probably haunted. And it reeks of death.

"Who could live in a place like this?" I ask mindlessly.

"You'd be surprised what kind of conditions humans can survive in."

I gulp. I've lived in some pretty shoddy homes in my day, but none compare to this. I imagine creepy critters have also taken up residence here, some probably having perished within the walls.

Joel parks the truck behind an abandoned camper van that's been swallowed whole by tall grass. He shifts in his seat to face me, one arm casually draped over the steering wheel.

"I'm locking the keys inside the truck with you in case shit goes south and you need to get away. Don't unlock the doors for anyone but me, and don't even think about leaving the vehicle unless I tell you to. Got it?" I go to protest, but he cuts me off. "Keep your phone on in case I call."

I decide there's no sense in battling this out with him. He's a freaking wall and as stubborn as a desert mule. I nod in agreement, but a tiny part of me has already decided to disobey.

Joel drops the key into my hand, his warm fingers skimming over my ice-cold palm. He reaches behind him and pulls his handgun from the back of his jeans. I know he carries a weapon but watching him switch the safety off and double-check that it's loaded is a whole other thing.

"You're not going to kill him, are you?"

He winks at me, then barrels out of the truck, slamming the door shut and gesturing for me to lock the doors, before jogging across the lawn and disappearing behind the building.

Twenty-One

Joel

I ROUND THE BACK of the house and search for an entry point other than the boarded-up front door. There's a sunroom off the west side of the building, it's slumped structure tipping away from the main building. I creep toward it, keeping my back flat against the wall as I sweep my eyes from side to side. The door isn't boarded over, but it's locked.

I bust the glass out of the top half with my elbow and reach inside to unlock the handle. The plank of rotten wood creaks open and an uninviting stench hits me like a ton of bricks.

"Jesus Christ," I mutter to myself and hold my breath while I take a cautious step inside, my head on a swivel and eyes and ears open.

The house is fucking filthy. Not only is it rough, but it's been overrun by junkies. Needles and dirty spoons litter the floor in the center of the living room. Soiled blankets are piled into one corner. There's a bucket overflowing with human feces in another and I can only imagine the condition of the bathrooms.

Something moves in the corner of my eye. I whip my head toward it and aim my gun at the ass end of a rat disappearing into a hole in the wall.

I fucking hate rats.

After clearing the main floor, I climb the set of stairs, the rickety wood steps groaning beneath my weight. I don't trust that they won't give out from under me, but there's a nagging in my gut that tells me I need to check it out. I pause briefly at a boarded-up window in the stairwell. Light filters through a crack between two boards. I squint and spot my truck still parked where I left it and the outline of Stella's silhouette in the passenger seat.

Good girl.

I make my way upstairs and stare down a long, empty hallway toward an open door at the very end.

I clear each room on my way, then take a step inside the last room and breathe in the musky, damp air, catching a whiff of body odor that grows more pungent as I approach a tattered mattress laying on the worn-out hardwood floor. Sheets stained with sweat, blood, and other bodily fluids are strewn about, and beside the bed is a single metal picture frame. I drop to my haunches and snatch the tarnished frame off the floor and inspect the photo.

A young girl with dark hair and big hazel eyes sits in a flimsy plastic chair in what looks like a police station. Her pale blue dress is filthy, her knees are scraped up, her fingers are knotted in her lap, and there's a white gauze bandage around her right palm.

Stella.

I slip the photo from the frame and tuck it into my back pocket as a heavy cloud of rage develops over me.

Wyatt fucking Danvers is living on borrowed time.

I grab my phone and dial Mac, bringing him up to date.

Then I abandon the stomach-curdling bedroom with a renewed sense of craze powering each step. Just as I hit the bottom of the stairs, I hear a creak in the floorboards. I pause and lift my gun in front of me. The sound came from the living room.

My heart beats calm and steady as I stalk quietly toward the adjoining room. My trigger finger is itching and I can't wait to get my hands on the piece of shit.

Another creak.

I cock my gun, the *click* piercing the stale air. I step away from the wall and turn to face the room, ready to pull the trigger.

My heart lunges into my throat when a pair of wild hazel eyes stare back at me in terror.

"What the fuck did I tell you?" I snarl and lower my gun. I'm so fucking angry right now I could bend steel.

"I ... I needed to see for myself," Stella explains, her voice shaking with nervousness. "I'm sorry."

Lava rolls through my veins as I stalk toward the only woman in the world who can infuriate me the way this one does.

"Jesus, Stella. I could have fucking shot you."

"I'm ... I'm sorry," she repeats, taking a step back with each of mine forward.

"No, you're not. But you will be." A wolfish grin splits across my face. I won't fuck her in here. The smell is enough to gag a maggot. But I will be teaching her a lesson.

My dick hardens at the thought of spanking her. She's going to pay the price for this, handsomely. I've warned her too many times, but she refuses to listen.

"Wha-what?" she stammers, slowly backing up toward the exit.

"You better run, baby. Fast."

She spins and bolts for the door, her dark hair whipping behind her as she races out of the building. I give her a two second head start before taking off after her, hot on her heels. I suck in a breath of fresh air, clearing the stench from inside my nostrils. She's quicker than I thought, but not quick enough. I gain on her, every long stride of mine spanning two of hers.

She presses the unlock button on the key fob, the headlights flickering just as she reaches the truck. But she doesn't make it in time.

I coil an arm around her waist and slam her body back into mine, the air knocked from her lungs on impact. She kicks and screams, flailing her tiny limbs as I propel us forward, sandwiching her between my body and the hot metal of my truck. Her palms land flat on the passenger door, her cheek pressed against the unforgiving surface. I rock my hips into her, my hard cock straining painfully against my jeans.

I bury my nose into her hair and inhale, then snarl into her ear, "I'm not your past, Stella. You'll never be able to outrun me. Unfortunately, for you, I'm fucking angry right now and need an outlet. You chose the wrong time to disobey orders, princess."

She grinds her ass against me, teasing my dick with her soft curves. Her voice cracks when she says, "You don't scare me."

Fuck, she feels good.

I brush her hair over one shoulder, exposing the velvety skin beneath her ear. I've been dying to sink my teeth into her again. Wetting my lips, I clamp down on the tender flesh of her neck, hard enough to leave a mark, but not hard enough to draw blood. Always like that. I'll never hurt her in a way she doesn't crave.

"Ah," she arches her back, her fingers curling inward against the metal.

"Do you remember what happens to bad girls?" I growl against her neck, then lick away the sting of my bite.

She moans in pleasure. It's such a sweet sound, one I could listen to on repeat and never grow tired of. I slide one hand beneath her sweater and pinch a hard nipple through the thin fabric of her bra.

"I asked you a question, Stella. I suggest you answer it before I take your silence as permission to do as I see fit."

A tiny whimper escapes her, then she pants out, "N-no."

I slip my free hand down the front of her leggings and into her panties. My fingers glide over her smooth, plump pussy lips, and I slip my middle finger between her slick folds, strumming her clit. Her knees wobble and her body temperature rises as she breaks out in a cold sweat.

"They don't get to come. And baby, you've been very, *very* bad."
I push past her tight entrance and crook my finger, applying pressure in that fleshy, soft spot I know drives her wild with need.

She bucks against my hand. "No, please. I'll be good, I swear," she promises, but I know it's a lie. She enjoys this game just as much as I do.

"Begging is for those who have nothing left to offer. But you, princess, have plenty to offer me." I grind my hard cock against her ass, then apply more pressure to her swollen bud.

"Oh god," she cries out. "What do you want, Joel? Please," she pants.

A sinister chuckle vibrates from deep within me. She knows what I want. The problem with what I want is that once I get it, nothing else will ever be good enough. No *one* will ever be good enough.

I withdraw my hand and lick my fingers, mixing my saliva with her sweet nectar. She watches me with wide eyes and rapid breaths. I drag my fingers over her bottom lip, smearing her juices and my saliva over her mouth.

"Suck," I order. She purses her lips together and shakes her head. "Taste it, Stella. Taste how delicious you are. How good we are together. Tell me it isn't the most intoxicating fucking cocktail you've ever had."

She wraps her lips around my finger and sucks so hard, her cheeks hollow out. I pull my finger from her mouth with a *pop* then take a step back from her, shuddering at the loss of contact. She spins and leans her back against the truck, her breathing wild and uneven. We stand there staring at each other the way we've done a thousand times before I scoop my keys from the ground and open the passenger door for her.

"Get in," I order.

She glowers at me, sour from the orgasm I refused to gift her. "Fuck you, Joel," she spits.

"Maybe later, baby. For now, get in the goddamn truck."

Fuck, I need a strong drink and to put some distance between me and Stella. Feeling her body pressed against mine, watching her eyes light up, the high noon sun beaming down on her dark hair and soft, tanned skin … *tasting her*. I might as well move into the shithole of a house with the rest of the junkies, because *I am addicted*.

If I'm not careful, I'm going to screw this job up. I was a millisecond from shredding those too-tight leggings to pieces and fucking her right here. If it weren't for the risk of Danvers lingering nearby, I would have done it too.

I watch impatiently as Stella hoists herself into the passenger seat, only slightly less awkwardly than the first time she climbed up into my vehicle. I could have offered her a hand, but I'm not feeling particularly generous at the moment. I round the hood of my truck, adjusting my hard-on before hopping behind the wheel, and face straight ahead with my fingers gripping the steering wheel so tight, my knuckles are bleached white.

A call comes through the Bluetooth just as I put the truck in drive. I hit the answer button and clip out, "What?"

It's Sloane. "Always such a delight." She pops her gum loudly.

"Did you call to piss me off? Or do you have something useful for me?"

"Well ..." Sloane draws the single syllable out. "Since you asked so nicely, I think I have something." Another annoying pop. "Wyatt Danvers ... thirty-one years old ..."

I already know this. "Just get to the goddamn point, Sloane."

She sighs. "Wyatt Danvers didn't exist until he was eighteen. Appeared out of thin air."

Stella straightens her spine and glares at me. She's still fuming, but there's uncertainty swirling behind those pretty orbs of hers.

"He hasn't put down any real roots since then. Kind of a drifter. No surprise that he tends to hang around Detroit." Silence stretches on while Sloane taps away on her keyboard. "Find anything in that dump?" she asks between pops of her gum.

I think about the small photograph I have tucked into the back of my jeans of young Stella sitting in a police station. *Where the hell did Wyatt Danvers get that photo? Was he there that day? Did he steal it from someone else?*

"Nothing right now," I respond, deciding against instilling any further fear into the hot mess sitting beside me.

"Alrighty tighty. Keep boss man and I posted if anything comes up. I'll keep hunting Danvers and let you know when I find him."

I pull onto the highway and drive like a bat out of hell. Stella sits quietly, too quietly, mulling over the new information we have about Wyatt Danvers.

But what she says next causes every muscle in my body to tense. She's not thinking about Wyatt Danvers. Her main concern isn't her psychotic stalker. It's Roger Donovan and the trauma he inflicted on her. She's still living in her past, despite having changed her name and starting a new life.

"I caught him hurting another girl," Stella admits, as if she should carry a single ounce of guilt for what that sick fuck did. I peek over at her and see her eyes welling with tears again. "I was eleven and I think she was a year or two younger than me," she explains quietly as she stares down at her fingers knotted in her lap. Right now, she looks just like that little girl in the photo. Long, dark hair whipped from the wind, fingers knotted in her lap, a desolate look on her face. When she turns her gaze to me, I can't help the flood of sadness that sweeps through me. "He had her pinned against a wall. He was ... touching her. I didn't know what to do, so I just hid and watched."

I set my hand on her thigh and give it a gentle squeeze. "That's not on you, Stella. You need to believe me when I say you're not to blame for any of this."

She sniffles. "That girl went missing a few weeks later."

"That's not—"

She cuts me off. "No. It's not my fault, but I should have told the cops what happened. I think Roger was responsible for her disappearance, and I could have helped. I could have given them some sort of lead. But instead, I chose to run and hide like a coward. And even now, as a grown woman, I can't find it in me to tell them. What does that say about me, Joel?"

"It says that you were too fucking young to know what to do. You were a child and you were terrified."

A long silence stretches on before Stella asks, "Can I call Harper? I haven't heard from her since we landed."

"Sure, baby. You never need to ask permission to call your friend. I may be an asshole sometimes, but I'll never keep you from the people you care about."

She shoots me a weak smile, and not a minute later she's on the phone with Harper, having her ear chewed off by the bubbly blonde. Stella giggles more than once, her mood shifting, which also means Harper's just fine. Which means Zak's behaving himself.

A text comes through. Speak of the devil.

Shep: Get me the fuck outta here, Stone. She's driving me mental.

Stella eyes the message that popped up on the screen on the dash and the corner of her mouth tips into a grin.

"Uh huh. Listen, Harper. I've gotta go, but I'll call you later, okay?"

I hear Harper protesting just as Stella ends the call and turns toward me.

Flashing her a thousand-watt smile, I ask, "Problem, princess?"

"Your good buddy Zak called Harper high-maintenance then locked her in her bedroom. Clearly, he's not very bright if he's choosing to pick a fight with her. She'll chew him up and spit him out just like every other man that dares cross her path."

"Is that so?" I respond curiously. The thought of Zak Shephard having his ass handed to him by a feisty blonde is more than just a little entertaining. What I wouldn't give to be a fly on the wall.

"Yes, that's so. She has ..." Stella's brows pinch tight. "Special tools, I think. *Magical* tools that turn grown men into babbling babies," she says whimsically.

"Well, clearly her *tools* aren't working on Shep." But even though Zak's not a babbling baby, I've never seen a woman ruffle his feathers the way Harper does. Shep's the gentleman of the three of us—the cool, calm, collected one who lays his coat down over puddles and helps old ladies with their groceries.

"You better warn him to sleep with one eye open," Stella quips, and I'm not entirely sure if she's joking or not.

"Zak can handle himself. He's a big boy. Tell Harper to play nice in the meantime. I'm not pulling Zak off duty until we have Danvers, so she might as well get used to having him around."

Shaking her head, she says, "I'm not telling her that. I value my life. But feel free to pass the message along to her yourself. It'll be your funeral."

Conversation grows easier with each passing minute. The drive back to my place is, dare I say, pleasant. I've never enjoyed the company of a woman beyond the time it takes to get my dick wet. But with Stella, it's ... natural.

But it'll all come crashing down eventually. She'll put those walls back up and push me away, just like she always does. And I'll be left standing there like an idiot with my cock in my hand, waiting for the next opportunity to get to her.

It's a sick kind of game I'm playing. One of tricking her into disobeying, or causing her to crack, just so I have an excuse to touch her again, to put her back together. But I'm afraid every time she breaks, there will be more and more pieces to pick up. Eventually, she'll get tired of shattering and do what she does best.

She'll run. And next time, I think she'll make damn sure she isn't found.

Twenty-Two

Stella

I BREAK FREE FROM my dream, shoot up in bed, and bring a hand to the small bruise on my neck, reminded of the way my pussy throbs when Joel sinks his teeth into me. The way his cock pressed against my backside while he pinned me against his truck. How his skilled fingers seem to find that special spot inside of me every single time. It's unnerving ... that he seems to know my body better than I do.

But I'm violently ripped from my state of arousal when I hear the faintest of whispers, like the rustling of fabric. My heart pounds in my chest, and all the blood in my body rushes to my head as I'm completely engulfed by my worst fear. Panicked, I feel around the bedside table and flick the lamp on. My eyes quickly adjust, and I jerk back in shock.

"Jesus, Joel. You scared me," I say breathlessly as I clutch the sheet and tug it up over my bare chest. I typically sleep in shorts and a T-shirt, but something about being in Joel's home ... I don't know ... I feel like I can let my guard down.

But regret is quickly flooding my system, and he doesn't respond to my freaking question and now I'm freaking the fuck out and he's staring at me unblinking and oh my god, I don't know what to do.

I mentally slap myself for being completely irrational and focus on the man staring silently at me while I fight an internal panic attack.

Joel doesn't even blink. His only movement is the slow, rhythmic rise and fall of his chest as he sits still as a statue in an oversized chair in the darkest corner of the room. There's an unexplained anguish to him right now, like his own thoughts are cloaking him in misery.

"Please say something." I ball the sheet tighter. Something isn't right, and the way he's looking at me ...

"Don't," he says with warning, his voice deep and gravelly, like he just swallowed a fresh handful of rocks.

"Don't what?"

His huge body is practically overflowing out of the chair, his long, jeaned legs spread wide in front of him. I glimpse his enormous hands stretched out on the arms of the chair, his fingertips white from gripping the navy fabric like it's taking every ounce of restraint to not lunge at me.

"Joel, you're making me nervous. What's going on?" I curl my knees up to my chest beneath the covers and make myself as small as humanly possible.

"Lay down," he demands without expression.

My head whips side to side. "No."

"Now!" His voice booms, startling me.

I glance at the door and consider making a run for it, but there's no way I'd make it past him. He's too big. Too fast. He's already proven that. I abort that plan and do the only thing I can. I obey.

Laying my head on my pillow, I chance a peek at the foot of the bed where Joel now stands, looming like a giant shadowy apparition from a nightmare.

Then I feel the smooth satin sheet slipping away, brushing coolly over my nipples as Joel strips me free of the only barrier between him and my naked body. In a desperate attempt to save myself from unimaginable embarrassment, I tug back on the sheet.

"Stella," he says my name like a warning. I can't see his eyes, but I can see his jaw slide in irritation in the dim light.

Every alarm in my head begins wailing as a thousand tiny red flags stand at attention. I release my grip, my self-consciousness rearing its ugly head as I'm bared to Joel, completely exposed. I reach for the lamp to flip the light off, but yelp when two large hands wrap around my ankles and drag me down the bed.

"Don't hide from me. Not now. Not ever," he snarls.

"Joel, I—"

"Shut up, Stella."

I swallow the words I want to say and watch anxiously as Joel cups both of my calves in his hands, bends my knees, and sets my feet flat on the bed, my heels brushing against my bottom. His blue eyes never leave mine.

Until they do.

And oh god does it burn when his heated gaze sears a path all the way down my body and straight to my exposed center.

His lip twitches, and I want to sink into the mattress and disappear forever. I know he's seen this part of me already when I was in the bathtub, but that was different. I was in control ... I think so, anyway. But right now, there's something about Joel that's unsettling. Disturbing.

"Look at my good girl," he purrs, but not in a cute kitten kind of way. More like when a lion purrs as he devours his freshly hunted prey. "Already so wet for me."

I say his name, but he doesn't hear me. He doesn't see me. I'm not human to him anymore. I'm a meal. Something has shifted in him, and as much as I'm turned on by it, I'm also freaking terrified.

"Tell me to stop." His eyes dart back up to mine, so full of anguish and hunger and desire. I could drown in those baby blues, swallowed whole by everything that is Joel, and I don't think I'd even try to save myself. I'd just let my soul sink to the bottom and collapse gently onto the ocean floor until death eventually comes for me.

Shaking my head, I manage a garbled, "I don't want you to stop."

His pupils blow wide and I know for certain what he's about to say will alter my perception of reality.

"This is the only chance I'm giving you to run, Stella. Once I'm inside of you, you're mine. I will own you. Every fucking part of you. Every kiss. Every orgasm. Every breath you fucking take. Even your pain will be mine, and mine alone. And just when you think I've had enough, I'll take your future too. Your bright, beautiful future, and I'll blend it with mine in every way possible. Our darkness will be so intertwined, you won't be able to tell whose demons are whose." He wets his lips, then adds once again, but this time with finality, "Tell me to stop, Stella."

I shiver at his words, his promise to dominate every aspect of my life sitting heavy in my heart. His hands are still on my calves, his thumbs tenderly drawing circles. I know I'm about to head down a path of assured destruction. I'm about to skip blindly toward the monster lurking in the shadows then leap straight into his arms. But I've never wanted anything more than to vanish into the dark with him and let him eat me alive.

My bottom lip trembles from the weight of the situation. There's not a doubt in my mind ... I want this.

"Use your words, baby."

"I'm not scared. I want it. All of it."

Joel scans my face for any hint of a lie, his expression darkening with each nanosecond that ticks by.

"I won't hurt you," he promises. "Not in any way you don't want me to. But I've been holding back, and it's taken every ounce of my restraint to not rip you to pieces, just so I can put you back together the way I choose."

Hot tears prick behind my eyes. I'm not sure if it's the thought of being owned the way I know Joel will own me, or if it's because I'm absolutely terrified of how much it will hurt when he decides he's had enough.

"I'm already broken, Joel. Do your worst."

His thumbs stall as he studies me. Then he kneels and brings his mouth to my foot, planting a soft kiss on the top of it. His lips are hot, feverish almost.

I claw at the sheets beside me as he plants another kiss a few inches higher, climbing the length of my leg with his hands skimming lazily behind his trail of adoration. It's pure torture, having him this close and taking his time when all I want is for him to fuck me into next week. A shiver rolls down my spine and a flurry of goosebumps scatter across my skin.

His hot breath tickles my pussy, but he doesn't touch it. Instead, he drags his tongue across my stomach, from one hip to the other, just as I had done with my hand in the tub, then he retreats back down my other leg, his hands dipping beneath my ass and squeezing as he makes his descent.

Then he stands and pulls his shirt over his head, exposing his perfectly sculpted stomach and chest and all those dark tattoos. My body temperature spikes and my mouth fills with saliva as I study him in the dim light. Everything about Joel is hard and intense, but there's a softness beneath that granite exterior, and I'm beginning to wonder if it's been there all along and I'm not the only one with walls.

Joel skillfully removes his belt, the leather whispering as it slides through the loops. He discards it on the chair and I'm overcome with another surge of panic.

Panic, because I've never wanted someone this much before and it's scaring the living hell out of me. Panic, because clearly, I'm a dumpster fire of emotions and need some serious therapy. Panic, because Joel's huge and beautiful and terrifying and I'm running full speed toward his black abyss.

"You're unsure," he states, freezing when he senses my hesitation.

Swallowing the boulder in my throat, I tell him, "You have a look in your eyes."

He angles his head, and I swear I see a flicker of amusement cross his face. "What look?"

"Like I'm about to be your dinner."

Then he grins a devastating, wicked grin and tugs his pants down his legs. His black boxers are the only barrier between us now, and they're struggling to conceal the giant bulge behind them.

"Does that make you nervous?" he asks, sardonically.

"No," I lie.

"Hmm. You look nervous." He drops his boxers to the floor and his rock-hard cock springs free before my eyes, the tip glistening with a bead of cum that I'm desperate to taste.

I wet my lips, then ask, "Should I be?" He promised he wouldn't do anything I don't want him to, yet here I am, quite literally trembling with fear.

"Yes," he states plainly, then fists the base of his cock and pulls.

"Why?"

"Because I'm going to have my way with you."

Twenty-Three

Stella

J OEL KNEELS ON THE floor again and snatches my wrists in his hands, pinning them to the mattress on either side of my hips. His mouth is inches from my dripping wet pussy. He inhales deeply and I hold my breath, because what the actual fuck.

"Mm," he hums. "I've been a patient man, princess. But this ..." His hot breath fans over my clit. The muscles in my core tighten, my orgasm already building. "This sweet fucking pussy of yours is enough to push me over the edge. And *it's all mine.*"

I arch my back off the bed, drawing his attention to my breasts. I need him to touch me, to fuck me. My entire body is aching with desire. I buck when he drags his nose up my slit as if swiping a credit card, then flattens his tongue against my throbbing clit.

"Oh god," I moan.

His hands tighten around my wrists as I ball my fists at my sides and struggle against his grip. When he latches onto my clit and sucks it between his teeth, I cry out and buck against his face. It doesn't hurt, but the raw vulnerability of his teeth on that part of me ...

"Please," I beg, desperate for release. I'm already so close. I feel him smile against my pussy before lapping at my juices again.

My breathing diminishes into nothing more than tiny pants, and my eyes roll back in my head. I stretch and arch and try to break my hands free. I need to touch him, to run my hands through his thick hair, to feel his hot skin beneath my fingers.

But then he pulls his mouth away, and I throw my head back in frustration.

"Not yet, princess."

He climbs onto the bed and forces his hips between my thighs, capturing both of my hands in one of his giant paws above my head. His cock brushes against my thigh, leaving a small trail of warm cum.

"I'm going to fucking destroy you."

"I'm not afraid of you," I rush out.

Chuckling, he explains, "Your pulse quickens when you lie." Then he thumbs my wrist, reminding me that he's a human lie detector test. "Tell me you're afraid. Admit you're a liar."

When I don't respond, he bites the side of my neck. I hiss from the sharp pain, but it's like a hot-wire to my pussy. By the time Joel's done with me, I'm going to be a canvas of black and blue.

A work of art. Marked by him, I'll be the most beautiful I've ever been.

"I'm not afraid of you," I repeat, squirming beneath him.

Without warning, he reaches between us and smacks my clit.

He smacks my freaking clit!

"Ah," I gasp. Okay, I am afraid of him. But not in the physical sense. I'm afraid of him ripping my heart to shreds then walking away from the bloodied pieces, leaving me to glue what's left back together and praying it's enough to get me through this life.

Nothing this good lasts.

"Fuck, baby. You're so wet." His fingers find my clit, soothing away the sting of the slap.

I make some weird, strangled noise in my throat as Joel brings me near orgasm again before delivering another slap to my pussy. I jerk and buck my hips. But then the pain fades to pleasure, and I go fucking feral.

This time he licks the pain away and I melt into the mattress like butter on hot pavement while he sucks greedily on my engorged flesh.

"Tell me you're afraid, and I'll let you come."

My resolve softens to the firmness of an overcooked noodle, and I forfeit. "Fine. Yes. You terrify me. Everything about you fucking terrifies me," I admit, the truth freeing me of my shackles. Metaphorically, of course, because he still hasn't released my damn wrists. "I ... I hate that I can't defend myself against you."

He pushes one long finger inside of me and I moan in pleasure as he stretches me out. Then he brings his lips up to my ear.

"It's me who should be afraid, princess. You're fucking ruining me."

I whimper, his words cutting deep. He growls a deep, animalistic sound, then his mouth comes down on mine in a bruising kiss. His finger pumps in and out of me, his thumb working the most sensitive part of my body.

His kiss is possessive and hot and desperate as he grinds his hard body into mine, giving me his weight. The man weighs at least a thousand pounds and I fucking love it.

Then he breaks the kiss and sucks a trail over my collarbone, then down to my heaving breasts. It feels as though every press of his lips sears the word *mine* into my flesh, branding me as his.

When he sucks one nipple into his mouth, I struggle to catch my breath.

"Oh god." My head spins like I'm on a tilt-a-whirl, my entire world falling off its axis. He goes to my other nipple and repeats the process, tormenting me until I feel drugged, ready to pass out from whatever elixir he's dosed me with.

He drags his nose down my stomach, inhaling the scent of my body, then feasts on me like I'm the last meal he'll ever have, savoring me for when I'm nothing more than an old, faded memory.

When I'm near coming, he adds another finger.

More pain. More pleasure. The lines are so blurred.

"Not yet," he snarls.

I'm hanging on the edge, one foot hovering idly over the rocky waters beneath a deadly cliff. My legs are shaking and zaps of electricity are flying through my body, causing every tiny hair to stand on end.

I try to hold back, but ...

My orgasm blows through me like an out of control freight train, completely unstoppable. Joel licks and sucks and pumps his fingers inside of me, and every bit of tension in my body concentrates into one spot then explodes out of me in surges of color, like fireworks on the Fourth of July. My whole world comes crashing down at the hands of the man between my legs. I convulse and contract as he slows his movements to draw the pleasure out far longer than my body can handle, finger fucking me straight through my orgasm until I'm so sensitive I'm twitching uncontrollably beneath him.

Joel releases my wrists and brings his mouth to mine so I can taste my salty, sweet arousal on his lips. My fingers fly over his body, skating over every ridge and hard plane of muscle as I memorize every inch of him.

"Fuck," he mumbles against my mouth. "You're goddamn nirvana, baby."

I'm weak, totally spent, and way too sensitive, but I still haven't felt him inside me. I know it's going to hurt, in more ways than one. But he could push me to my every physical limit, and I'd still come crawling back for more.

I grip his firm ass, pulling his body into mine until I feel the tip of his cock nudging against my entrance. One small thrust and he'd be inside of me. I'm a prisoner to this man. I was made for him to do as he pleases. It's empowering, knowing I have this affect on him.

"Lift your hips," he instructs, then tucks a pillow beneath my bottom.

He grips his cock and slides the swollen head between my pussy lips, coating himself in my juices, then pauses at my opening.

"You have the power here, Stella. If it's too much, just say so and I'll stop."

My heart bangs loudly and a flush of heat rises to my cheeks.

I have the power.

I nod and suck in a deep breath as he rocks his hips forward and pushes into me in one slow and controlled thrust, but it's no less devastating than if he had slammed into me full force. My head drops back and I pinch my eyes shut, struggling to accommodate his size.

"Fuck, you're tight," Joel hisses, then slowly withdraws and pushes all the way back in so he's seated deep inside me.

I let out a small whimper and he stills, staring down at my scrunched-up face. A tear slips down my cheek, but Joel catches it with his lips and kisses it away.

"So beautiful." He props himself on one elbow, massaging my clit with his free hand. "Relax, baby."

My pussy clenches around him, and he eases back out of me, then pushes back in harder than before. He slowly picks up the pace as I adjust to him, and eventually I'm meeting his thrusts with the rock of my hips, another orgasm building.

I bring my hands up to his face, feeling his scruff beneath my fingertips, and kiss him.

He's holding back. I can feel it in the shake of his hands, see it in the desperation in his eyes. "Take what you need," I whisper against his mouth.

He shakes his head. "I don't want to hurt—"

Hushing him, I promise, "You won't." His brows furrow as he studies my face. "If it's too much, I'll tell you. Please. I want this. I want you, Joel. All of you."

His expression softens and he drops his forehead to mine, chuckling.

"What's so funny?"

Grinning, he says, "Nothing." Then nuzzles into my neck, his breath leaving a damp heat on my skin, and begins fucking me hard and fast. I dig my fingernails into his back as his balls slap against my ass. His cock galvanizes to steel inside me and I wrap my legs around his hips and hook my ankles as I hang on for dear life. He's so deep, so thick and hard and rough.

"Mine," he snarls. I nod my head frantically, blinking away the tears in my eyes.

I am.

His breathing grows ragged, his heart hammering against mine. Even though he's losing control, his thumb is still making perfectly timed circles exactly where I need it most. He doesn't falter. Not now. Not ever.

A dull ache builds inside me. "Joel. I'm so close." The words are practically knocked out of me between his powerful thrusts.

"Come for me, baby," he orders. "I want to feel that perfect pussy squeeze around my cock. Fuck, I want to fill you up in the worst way."

He thrusts a few more times before I cry out, his name spilling from my lips as my walls contract around him. A few more thrusts and I feel him pulsing inside of me, filling me with his warm cum. His head drops back and he lets out a primal grunt as he fucks me through his release. Not until he's completely drained does he settle deep inside of me and drop his forehead to mine. His eyes flutter shut and once again he gives me his weight.

Even though I can't breathe properly, I feel the safest I've ever been. He's every bit as solid as the stone walls I've built up around myself, but even more impenetrable. Nothing will ever get to me as long as I'm right here, with my big, brooding granite man.

My fingers drift lazily over his shoulders, up and down his smooth, strong back. We're a sticky, sweaty mess, and his cum is seeping out of me.

I love it.

But then reality bitch-slaps me and I begin to panic.

"Oh my god! We didn't use—"

Joel presses a finger to my lips, cutting me off. I've never been so reckless in my life. I don't know who he's slept with. No doubt women throw themselves at him. How many vaginas has his dick been in? Probably at least a million.

As if he hears my racing thoughts, he says, "I'm clean."

Oh, thank god.

He slips out of me with a hiss, and I suddenly feel empty without him. He plants a chaste kiss on my forehead, disappears into the ensuite, and returns a moment later with a warm, wet cloth.

He instructs me to sit up, slides into bed behind me with his back against the headboard, then pulls me against his chest so my head is resting on his shoulder. He reaches between my thighs with the cloth and cleans me up. I tense against him, uncertain if I should feel embarrassed or if this is the sweetest thing a man has ever done for me.

I decide it is.

"You're thinking too hard again," he says lowly in my ear. "I told you I'd own you once I've been inside you, Stella. But that also means I'll take care of you."

"I ... Oh god," I breathe out when he massages my clit with the washcloth. I can feel him smile against my neck as he kisses me and pinches my nipple with his free hand, rolling the sensitive bud between his fingers.

"I'm on the pill," I blurt out. He didn't ask about contraceptives before we had sex, but it's not like I initiated the conversation either. In fact, he didn't seem at all concerned when I brought up the fact that we didn't use protection.

He stills behind me, and I think he's going to punish me for my outburst, but instead, he murmurs, "For now," then continues to turn me into a trembling puddle of wanton waste.

My orgasm snowballs, growing and growing until I'm riding his hand, my hips bucking on their own accord. Joel tosses the washcloth to the floor, scoots us down the bed, lifts me onto his lap so I'm straddling him backward, and lays back.

"Ride it," he demands, then lifts his hips and pushes his cock all the way in.

My back arches and my thighs tense as I'm forced to accommodate his size without warning. He's deeper than before from this position, and I'm sure I won't be sitting right for a week. Rough hands grip my hips and guide me, rocking me back and forth, my ass pressed against his pelvis, my hands gripping his thighs for balance. I peek over my shoulder at him. The restraint on his face is obvious by the two little lines between his pinched brows.

"I said ride it, princess."

Twenty-Four

Joel

MY ENTIRE BODY SHUDDERS as Stella rolls her hips, my dick buried so deep inside her, I'm not just fucking her gorgeous body anymore. I'm fucking her soul. Her dirty, messed up little soul that I feel the instinctual need to protect.

And that ass ... Jesus. The woman has curves that only a man as sick as Satan could have created. The kind of curves designed to intentionally lure men into sinning. But I'm going to hell anyway, so I'll gladly worship the little she-devil until the Grim Reaper comes for me.

Stella's back arches, her round ass on display for me as she rides my cock like a good girl. I grip her hip with one hand, slowing her every time she picks up the pace. I'm a glutton for punishment, forcing her to rock slowly, seductively, even though all I want to do is slam into her. But I know if she starts riding me fast, I'll blow my load within seconds, and no way will I allow myself to come before she does.

My princess will always come first.

I trace the length of her spine with my free hand, my fingers leaving a trail of goosebumps in their wake, all the way to the base of her spine, splaying my hand wide over her lower back.

"Fucking beautiful," I tell her as she breaks out in a cold sweat. When I feel her pussy clenching and her orgasm cresting again, I roll her onto her stomach, kneel behind her, lift her hips and press a palm between her shoulder blades, shoving her face down into the mattress. Then I plow into her from behind, fast and hard with my balls slapping against her pussy.

"Oh god," she cries, her voice muffled by the bed as she grips the sheets at the side of her head. Her ass bounces and she begins meeting me thrust for thrust, shoving herself further onto my cock like the greedy little thing she is.

"Ah, fuck, Stella," I groan, reaching around and smearing her juices around her clit.

She cries out and comes around my cock, her pussy contracting so tight that I'm following right behind her, filling her up again.

I decide this is how I want her from now on—marked by my fingers and teeth, and so full of my cum that it's seeping out of her.

I don't pull out of her this time. Instead, I roll us onto our sides, settle in behind her, and pull her in close so her back's against my stomach and my arms are wrapped around her. She doesn't protest. Just wiggles in closer and releases a long, pent-up sigh.

A few minutes later, I'm dozing off when I feel her shifting. I tighten my arm around her and nuzzle into the crook of her neck, inhaling her. She smells of vanilla and sex and a little like me. "Where do you think you're going?"

She pauses and stares down at me. The bedside lamp provides just enough light for me to see the sleepy smile on her face. "I have to pee," she says quietly.

I give her a swat on the ass and release her, ordering her to hurry back. She saunters off into the bathroom, completely naked, and I lay on my back with my hands folded behind my head, grinning like an idiot.

But my moment of bliss is swiftly interrupted by reality. The PI is dead, mysteriously the same day we needed his help. We don't yet know how long Danvers has been stalking Stella, but we know it's been at least a few years, probably longer. And he's growing ballsier by the day, which is exactly what stalkers do.

It starts out with an innocent encounter, then morphs into scouring the internet for pictures, obsessing over social media and the like. Then it snowballs into driving by their victim's house and place of work. The obsession feeds off itself, picking up speed and surface space until it's an out of control animal and starving for attention. And then they snap, and that's when they make themselves known to their victim. That's when it gets really fucking dangerous.

But I won't let it get that far. Wyatt Danvers will never come within reach of Stella.

A grim feeling settles into my bones. Stella's felt like she's been followed since she was fourteen and forced to kill her attacker, Roger Donovan, whose body was never found. Is he still alive? Did little teenage Stella not quite finish the job when she smashed his skull in with a rock? Did the PI, who's been tracking Stella since she was just a child, happen to witness what went down that day and Roger Donovan somehow find him and tie up that loose end?

No. That wouldn't make sense, because Roger Donovan isn't the one stalking Stella. Wyatt Danvers is, and there's no way Danvers and Donovan are the same guy. Wyatt's in his early thirties whereas Roger would be at least sixty by now. And Stella's certain Donovan was dead when she left him out there that day, his skull smashed in and surrounded by a pool of blood.

So ... where's his body? Why is the PI dead? Who the fuck is Wyatt Danvers and why is he stalking my girl? She said he looked familiar, but that she couldn't place him. Has she seen him around while he's been creeping her? Is he a guy from college she turned down and couldn't take no for an answer?

Too many holes to fill in. Too many missing pieces.

When Stella reappears, I drag her close and drape my arm over her waist and pin her down with my leg over hers.

A moment later, she tilts her head back and peeks up at me. "I have a question," she says sheepishly.

"Mm," I hum, exhaustion slowly taking hold of me.

"Is there another woman I should know about?"

If I was drifting off to sleep before, I'm sure as fuck wide awake now. Propping myself up on my elbow, I stare down at Stella.

There's a pink hue to her cheeks, like she's embarrassed for asking me such a silly question.

Then it dawns on me, and I can't help the chuckle that bubbles from my chest. Sweeping a strand of hair off her forehead, I tell her, "If the maid that visits weekly counts, then yes. But other than her, you're the only woman that's ever stepped foot into my home."

She twists her mouth in thought, then presses on. "You could have a woman and *not* have her in your home, so that doesn't really mean much."

Smirking, I agree, "That's true. But no, princess. Haven't so much as looked at another woman since I laid eyes on you six weeks ago." That was a slipup, and Stella catches it.

Recoiling, her voice rising an octave, she screeches, "Six weeks? You ..."

Rolling her onto her back and nudging her knees apart, I settle between her thighs and pin her wrists above her head. She doesn't flinch or struggle, and I can't help the pride that rises in my chest. My girl's getting comfortable with me. She's letting her guard down.

"You listening, Stella?" She nods and sucks her bottom lip between her teeth. "Good. Because I won't lie to you. And if I ever hide anything from you, it's only because I absolutely had to." She nods slowly at that too. "You already know Giulia hired us, but you didn't know she had us follow you for a few weeks before she died. I was in Detroit, tailing you, even boarded that plane with you when you came to California. I've been watching you, but rest assured, I never once breached any ethical code of conduct or invaded your privacy beyond the means to keep you safe and report back to Giulia. So, yeah, I laid eyes on you six weeks ago and you flipped my entire fucking world upside down. I've got a mad obsession over you, baby, far worse than Wyatt Danvers ever will, and I'll lay my life on the line to protect you like the goddamn princess you are. Got it?"

Her eyes pool with water until it's leaking down her cheeks. Kissing away her tears, I drive my point home by telling her, "Get used to being watched, baby. Because now that you're mine, you'll never truly be alone."

Twenty-Five

Joel

A DOOR SLAMS. I sit up and rub the sleep from my eyes. *When the fuck did I pass out?*

"What the hell is this?" Stella stands at the foot of the bed, her expression sour and body tense. She tosses a piece of paper onto the mattress and glowers at me. "Where the hell did you get that picture, Joel?" She crosses her arms and pops a hip. Fuck, she looks sexy in my T-shirt. "Hello," she snaps. "I'm talking to you."

I still haven't shown her the photo I found in Wyatt Danvers's bedroom. She was already freaked out enough. But now ... now I wish I had told her, because the betrayal in her eyes is sickening, and I know I fucked up.

I groan and crawl out of bed, not caring that I'm naked and sporting morning wood. Stella's gaze flicks to my dick then back up to my face as she takes a giant step back.

"I found it at the abandoned house yesterday and decided to keep it to myself until—"

"Until what, exactly?" She screeches. "Until I was no longer riding the crazy train? Well ..." She cackles manically "I've got news for you, buddy. I've been on that train most of my life and it's not stopping anytime soon."

My mouth moves before my brain has a chance to catch up. "Clearly," I deadpan, then snap my jaw shut.

Stella's eyes narrow on me. "Really, Joel. Do you think this is funny?"

"Not at all," I respond without hesitation, then decide I should do something to diffuse the situation. "Look. I found the photo in the bedroom I'm presuming belongs—"

"Stop." Stella slices her arm through the air. Several silent seconds tick on, the only sound in the room Stella's labored breathing. "You should have shown me. Do you have any idea what that picture means?" She blows out a rough breath as her eyes gloss over with tears. Dropping her tone, she says, "That picture was taken that night."

"I know, baby."

Her expression sobers, but only for the length of time it takes for her panic attack to sink its teeth in.

She shakes her head, and here it comes ...

"How am I supposed to be a functioning human being when my entire world has been thrown into a freaking blender? Carlo needs me to sign a bunch of paperwork that I don't really understand.

Harper's losing her shit over everything. My brain is so fried that I can't even put my underwear on straight, let alone deal with this."

I pinch her chin and tilt her head back. Brushing my lips softly over hers, I say gently, "Reel it back in, baby. I promise, I'm going to handle this. Just breathe for me. That's all I need you to do. Now and forever ... just breathe."

She sucks in a few gulps of air, her eyes never leaving mine. When I trace my thumb over her bottom lip, she visibly relaxes.

"Good girl. Now, listen. Sloane's already looking into every person that went through the police station that day. I assure you, we're leaving no stone unturned. We'll figure this out. But for now, I need you to go cook us breakfast while I make a few quick phone calls. Can you handle that for me?"

Stella peeps the photo laying on the bed behind me one last time, then nods, her tears already drying. Then she vanishes down the hall and I snatch the photo up and glare at it. Every nerve in my body is screaming that this photo is a crucial part of the mystery of Wyatt Danvers.

Grabbing my phone from the nightstand, I call Sloane to check in. She has nothing. Yet.

Next, I call Zak, who informs me that Harper is not only a pain in the ass, but that she attempted to escape out her bedroom window like some modern-day Rapunzel and is now hobbling around with a sprained ankle and perma-scowl.

Finally, I call Liam. Besides his usual grunts and groans, he has nothing to share.

So, I leave the bedroom and head to the kitchen where I find Stella whipping cabinets open and closed, searching for god-knows-what.

I lean against the wall and watch her reach up on her tippy toes for something on the top shelf. My T-shirt rides up her backside, giving me the slightest peek at the delicious crease beneath her ass cheeks. As usual, she's wearing simple black lace panties.

I lick my lips, my appetite for her nowhere near satisfied. If anything, having her last night only made me realize what I've been missing out on. Now … there's no stopping me from taking what I want, when I want it.

The tips of Stella's fingers skim the can of coffee she's reaching for, pushing it further out of reach. She mutters a curse word, then stretches as far as she can. I quietly prowl toward her, like a lion approaching a gazelle grazing innocently in the pasture.

Stella freezes, the muscles in her back tensing with every step I take. It appears that my meal senses imminent danger.

When I place my hands on her hips, she jumps, the fear rolling off her in waves. But then she presses her palms flat on the counter and peeks over her shoulder at me.

"What are you doing?" she asks, her eyes hooded and face free of makeup. Fuck, she's beautiful.

I grind my hips into her, my cock pressing against her lower back. Sweeping her hair off to one side and tugging my shirt down over her shoulder, I bring my lips to her neck to taste the salty, sweet skin that I've been craving since the second I opened my eyes.

"Mm," I hum as I kiss and suck my way from her shoulder up to the sensitive spot below her ear. "I'm starving, princess. But not for food."

She lets out a soft moan and drops her head back onto my chest as I take my time savoring every inch of her. I lift the hem of her shirt and my hands skim over her ribs, cupping her tits and rolling my thumbs over her hardened nipples.

"You're fucking beautiful like this. So warm. So soft and sweet." I pinch both of her peaks and she arches her back. "So needy." When she lifts her palms from the counter, I snatch her wrists and force her hands back down to the cold surface before her. "Move a muscle without my permission and you'll be punished. And you remember what happens to bad girls, don't you, baby?"

She bites down on her bottom lip and nods.

"Use your words, Stella. I won't ask again."

"Yes, I remember," she breathes out.

"That's my good girl."

I release her wrists and drag my hands up her arms, relishing every goosebump as she reacts to my touch. I squeeze her shoulders, massaging her tension away, then work my way down her back until my fingers reach the hem of my shirt again. Molding my body against hers, I hook my thumbs into her panties and growl into her ear, "I bet you're already wet for me, aren't you?" She grinds her ass against my cock, disobeying my order to not move a muscle. "You're going to pay for that."

Pushing a thumb through the flimsy lace, I rip one side of her panties free from her body and the scrap of material slides to the floor. I have intentions of shredding every last pair of panties in her wardrobe, and at this rate, it'll be sooner rather than later.

Stella lets out a yelp when I roughly grip her hips and pull her ass into me.

"Face on the counter," I demand.

"Joel, please—"

Before she has a chance to finish, I tug the shirt up her body, wrap her hair around my wrist and press her face into the counter between her hands. She hisses when her bare breasts press flush against the cold granite. Then I kick her legs apart, separating her thighs.

Her eyes widen when she realizes exactly what I have planned. Shaking her head, she pleads, "No, please don't. I listened. I didn't do anything wrong."

I lean back and glimpse her pretty pink pussy peeking out from behind. Priming her ass cheek with my palm, I tell her, "If you take your punishment like a good girl, I'll let you come. If not, well ... you know." Her knees begin to wobble, but I can practically smell her arousal already. "I'm going to spank you ten times. You're going to count for me. Ready, baby?"

"N-no," she stutters. "Please, Joel. I won't do it again."

"Do you trust me?" I ask her, ignoring her empty promises.

"I ... I don't know," she admits hesitantly.

My hand stalls on her ass and my grip tightens in her hair. I lean forward and press a soft kiss to her ruddy cheek. "How about a safe word?" She lets out a soft whimper. "Speak, Stella."

"Okay. A safe word."

"You tell me what it is, and you have my word that the second you so much as whisper it, we stop."

Her lower back glistens with a sheen of sweat as her breaths come in short pants, fogging up the polished, black granite in front of her face. "P-pickles."

"Pickles," I deadpan, a smirk tugging at the corner of my mouth. This girl continues to surprise me.

"Yes, pickles."

Chuckling, I agree, "Alright, pickles it is." I smooth my hand over her round bottom once more before bringing my palm down on her bare flesh with a sharp *crack*.

"Ah, fuck," she cries out and her body jerks forward.

Gently soothing the red handprint, I remind her, "Count."

"One," she rasps out.

I raise my hand and bring it down again, this time harder.

She bucks and cries out again. "Two." Each swift crack is followed by a throaty moan that makes my dick throb. "Three." Another smack. "Four."

With each spank, her pussy glistens more and more until eventually, she's so wet that it's coating the insides of her thighs. Gently stroking my hand over the blooming welt, I groan, then continue on.

When she gets to seven, I reward her bravery with a few strums of her clit.

"You're enjoying this a little too much, princess." She moans and bucks against my hand. Smearing her juices around, I lean over her so her back is flush with my stomach and graze my teeth over her jaw. One wild hazel eye stares back at me.

"Wha-what are you going to do?"

A wicked grin splits across my face as I push one finger inside her. "First, I'm going to finish punishing you. Then, I'm going to fuck you."

Her entire body breaks out in bumps when I remove my finger from her pussy and return to her red ass cheek. "Three more, then you can come."

My palm tingles and I know she's going to be sore after this. But I'm nothing if not a man of my word.

"Eight," she cries out but doesn't flinch this time. A tear rolls over her nose and pools with the others on the counter beside her face. "Nine." Another sob. Then finally, "Ten."

As soon as it leaves her mouth, I drop to my knees behind her, worshiping her like the fucking goddess she is, and lap at her wetness, licking her clean. Gripping her ass with both hands, I spread her cheeks and suck on her clit until she's grinding against my face, chasing her orgasm.

When she's near coming, I spin her around and lift her onto the counter, so her ass is perched on the edge. Propping her bare feet on my shoulders, I shove her chest and she leans back on her elbows.

"Oh god," she moans, her head dropping between her shoulders as I eat her out. Her hand drives into my hair and she rides my face. "Fuck, Joel."

I insert one finger, then another, and curl them inside of her so I'm hitting her sweet spot, pumping her with each circle of my tongue over her clit. She comes harder than ever, crying out as her hips rock uncontrollably and she soaks my face as she finds the type of release I knew I'd eventually get from her. Her wetness coats my beard and drips down my neck and bare chest, and I've never been so hard in all my fucking life.

But only two-thirds of my promise are complete. She was punished, she came, and now I need to fuck her.

I stand and stare down at her. She's embarrassed by her body's reaction. I can see it in the flush of her cheeks. I coax her legs around my hips and her arms around my neck and our mouths meet in a clash of teeth and tongues as we desperately claw at each other. Lifting her off the counter, I walk us to the bathroom, my cock bobbing painfully inside my boxers. Without setting her down or removing our clothing, I turn the shower on and step beneath the hot spray.

"Joel," she mumbles into my mouth, breaking our kiss. "I ... I don't ... I've never ..." Her thought comes out in tiny stammers, as if her brain is moving so fast, she can't form words.

Gently setting her on her feet, I drop my boxers to the floor of the shower and lift her shirt over her head and discard it. She hisses when I press her back into the cold tile and grind my hips into her.

"Just shut up and stop thinking. For once in your life, just *stop thinking*."

She sucks her bottom lip between her teeth and stares up at me with angst, her eyes a swirling pool of uncertainty.

I kiss her sweetly on the forehead, then spin her around and pin her against the wall. Locking her wrists behind her back in one of my hands, I let my other roam freely over her curves. She lets out a small whimper when I graze my fingers over the tender welt on her ass. My hand roams over her hip, down the length of her thigh to the back of her knee. I lift her leg and force her to set her foot on the built-in bench beside us. Her ass is jutted out, her back is arched beautifully, and her wrists are captured behind her back.

She's completely at my mercy like this.

Dipping my middle finger into her pussy, I whisper, "Still thinking, baby?"

She responds with a shiver and a silky moan that makes my cock jump. Sliding the length of my dick into the crevice of her ass, I growl a string of incomprehensible words.

"No. Not thinking. Just ... oh god," she cries out when I insert two fingers inside her.

"Fuck, Stella. This cunt is fucking perfect. So tight, and always soaking wet for me. Who does it belong to, princess?"

"You. It belongs to you," she breathes out.

Rewarding her good behavior with my thumb to her clit, I tell her, "That's right. Me. It's mine. Nobody will ever own it like I do, will they?"

"No. Nobody will ever own it like you do. It's yours, Joel. *I'm* yours. All yours. Please, just ..."

I withdraw my hand and insert my fingers into her mouth. "Taste what I do to you." She complies, wrapping her lips around my fingers and sucking them clean. "Tell me what you want."

"You. I want you. Please."

"Mm. I love when you beg for my cock." Slipping the head of my cock through her juices, I rock forward and plunge into her tight pussy in one heady thrust.

She cries out, her tight walls stretching around me. Gripping her wrists in a battle to compose myself, I slowly slide all the way out, my dick glistening with her arousal, then slam all the way back in, filling her completely.

"Fuck, you feel so good." I fuck her hard but slow, relishing the way her muscles contract with each thrust, pulling me in deeper and deeper. "Such a greedy pussy."

Her mouth opens and closes but all that comes out is labored breaths and garbled moans. I pinch her clit and her hips rock back, meeting each of my thrusts with desperation as she climbs higher and higher.

"You take this dick like such a good girl." She stares back at me over her shoulder and just seeing her like this is enough to make me come. "I need you to come, baby. Prove to me that I own you."

Our wet skin slaps as her climax rips through her and her knees buckle. I hold her upright and plow into her four more times before spilling into her, spurt after satisfying spurt.

"Fuck," I grunt, coming so hard I think my dick might fall off.

I release her wrists, slip out of her, and scoop her limp body into my arms. I collapse onto the bench with Stella cradled in my lap and kiss her. She sags against me, our hearts hammering wildly against each other.

Stroking her damp hair, I realize there's no better feeling than this. No better feeling than fucking Stella and then wrapping her up in my arms. Something in my chest cracks and light streams through, warming a part of me that's been cold and lifeless for so long.

She lays her cheek against my chest and listens to my hammering heart.

"You're thinking again," I accuse.

"I'm scared," she mumbles.

I trace my fingers up and down her spine, soothing her. "I'm not going to let anything happen to you."

She shakes her head. "It's not that. It's ... other things."

Peeking down at her, I ask, "What is it?"

A heavy sigh leaves her lips. "I spent years pushing men away. I never had anything more than unfulfilling one-night stands. And when I say unfulfilling, I mean ..." Her sentence trails off.

My gut clenches. I don't need to be reminded that other men have touched her before me. I think about it all the time, and the thought makes me fucking sick to my stomach. Jealousy is an ugly bitch I haven't been able to wrangle into submission since I first laid eyes on Stella.

"I'm afraid of what you're doing to me. I've never ..." Frustrated with herself, she blurts out, "I don't know what I'm saying."

Cupping her jaw in my hands and stroking her cheeks with my thumbs, I reassure her, "I'm not perfect, baby. I'm going to fuck up a time or two, but I promise I will never hurt you."

She stares up at me, her hazel eyes watery and bright. "How can you make a promise like that, Joel? We hardly know each other and

I've already crossed a line I'm not sure I'll ever be able to step back over."

I sit with that for a minute, because she's right. We barely know each other. But that's just it ... I barely know Stella, and yet I'm able to confidently make a commitment to never hurt her. To protect her for as long as I roam this miserable planet.

"Then we'll cross that line together. We'll be in danger *together*. Because you're a fucking storm, Stella. You showed up in my life, kicked up all sorts of dust, and sucked me into the center of all of it. We're not so different," I tell her, thinking about all the hookups I've had over the years, and how empty I felt afterwards. "I don't know what it is about you, whether it's your incessant need to be irritating as fuck, or your desire to fight me on every little thing, but I've never felt a pull like this before."

She blows right past my admission. "I'm not irritating. You're just incapable of dealing with a woman who's smarter than you."

Chuckling, I say, "See? Fighting me on every little thing." I'm not sure if it's that fiery attitude of hers, or the fact that she's sitting naked, soaking wet, and dripping my cum, but my cock springs back to life against her ass.

She feels it and her eyes widen. "You can't possibly be ready again."

I shift her on my lap, so she's sitting facing me with her feet planted flat on the bench on either side of my hips, and slowly ease myself inside of her. Exactly where I belong.

Her hands grip my shoulders and her head drops back as I lift her hips and slip inside of her, our juices a sticky, messy disaster coating both of our thighs.

"Oh, fuck. You're so deep," she hisses, her fingers finding purchase in my bare shoulders.

Studying her face, I memorize every fine detail. Every cute freckle dotting her nose. The thick, dark lashes that frame the most unusual shade of hazel irises I've ever seen. The high arch of her brows. The sharp angle of her cheekbones. Those full, pink lips.

Quickening my pace, I thrust into her harder, pushing her toward the edge and following closely behind. She cries out. I meet her there, grunting out my release just as she tumbles over the cliff.

We catch our breath and I help her to her feet. wash her hair and body, taking extra care around the raised handprint on her ass. She squirts a glob of shampoo into her hand and giggles as she reaches up and washes my hair. There's something about that mischievous little smirk of hers that makes my rib cage tighten around my lungs and squeeze out all the oxygen. Watching her genuinely enjoy herself, being so carefree, is a whole other layer of the onion I intend on peeling back.

Twenty-Six

Stella

E VERY SINGLE MUSCLE IN my body screams out in protest as I stretch beneath the covers. But then it dawns on me. I'm in bed in the middle of the day, napping, with a giant, tattooed Navy SEAL snoozing peacefully next to me.

I've been fucked to within an inch of my life, have had more orgasms in a week than I have in ... ever. And I haven't a clue what I'm going to do with the rest of my life. I've decided to not go back to Detroit, but I'm not sure if I want to stay in California either.

I roll onto my side and stare up at Joel. His hard features are slack, and he almost has a boyish look to him when he's sleeping, like all that gruffness and terrifying broodiness fades away while he's unconscious.

But then his blue eyes crack open a sliver and peer down at me, and all that intensity returns.

I smile sweetly at him. "You're much cuter when you're sleeping."

"Mm. You're much cuter when you're stuffed full of my cock," he responds, a sly grin on his handsome face.

Jeez, he's forward.

I shove my embarrassment aside and trace a lazy finger over the tattoos on Joel's ropy forearm. A single black eye stares back at me, its inky iris surrounded by a billow of smoky clouds, a stopwatch, and a lighthouse. I follow each dark line before moving up to his bicep.

So many muscles. So many tattoos.

There's a mountain range with a full moon hanging high above one of the peaks—a starry sky its moody backdrop. I try to count the cluster of stars but lose track when I come to two that look fresher than the rest.

"These ones are new," I observe. "Why?"

He stares down at me with hooded eyes and a muscle in his jaw slides. God, he's so beautiful, he could make angels weep. We've spent several days at his house binge-watching stupid dramedies and true crime documentaries, eating, and sleeping. *Screwing.* I've studied his tattoos several times in an attempt to understand them, but they're as mysterious as the man himself.

"It's how I remember them," he says lowly.

I drag my finger up to his collarbone and trace it to his other shoulder, then down his bicep. "Remember who?"

I watch his Adam's apple bob as he swallows hard. Then his next words come out strained. "The ones we couldn't save."

Hot tears prick behind my eyes and I prop myself up on my elbow and try counting the stars again through blurred vision. I make it to thirty-two before Joel pinches my chin between his thumb and forefinger and pulls me down for a long, sultry kiss. His throaty moan vibrates straight to my pussy, which is far too sore and sensitive for anything right now.

"What about the ones you *did* save, though?"

He watches me count the stars again. "I know what you're trying to do, to convince me that we're doing something noble and brave. But the ones that matter the most are the ones we didn't get to in time. Innocent people. Mostly women and children who were gone before we knew they even existed."

"So, when you said your team does jobs the military can't ..."

"We specialize in bringing down human traffickers but do other odd jobs when needed, like this one."

Being referred to as a job hurts a little, but I know that's what I am for Sweetwater. But then confusion replaces that hurt and I ask, "Why can't the military bring down human traffickers themselves?"

Joel captures my wandering hand in his and laces our fingers together. My hand is half the size of his, but somehow, they fit perfectly, like two puzzle pieces.

"You'd be surprised who runs these rings. Other governments, underground officials with more money and power than brains. If they found out who was responsible for bringing them down, it could start a war. So, we go in and take care of things quietly. Discretely. It's not a perfect system, but I like to think we're on the right side of the law. Some of us are pretty fucked up from our time in the military, but our morals are still intact. Mostly."

What Zak told me about Joel's PTSD springs to mind. I know in my heart that Joel's good. I feel it in my very being. He may be rough around the edges and push limits sometimes, but his morals are still firmly intact. If I'm being honest with myself, which let's be real ... that's rare, I trust him, regardless of whether or not I say I do. I know without a shadow of doubt that he would never intentionally hurt me.

Then I think of Zak, who's just as scary as Joel, but more the quiet type, more polite. Intelligence rolls off him in waves, and you can tell he's extremely capable—a smooth operator, for lack of better words. And no doubt a ladies' man. I wonder for a brief moment how him and Harper are coping.

But then my thoughts slide to Liam. There's something dark manifesting inside of him. Like he's seen or done something that haunts him. And that knife he plays with ... I shudder.

"So, these two stars ..."

"One for a twenty-three-year-old woman named Crystal, the other for a twelve-year-old girl named Anna."

A lump forms in my throat. *Twelve years old.* What horrors did that poor child experience before they ripped her life out from under her? I don't think I could handle knowing.

"Did you catch the people who took them?" I ask, praying to God they suffered more than all their victims combined.

Joel's gaze darkens. Beneath his muscular chest, his heart beats loud and steady. "Not yet. But we will."

"I know you will. I just can't imagine what ..." I can't finish that sentence.

"The world is full of evil, Stella. Just because the devil resides in hell, doesn't mean he won't send demons to do his dirty work."

"Harriet once said something similar to me. I would have been about sixteen, seventeen maybe. She told me some people are born evil. That the devil tainted their souls before they ever took their first breath. There was no hope for these people. They were damned from the moment they were conceived."

Silence stretches on before Joel asks, "Do you believe that too?"

I sigh and drop my head to the pillow and stare up at the ceiling. Joel slips an arm under my pillow, the other around my waist, and pulls me in close, burying his nose in my hair.

"I'm not sure what I believe anymore."

Something buzzes beside the bed. Joel groans, then reaches over for his cell phone.

"What?" He snaps into the device.

I hear the faint sound of a woman's voice. It's Sloane. Joel lays still and silent beside me, listening to every word she has to say.

Then he sits up abruptly, propping his back against the headboard. Glaring down at me, he growls into the phone, "Get me *everything.*" Then he ends the call.

Clutching the sheet tightly to my chest, I ask, "What is it?"

Joel rakes a hand through his already messy hair and hits me with a look so pitiful, I recoil. "Sloane looked into the PI some more. He never had a drug problem."

"But he ..."

Joel nods and blows out a ragged breath. "Someone killed him and tried to make it look like an accidental overdose."

I slap a hand over my mouth.

"Stella." I spring from the bed and begin pacing the room. Joel meets me there and holds me at arm's length. "Is there any chance at all that Roger was still alive when you left him out there in that forest?"

"I ... I already told you."

"I know, baby. But his body was never found."

My mouth opens and closes and my brain feels like it was just shoved through a meat grinder. "He had to have been dead. I hit him ... over and over and over ... I hit him so much. Oh god ... there was so much blood, Joel." Violent sobs wrack my body, and I nearly collapse to my knees. But before I hit the floor, Joel scoops me up and cradles me in his lap on the edge of the bed. I bury my face in his chest and lose myself to my emotions. *Again.*

"Shhh. It's okay." Joel rocks me back and forth, smoothing my hair down my back. "I believe you. I do, I promise. But it would make sense if he somehow survived and took off."

"No," I cry, shaking my head. "There was ... the blood. The bone. It was too much."

"Okay. It's okay. We'll figure this out. Sloane's looking into Harriet."

I snap my head up and stare at him in shock. "What? Harriet? No," I sniffle and shake my head. "There's no way Harriet's involved."

Joel's eyes dart back and forth between mine. "You'd be surprised—"

"No. Harriet had no idea. She couldn't be involved in this."

"We're still going to look into her, but if you're certain ..."

"I'm certain."

Twenty-Seven

Stella

DAYS TICK BY AND I feel like I'm starring in some cheesy, never-ending horror movie, but instead of a movie, it's my life. My system is stuck in overdrive, and pretty soon, I'm going to crash and burn.

Joel's kept me busy, and by busy I mean contorted into every sexual position possible while he fucks me into oblivion. But I've been going a little stir-crazy. We haven't left the house in days, except once to step outside to grab the grocery delivery Joel placed.

Zak's still at Harper's, despite her valiant efforts of throwing him out on his ass. Liam's still posted up at Casa del Sol, probably wandering the halls aimlessly while fiddling with his knife out of pure boredom. And Martina's still stuck in some hotel somewhere, flanked by a group of contracted security guys.

Just because the devil resides in hell, doesn't mean he won't send demons to do his dirty work.

Joel's words play over and over in my head. Roger was a demon, undoubtedly contracted by the devil himself, but there's no way he survived those blows to the head. There was too much blood. His body was too still. I saw him lying there, dead, with my own two eyes.

And Harriet wasn't involved. Sloane looked into her and confirmed that there's no way she took part in Roger's sick games. She also confirmed that the PI was murdered right there in the hospital. But conveniently, the hospital surveillance has been nonoperational for several weeks, the system due for upgrades apparently, and nobody saw anything or anyone strange go in or out that day. The police have been notified, but Joel said they likely won't find anything. The case will go cold, and Wyatt will get away with it.

So until Sloane can track him down, we're sitting ducks, just waiting for Wyatt to make his next move or slip up.

I massage my throbbing temples and take a few deep breaths. I feel like I've been hit by a dump truck, and haven't been able to sleep properly since I found that photo peeking out of the back of Joel's jean pocket. I haven't a clue who took it, and I'm racking my brain trying to visualize the police station and the angle of the photo, but continue to come up empty.

I pad out to the kitchen in nothing but the gold bracelet Giulia left me, comfy cotton undies, and one of Joel's T-shirts while Joel takes a shower. I fill a glass with water from the tap and slug it back.

It does nothing to cool the burning sensation in my throat. I refill it and take another gulp.

Leaning against the counter, I stare down the hallway at Joel's bedroom door. An unusual warmth blooms inside me.

I've hated myself for years. I've been on the run, watching over my shoulder ever since I was fourteen and lied to the cops about that night. Then I turned eighteen and walked into a government office and changed my legal name from Emma Romano to Stella Clarke. I learned then that I had a knack for manipulating people. But even then, I didn't feel safe.

Over and over again, images of Roger's bloated body, rigor mortis setting in, flash behind my eyelids. Visuals of his rotten flesh being picked at by coyotes and vultures have become a daily thing for me.

His body was never found.

It's likely he was dragged off by hungry wildlife and eaten, piece by disgusting piece, over a matter of weeks. I'm certain the cops would have found him if I hadn't gotten turned around out there in the forest. But then there's the matter of his missing van. It was also never located. And now I'm second-guessing whether he did survive, if I underestimated how hard I hit him, or how much blood there was.

But all of those feelings of fear and uncertainty, all of those haunting images vanish when I'm with Joel. He's like a big, grumpy security blanket, all rough edges and tattered threads. But then there are these moments where his tough exterior flakes away and I'm wrapped up in his safe haven.

I set the glass down in the sink and turn to look out the window that overlooks the vast property. It's dark out now, but the backyard is well lit with twinkling strings of lights. One of the motion sensor lights flick on.

I take a cautious step backward, my legs suddenly wobbly and heart beating erratically in my chest. Joel had told me the motion sensors are set to detect anything over a certain size to avoid turning on every time a squirrel scampers across the yard. I shake my head and remind myself that I'm safely locked up in Joel's home. Nobody can get in.

There's movement beyond the kitchen window, and I step forward and peer out the small pane of glass over the sink, my breath creating a circle of fog in front of my face. I swipe it away and squint at the shadowy tree line.

I place a hand to my chest and blow out a breath of relief, laughing at myself for being utterly ridiculous. A female deer stares back at me, her giant doe eyes black and shiny, her jaw working over and over as she ruminates.

I tiptoe over to the patio doors off the dining room that lead to the backyard and watch her closely. I consider grabbing my phone to snap some photos, but by time I retrieve it, she'll probably have moved on.

The keypad beside the doors blinks at me tauntingly. I've watched Joel punch his code in a few times now. I know it's eight digits and I'm pretty sure I remember it.

Holding my tongue just right, I punch in eight digits. There's an annoying squawking sound and a flashing red light that tells me it's wrong.

I try two more times, and nearly jump with joy when it flashes green, *system unarmed* printed in bold across the tiny screen.

I carefully slide open the patio door and step onto the cold stone patio in bare feet. The cool night air slaps against my skin and I rub my arms to chase away the chill. Sure enough, off in the distance, there she is.

"Hi, beautiful," I whisper as unthreateningly as possible, then make some unidentifiable clucking noises. She takes a step back, eyeing me warily, but she doesn't run.

I know she's not going to come any closer, so I take a step toward her. She perks up, her ears twitching and rotating. I take another step forward, and another motion light comes on, nearly blinding me. I wince, casting my hand over my eyes like I'm blocking out the sun as the doe vanishes into the dark shadows of the trees.

I release a sigh and turn to head back inside, but just as I reach for the door, something rough clamps over my mouth, and I'm jerked backward so fast I don't have a chance to react.

"No! Joel! Help!" But my cries are muffled by whatever's covering my mouth. I inhale something sweet, the tip of my tongue tasting the damp fabric smothering my face.

A set of unfamiliar arms galvanize around me, dragging me further and further into the darkness. Hot, dragon breath scorches my neck as my attacker snarls something in my ear.

Then everything goes black.

Twenty-Eight

Stella

MY THROBBING HEAD LOLLS to the side as I wake from my chloroform-induced slumber. I'm not sure how long I've been out, but I'm not ready to open my eyes yet, so I just listen.

There's a steady dripping sound, like fat rain drops splattering on your windshield right before the storm rolls in. It's directly above me, I think. I allow the soothing rhythm to take me as far away as possible from wherever I am.

I imagine being nestled away in a forest somewhere, tent camping, with nothing but the warmth of a campfire and Joel's giant body to shield me from the chill of the evening air. Over the years, I've conquered my fear of the woods despite what I went through. Even though I knew Roger was dead, I refused to allow him to win. And I know that with Joel, it wouldn't bother me to be lost somewhere out there with the trees and soil and leaves and woodland animals. I'd welcome it, actually, because I know I'd be safe with him.

He seems like the type of guy who would camp. Surely he knows how to survive in the wilderness. Maybe I could proposition him when I see him. I could cut him a deal. He takes me camping for a weekend, and I don't argue with him about a single thing for a full twenty-four hours.

It's a bargain, really.

But as the dripping sound slows, so do my whimsical thoughts. My eyelids scrape against my eyeballs like cheese graters as I peel my lids open and take in my surroundings. I sit upright, groaning as my aching body rights itself and wincing at the renewed pounding in my head. My pupils adjust to the darkness, and panic rips through me with claws so sharp, I'm sure I'll be shredded to pieces.

I'm on a dirt floor. My wrists are bound behind me, secured to something solid. As if my nose gets the memo that I'm in imminent danger, it picks up the stench of the death that wafts around me and my stomach churns like a violent hurricane in the middle of the ocean. I swallow the bile rising in my throat, refusing to add chunks of vomit to the mix.

A chill rolls through my body and I try to calm the trembling, to force my muscles to still, but I can't. I'm freezing cold and locked away in a dark, damp basement.

Seconds later, a square hole in the ceiling parts way and bright light filters through the opening, blinding me. When my eyes adjust once again, a fresh wave of fear crashes over me as a dark figure looms in the doorway, his presence filling the space with something

far more ominous than the pitch black I've been banished to.
Something evil and depraved.

My teeth chatter audibly, and I strain against the bindings holding my wrists behind my back. I dig my heels into the dirt floor and
press my spine into the cold, unforgiving structure behind me.

The dark figure steps forward and every nightmare I ever had,
every terrifying thought comes crashing down around me. My
heart hammers in its cage, threatening to break free and make a
run for it.

*This can't be happening. Wyatt Danvers can't be standing in
front of me right now.*

"Oh, sweet, sweet Emma. Did you miss me?"

No, no, no!

Wait ... Emma? I rake my eyes from his worn-out boots, up
the length of his baggy, filthy jeans stained with varying shades of
brown and red, and land on a set of familiar green eyes. *Snake eyes.*

"Wh-who are you?" My lips tremble. I can't stop the shaking.
Why can't I stop the shaking?

He angles his head at me. "You don't recognize me?" He sounds
offended by my lack of recognition. I know it's Wyatt Danvers, but
I don't know what he wants from me.

When he swipes a bloody hand through his hair, that's when it
all clicks into place. He was in the police station that day. He didn't
steal that photo of me ... he took it himself. I'm certain of it.

I shake my head and pinch my eyes shut, praying that when I
open them, he'll be gone, and this would have all been another
nightmare. But it's not a nightmare. And he's not gone. I can still

smell him. *Feel* him. There's an evil aura to him, and I don't think I'll ever be able to rid myself of the haunted feeling I've felt ever since that day. His demonic presence has latched itself to me, and I'll never be free again.

"Hm," he hums. "You're quieter than usual." He strokes his wiry beard with the back of his knuckles.

I stare up at him, blinking until my eyes burn, still not entirely sure if this is real or not. But when the back of his hand connects with my cheek and my head whips to the side, I know this is my reality.

I spit my hair from my mouth and whimper, a small trickle of blood meets my lips. I lick it, allowing the metallic tang to remind me that I'm still alive. I'm still here.

This is not over.

I turn my face back to him, my neck creaking in protest from the movement, and glare up at him. His chest heaves, his breathing irregular and ragged. He's freaking mentally unhinged.

"Say something. I dare you," he challenges, waiting for an excuse to strike me again. My silence irritates him, so I pinch my lips into a tight line and stare straight through him. "No? Nothing? Well, I know one way to make you scream."

He reaches down and grabs my ankles with his sticky, bloody hands and drags me across the dirt floor. But my arms are still bound to something behind me. I cry out in pain when fine gravel scrapes my bare back as Joel's shirt slips up. My spine stretches to an impossible length and my joints pop as sharp pain radiates throughout my entire body. Then he drops my feet and my heels hit the ground with a nauseating thud.

I lay splayed out before him with nothing more than Joel's T-shirt and my undies covering only the most intimate parts of me.

"Mm," he hums, and my stomach lurches. I watch in terror as he snaps his chops like a feral animal. His eyes flash with sick desire as he stares directly at my cotton-clad center.

Then he crawls toward me on hands and knees, his sights set on the space between my thighs.

"No!" I scream and kick, my foot slipping and connecting with his chin. It's enough for him to take pause, and I shove myself back against the wall into a crouching position, frantically wiggling until the shirt falls back down into place and covers my bottom.

Wyatt cups his jaw and straightens his posture. "You stupid little bitch!" Then he lunges.

I shriek, bracing myself for the impact. He pries my thighs open, his dirty fingernails digging into my flesh, then drags me down onto my back, pinning my thighs beneath his knees.

"No," I cry out, fighting and squirming and kicking like my life depends on it. But it's the same position Roger had me in that day. It's the same revolting feeling of him looming over me, crushing me with his weight. And it's those same green snake eyes staring down at me with sick depravity.

I'm completely trapped. I'm a tiny ball of flesh and bones and organs that he could do as he pleases with, just like Roger did so many years ago.

His foul breath skitters across my face like a million tiny bugs and I gag at the sour stench of his stomach contents infecting my system.

"You're going to pay for what you did to him," he snarls. "And when I'm done with you, I'm going to find your pretty little blonde friend and do the same fucking thing. I'm going to fuck you into the dirt, Emma. Just like my father did so many years ago. Then I'm going to dispose of you the same way you left him—face down in the forest with your skull smashed in."

My eyes widen in horror as all the pieces click together.

My father. Wyatt Danvers is Lucas Donovan, Roger's son. I had heard Lucas went missing when he was younger, but never looked into it for fear of the police watching my every move, waiting for me to show them some sign that I was involved in Roger's disappearance.

"L-Lucas?"

"Shut the fuck up!" He bellows in my face, and tiny pin needles of saliva burn my skin like acid.

I whimper and struggle beneath him, but with every passing second, the overwhelming feeling of doom rises in my chest, swallowing any hope I had of survival.

"You've been fucking him," he snarls in accusation, as if I'm his and have been caught cheating. "You've been fucking your bodyguard, haven't you, Emma? You filthy little whore." His scowl deepens and he reaches between us to run his dirty, boney finger over my cotton-covered opening. I cringe, every cell in my body repulsed by his touch.

A disgusting smile splits his face in half, baring his rotten teeth at me like the menace he is. He's vile. He's fucking evil.

Just because the devil resides in hell, doesn't mean he won't send demons to do his dirty work.

Wyatt pulls a knife from somewhere behind him, the steel blade glinting in the light that's filtering through the square hole in the ceiling.

"Have you ever watched a pig being slaughtered, Emma?" he asks, his green eyes wide and crazed as he holds the knife in front of his face, almost as if admiring the way it shimmers in the light.

I don't respond. I can't. I'm frozen in fear.

"The sounds they make ..." He shudders, and I feel his erection solidify between us. "The squealing. Mm. A symphony of sheer terror and pain. I'm going to make you squeal like that, Emma." He lowers the blade and I feel the cold, sharp tip scrape over my ribs. I suck in a breath and hold it, terrified that if I make any sudden movements, he'll sink the blade into me. "You'll be my very own little piggy that I get to play with as much as I want before sticking you."

Joel. Oh god, Joel. Please find me. Please find me before the devil takes another piece of me for himself.

Please ... just ... find me.

Then another damp cloth appears in front of me and I'm plunged back into darkness again, but this time, I'm not sure I'll wake up.

"*I think she's still in shock,*" the lady officer whispers to the male officer who questioned me at the scene of the crime.

The scene of the crime.

That's what they're calling it. It makes me feel so ... criminal. But I force myself to pretend I'm not guilty. If I feel guilty, then I'll look guilty. And if I look guilty, then they'll start questioning my story.

And Harriet will end up heartbroken. And I'll end up in deep, deep doo-doo.

I rise from my chair and excuse myself for the umpteenth time to use the washroom. They must think I have bladder issues because the looks I get when I come back out of the bathroom are anything but cavalier. Truth is, I've washed my hands so many times since being escorted to the police station that my fingers are cracked and bleeding. But no matter how many times I scrub and scrape at them, cleansing them of any microscopic chunks of Roger's flesh and blood, I still feel filthy.

But that's not the only evidence my body harbors. There's a whole mess of it in the cavern between my thighs. The only way to rid myself of the feeling of Roger being inside of me is to soak in an acid bath and burn away every inch of skin he touched.

I glance over at Harriet, who's speaking in hushed tones to an officer. She looks ten years older. Her eyes are puffy and dark. Her face is pale and weathered. She's exhausted from worry and I can't help the pang of guilt hitting me dead center in my stomach.

I return to my seat in the waiting room and absentmindedly pick at my fingernails. I hear a chair across the tiny room scrape along the tile floor and I cringe, the sound grating at my raw nerves like nails on a chalkboard.

I peek up. There's a boy about my age, maybe only a couple years older but much taller, seated across from me. His clothes are clean and tidy. His hair is trimmed neatly. He looks ... nice. Like maybe his parents take good care of him.

"Hi," the strange boy greets.

"Hi," I respond, my voice still raspy from earlier.

He smiles gently, but I can tell it's forced. "I'm Lucas."

I smile back. "Um, I'm Emma." He seems friendly. Normal. I could use some normal right now.

He rummages around in the backpack sitting at his feet, then stretches his arm out in front of him. "Candy bar?"

My stomach growls. I haven't eaten since breakfast and it's now well past midnight. I lean forward to accept his offer, nodding a thanks. I unwrap the bar and take a greedy bite as tiny crumbs fall down the front of my dress.

"Why are you here?" Lucas asks curiously.

I dust the stray crumbs away and respond, "Um, a friend of mine is missing." All that's left my mouth since that van ride has been lies, and I know for certain this won't be the end of it. Roger was never my friend, and we were never attacked, but at least the missing part is true.

"I see," he says plainly.

"Why are you here?" I ask, curiosity niggling at me. He doesn't look like the type to be in trouble. He looks like a good boy. He'd never survive in the system. Maybe he's the son of a cop or someone who works here.

His eyes narrow on me, all the warmth in them now gone. Suddenly, the friendly boy is no longer friendly. "None of your business," he snaps.

I slump down in my seat, unsure of what I said to offend him. Lucas pulls a cell phone out of his bag and starts typing I stare at the back of the phone, wondering what it's like to have parents that cared enough to get you a phone at such a young age.

I force the thought away because I'll never know the answer to such a silly question.

Then I distract myself with the sounds of the buzzing police station. The tapping of someone's fingertips flying over a keyboard. The scratching sound of the little radios officers have clipped to their vests. The slam of a door down a nearby hallway. The shutter of a camera.

Lucas doesn't speak another word to me. Doesn't look up at me. Doesn't say goodbye when an officer leads him away It's like the conversation never happened.

I have no idea how I'm going to get through all this. I keep telling myself I only have to survive four more years, then I can do whatever I want. Move wherever I want.

Just four more years.

Twenty-Nine

Joel

I STEP OUT OF the shower and sling a towel around my waist. The only reason I didn't drag Stella in here with me was because I knew she needed some rest. She's sore, no doubt. And my little princess needs some time to heal.

I force away my erection, because the stupid bastard clearly doesn't know when he's had enough, and go in search of Stella. The last I had seen her, she was passed out in bed, the cutest little snores leaving her pretty, pink lips.

But when I get to the bedroom, Stella's clothes are piled on the floor, and her phone is on the bedside table. I go to the closet and slip on a pair of sweatpants, noticing my T-shirt from earlier is missing. That means she's lounging around somewhere in *my* home, wearing nothing more than *my* shirt.

Mine. Mine. Mine.

"Stella?" I saunter through the house, checking each room on my way to the kitchen. The halls are lit by only the soft glow of the nightlights I've installed throughout. "Baby?" I check all three bathrooms, all the bedrooms, the living room, but she's nowhere. I circle back to the kitchen and eye the empty glass in the sink.

A green light catches in my peripherals. I glance at the keypad by the patio door and race over to find it unarmed. I search outside, turning on all the lights, but find nothing.

"Fuck!" I circle the island and check the garage in case she slipped out to get something from my truck. But her little, black cross-body bag is still here, and so are my truck keys. "Stella?" I shout, searching frantically, unease trickling into my veins with every second that passes where I don't have Stella in my sights.

Silence. Deafening, bone-chilling silence.

I grab my cell phone and dial Mac. Neither him nor Sloane have heard from Stella. I call Liam next. He grumbles into the phone, still half asleep. He knows nothing. My final call is to Zak, and I say a silent prayer that Harper has heard from her. My blood turns to ice when Zak tells me the last thing I want to hear.

"Haven't heard a peep, Stone."

An all-consuming monsoon of rage crashes over me. The only feeling greater than anger ... *fear*.

"She's fucking gone," I shout into the phone and slam my fist into the granite counter, cracking the stone surface with my bare knuckles. The pain radiates up my arm and into my chest, but no amount of agony can surmount the hollow ache in my chest, the one that tells me I may have just lost the single most important thing in my life.

I call Liam back and tell him to get his ass up and ready. Wyatt Danvers is a fucking dead man. He fucked with the wrong guy and took the only thing that I give a shit about. I will rip this entire world apart until I find Stella. And then I will nail Danvers to the ruins and burn it all to the ground.

Pacing the kitchen, I catch my reflection in the patio doors.

Why the fuck did you disarm the system, baby? What the hell were you thinking?

Glaring at myself in the glass door, I think of all the reasons Stella might have needed to go outside. There are none.

A furious roar rips from my throat as I drive my fist into the glass pane over and over again, its bulletproof density barely budging beneath the onslaught of my rage. Then I flip my entire fucking house upside down, searching for any clues as to where Stella might have ventured off to.

I know Danvers couldn't have breached the security system. All of Sweetwater has been set up with the best of the best. It would take a fucking computer genius to get through the tech, but from the inside, it's as simple as punching in an eight digit code.

A half hour later, Liam bursts in through the garage door and I hear the dull thud of a duffel bag filled with weapons hitting the hardwood floor. It's music to my goddamn ears.

My teammate glances around the space, noting the busted lamps and overturned furniture. But he doesn't speak a word about it, because he's well acquainted with this feeling and knows what I need.

"What's the plan, Stone?" he asks while we make quick work of strapping fifty-plus pounds of ammo and weapons to our bodies.

"She has a tracker," I grate out through clenched teeth.

Liam quirks his scarred brow. "You put a tracker on her? How the fuck did you manage that?"

"Giulia had Mac install it in the bracelet she left Stella." I have no fucking clue why she felt the need to have Sweetwater track her daughter, but clearly, she knew something we didn't. And I have a nagging sensation in the pit of my gut that tells me it has something to do with the PI and Roger Donovan.

My phone rings. I answer immediately and put it on speaker so I have free hands to finish suiting up.

Mac cuts straight to the point. "We have a location."

"Where?"

"Sending it now." My phone chimes a second later. "Let's hope to fuck she hasn't lost that bracelet."

I grind my teeth, my jaw working as I recall seeing it on her wrist when she was asleep. In my bed. *Fucking safe*. Stella hasn't taken that bracelet off since the day of the funeral, except to bathe. Occasionally, I catch her fiddling with it and muttering something under her breath like she's having a private conversation with her dead mother.

Liam hops to his feet, dressed head to toe in his fatigues with Linda, his favorite sniper rifle, strapped to his back like a small child. I check the coordinates Mac sent me.

"Middle of fucking nowhere," I murmur when I realize Stella's bracelet was last located somewhere in a petrified forest about an hour north of here. At least she's still close by.

Liam loads our ammo and guns into the back of my truck, and we peel out. My teammate's ominous presence mingles with my rage, and between the two of us, the cab of my truck is overflowing with dark energy.

I'm coming for you, baby. Just hang on.

My phone rings and I stab the answer button and listen to Mac as Liam's gaze bores into the side of my head. "You're not going to believe this."

"Cut to the chase," I snap.

"We looked into the PI some more." I grip the wheel tight, my patience wearing thinner by the second. "He was the one who moved Roger's body. He witnessed what happened to Stella and took care of the body and all the evidence himself, the van included. All at Giulia's request."

I slam my palm down on my steering wheel. I fucking knew this had something to do with Roger Donovan, but we couldn't put it together. There were too many holes.

"Easy, Stone. That's not the worst part."

Alarms begin wailing in my head as hot lava flows through my veins, singeing the remaining composure I have as every desire I have to rip Wyatt Danvers's head from his useless body is multiplied by a thousand.

"Wyatt Danvers is Lucas Donovan—Roger Donovan's son."
Mac's voice trails on, but all I hear are the blood-curdling screams
of when I tear Wyatt limb from limb. "You still there, Stone?"

"Yeah boss," Liam speaks on my behalf.

Mac continues. "Lucas inherited a property when Roger Donovan was officially declared dead. That's where you're headed right
now. Lucas was born in California in a house on that very land.
Eight years later, Roger moved his wife and kids to Michigan where
he worked as a social worker, and that's when Roger stepped into
Stella's life."

I map the timeline out in my head.

Emma Romano was raped by Roger Donovan at the age of
fourteen. She killed him in self-defense and lied to the cops to
protect Harriet, who Emma believed was in love with Roger.
Roger's body and vehicle vanished before the cops could find it,
having been moved by the PI Giulia hired to watch over Emma.
Lucas Donovan somehow meets Emma, whether she knew he was
Roger's son or not, and that's when his obsession began. Emma
turns eighteen, changes her identity to Stella Clarke, and starts a
new life. All the while being stalked by Lucas—Wyatt—her rapist's
son, who happened to be born on the property that Stella's tracker
is leading us to.

Why would Roger hang on to that property if they moved all the
way to Michigan? Why not sell it?

Thirty

Stella

"Oh, princess," Joel drags his nickname for me out, his voice echoing through the thick forest as his footfalls grow louder and louder with each step.

I know I'm dreaming, but I squeal and laugh anyway, my heart pounding wildly in my chest as I force my legs to move faster. To carry me to safety.

I spot a large shrub a few feet to the left. Glancing over my shoulder, I see no sign of Joel, so I duck behind the shrub and drop my hands to my knees and catch my breath. He's too fast. I can't outrun him.

"Oh, princess," he calls out again, this time closer. "You're being a very bad girl. And you know what happens to bad girls."

Oh god, do I.

But if there's one thing I've learned, it's that being bad is so much more fun than being good.

I search the forest for any spot to hide out. Maybe if I can find a good enough hiding place, he'll pass by, and I can run back in the direction I came from and put some distance between us.

Sucking in a few more breaths, I bolt for another bush about a hundred feet away. Dead leaves and sticks crunch beneath my feet as I push my body harder than ever until I'm safely tucked behind the greenery.

If I can't get away, he'll spank me again. And I'm afraid this time will be worse than last. Biting my lip, I clench my knees together to dull the ache between my thighs. Maybe I should let him catch me. Maybe I can convince him to go easy on me.

The sound of a twig snapping makes my heart lurch. I hold my breath, listening carefully for any other sounds. Then a puff of warm, minty air skates over my shoulder.

"Gotcha," he growls.

I scream and propel my body forward to run, but an iron arm coils around my waist and drags me back into a hard, familiar body. I lift my legs and kick and thrash, but it's hopeless. Once the beast sinks his teeth into his prey, it's game over.

"No. Let me go," I screech, clawing and scratching at his arms.

A deep chuckle vibrates against my back. "Hmm," he hums as he drags me backward, then drops me to the dirty forest floor on my back, his big hand cradling the back of my head to cushion the blow. Joel's heavy weight comes down on top of me, pressing me into the dead leaves and cold soil. "I think I want to keep you," he snarls into my ear, then bites down on my shoulder, eliciting a loud cry from me as wet heat pools in my panties.

"You don't get to keep me." I bite back a moan when he licks the sting of his bite away, dragging the tip of his tongue all the way up the side of my neck, across my jaw, and to the corner of my mouth. I claw at his chest, but he snatches both of my wrists in one hand and pins them above my head.

"Such a bad girl, running like that. I warned you, baby, but you didn't listen. So now what?"

"Now you let me go. Please, Joel."

Rough fingers skate beneath my shirt, roaming over each of my expanding ribs as I suck in panicked breaths, then he palms my breast and flicks his thumb over my hard nipple.

"Fuck, you're beautiful." The rumble of his voice does something to my insides. The desire behind his eyes is thick, dark, and unrelenting. Every time he looks at me like that, I know I'm toast. "And I bet you're soaked right now, aren't you, princess?"

I clamp down on my bottom lip to refrain from moaning when he rolls my nipple between his fingers, but I can't stop the buck of my hips.

But then the stench of something sour and acidic assaults my senses. Joel's hard body morphs into something rounder and heftier. My eyes fly open, and suddenly I'm staring up into a pair of green snake eyes, rotten decay emanating from a black hole in the face that haunts me eternally.

And that's when I realize I'm not dreaming at all.

I'm in hell.

Thirty-One

Joel

I CUT THE HEADLIGHTS and roll to the edge of the asphalt where the road meets the tree line. Liam pulls out two sets of night vision goggles and we abandon the vehicle. With every step into the darkness, the weight on my shoulders grows heavier, like I'm carrying the entire fucking world around.

But that's just it … Stella's my entire world now, and it's my fault she's been taken.

Death is all around us, the forest having been burned by a wildfire years ago. The trees still standing are merely blackened bones of the beauty that once existed. And there's not a sign of life in sight.

We creep through the deadened forest, our eyes and ears on high alert. The smell of the fire still lingers thick in the air. Ash fills my lungs with every calculated breath we take. We walk for what feels like days, the little red GPS dot on my phone a tiny beacon of hope. The closer we get, the hotter my insides burn.

Liam comes in over the comm in my ear. "Got something."

I spot him in the distance, standing at the edge of what looks like a small clearing. It's like someone chopped the trees down before the fire sucked the life out of the rest of the forest. I creep toward him, dread settling deep in my bones.

I stop beside Liam and stare out at the open space. The perimeter is lined with rocks that would take a decent-sized man to move by hand. I scan the clearing, counting fifteen intentionally placed stones.

"What the fuck is it?" I mutter under my breath.

"It's a graveyard," Liam responds dryly. "Look closer."

I drop to my haunches in front of one of the stones and dust the ash off with a gloved hand. Narrowing my eyes, I read a date of more than thirty years ago hand carved into the face of the rock. Wyatt Danvers—Lucas Donovan—was a baby then, so he's not responsible for whatever the fuck this is.

Somehow, I just know this is the work of Roger Donovan.

"Jesus Christ." Liam's right—it's a fucking graveyard. I stand and take a few steps back. A dark presence surrounds us, calling us deeper into the forest, welcoming us into the pits of hell. "Let's keep moving." I need to find my girl and get the fuck out of here. Fast.

Puffs of hot air leave my mouth as we creep through the forest on foot. Condensation from my breath evaporates in front of me, the cold night air the only thing keeping me from bursting into flames and burning this place down all over again.

A small flicker of light in the distance catches my eye and I check my phone. We're only a few hundred feet from Stella, and the red dot indicates she's somewhere in that direction.

I keep my voice low in case there's anyone out here lurking in the shadows. "Twelve o'clock," I bite into my comm, alerting Liam of what I see.

Liam nods and disappears into the dark while I crouch low and move cautiously toward the building, my gun aimed and finger on the trigger. A log cabin comes into view, not old enough to have survived the fire, so I know someone built it afterwards.

"No vehicles nearby," Liam informs me after rounding the back of the building. "Limited visual inside."

I creep closer, my heart pounding so hard I can't hear myself think. The only thing I know is that I need to get Stella out. I need to see her. I need to feel her. Taste her. God only knows what that sick fuck has done to her already. I will wrap my hands around his throat and squeeze until the life drains from his eyes. Until the light flickering behind his pupils burns out.

"Hold on," Liam rushes out.

I pause. "What is it?"

"I have a visual on Danvers." I glance over at Liam, and realize he has Linda aimed through a window in the side of the cabin.

My feet move on their own accord, and I sprint toward the half-assed wooden structure. She's in there. I can feel it.

"Stone," Liam barks out. "Stone," he snarls again, this time louder and with warning. "Don't fucking do it, brother. You don't want to go in there."

But I'm already nearing the front door and prepared to bust through it and rip that fucker to shreds.

"He's mine," I growl. There's nothing that could stop me now. I'm a fucking force. Not even God himself could reach down into earth and stop me from getting to her.

Danvers better start praying because I'm going to peel his skin from his body and feed him to himself until he's shitting out his own flesh and blood. I will cut every useless organ out of his cavity and grind it into the earth beneath my feet. I will ram my gun so far up his ass, that he'll be chewing on the shitty end of my rifle. Then I'll blow his fucking brains out.

I skid to a halt when I spot something hanging in one of the windows. It's a mass of dark hair and crimson red. Every muscle in my body turns to stone. My chest cracks open and my blackened heart shatters into a million pieces.

"Stay there, Stone. Don't go in," Liam's voice cuts through the screaming in my head.

I stumble backward, away from the cabin, catching my footing before I fall to my ass on the ground.

I'm too late. I'm too fucking late. Stella, my perfect fucking princess. I'm so sorry. I'm so goddamn sorry.

Dark, tangled hair covers the face of the severed head hanging in the window. Thick, sticky blood drips slowly, constantly, from her neck. A pair of mutilated breasts are set on display on the windowsill beneath her.

All the air in my lungs turns to acid, burning on its way out. The ringing in my ears penetrates my brain like a sharp sword. My rifle hits the ground just as someone grabs me and drags me backward into the shadows. The darkness ... it's where I belong now.

I fall to my knees and fist the ash of the dead trees in my hands. Rearing my head back, I cry until the remaining pieces of me have broken. There's nothing left of me now. I'm too fucking late. She's gone, and it's my fault.

I drop my chin to my chest, hot tears flow down my cheeks and saliva strings from my mouth.

Then my NVGs are ripped off my head, plunging me into inky blackness. I look up again toward the light and she's all I see. My beautiful Stella, the soft glow of the light within the cabin illuminating her head like the warm halo of an angel.

My fucking angel.

Someone moves in front of me, blocking her from my view. They drop down to eye level with me and start slapping my cheek repeatedly. I don't feel it though. I feel nothing. There's just this gaping hole someone carved into my chest.

"Stone." They say my name over and over.

I stare through him into nothingness. I didn't get to her in time. I didn't save her. She's fucking gone.

"Stone," he says again, knocking me in the side of the head with the butt of his gun. I realize it's Liam but I can't see him. I hear him shuffling around, then something glints in front of me. I stare down at the knife in Liam's hand. "We're going in together. We come out together. Let's end this fucker."

I shake my head, unable to move any of my limbs. It's all for nothing. It's all pointless now.

She's gone.

Liam's voice comes out gruff and strained, like he's holding back emotion. "Don't let it end like this. You need to finish this job. He's all yours, brother. I've got your back."

I muster every ounce of strength and take the knife from his hand, then stand on unsteady feet. The world spins around me but Liam keeps me upright.

I promised Stella I would protect her and I can't do that anymore. But I can make sure Danvers suffers at the hands of the man who needed her more than the oxygen he breathes. The man who will meet her on the other side someday very soon. The man who loved her the second he laid eyes on her.

She was my salvation. She was the only reason I existed. God put her on this earth for me. She was my light, and I was her darkness. But the darkness cannot exist without the light.

I cannot exist without her.

Blinking away my blurred vision, I bring the cabin back into focus. Danvers is on the other side of that door somewhere, and he's going to fucking pay. I stalk toward the building, Liam hot on my heels. The metallic stench of blood mixes with the heavy scent of ash and death. Soon, Danvers's blood will join it.

Placing one hand on the doorknob, I close my eyes and picture Stella's sweet smile. The way her hazel eyes turned a brighter shade of green when she was excited. Her soft pink lips that she'd suck between her teeth when she was nervous. Her sweet little giggle that I never got to hear enough of. Her quickening pulse in her neck and wrist when she'd try to lie to me about something. The way she looked at me when I told her she was mine.

Forever and ever, baby. Even if that means I have to carve your name into my hollow corpse before I die.

Thirty-Two

Joel

THERE'S SOMETHING TO BE said about a man in love. Mostly, they're fucking idiots who don't stand a chance in hell at surviving this life. Not that any of us do. Death always comes for us, some sooner than others.

But the strength it takes for a man who's lost that one person he loves most, the only fiber holding his being together, to keep pushing through ... well, *that's something*.

Having your heart ripped out and shredded at the hands of Satan can really fuck with your mental state. Right now, heartless and completely shattered, I'm not entirely sure if I can trust myself to make the right decisions.

But fuck what's right. There is no right. There is no wrong either. There is just choice. And Wyatt Danvers has made his choice, and so have I.

I turn the knob and stagger into the main room of the cabin. Liam rounds in behind me with his rifle aimed as I grip the handle of the knife tight, ready to plunge it into Danvers the second I set my eyes on him. But I won't kill him. Not yet, anyway. But by the time I'm done with him, he'll be begging me for the sweet release of death.

But then I hear it. A voice. *Her* voice. And I know I've either lost my mind, or her ghost is calling out to me. I storm into the room where Stella's head hangs like a trophy in the window.

She's gone. She's gone. She's gone.

Liam comes into my ear, "Stone, get in here. Now."

I'm frozen still though, staring emotionlessly at the back of her head, her hair caked with sticky, drying blood. Liam appears in front of me, grabs me by the arm, and drags me into another room.

Jesus fucking Christ. If I thought her head was enough, I was wrong. Her body is what does it. It's the final nail in my coffin.

There she is ... splayed out on a table, sliced and diced so deep her intestines are dangling over the side of the table. On the floor beside her are three plastic buckets, all filled to the brim with the crimson essence of her life.

I take one step toward her. Then another. And that's when I see it.

A black scripture on the inside of her arm.

A flicker of hope sparks within my hollow cavity. Stella has no tattoos. Her beautiful canvas is completely blank, untouched by a needle and ink. Liam bumps my arm and points to the next room. The only room we haven't checked.

Knife in hand, I shoulder through the doorway and find an open hatch in the floor. From somewhere beyond it comes a shuffling sound and muffled cries.

Her cries.

Another flicker of hope, this time fueled by something more potent than any fire propellant. I waste no time storming down the stairs and grabbing the useless waste of flesh by the back of the shirt and hauling him off whoever's beneath him. And then I stall, that flicker of hope now a raging flame burning white hot. Fire doused by gasoline spills through my veins, its smoky clouds shadowing my better judgement.

I drop to my knees in front of the woman I failed to protect. The woman who moments ago, I saw hanging in the window, her face distorted and covered by matted hair and thick blood, masking her beautiful features behind a veil of death.

"Joel. Oh god. Please be real," she whines, her bottom lip fat, bloody and trembling.

I reach out and swipe a drop of blood from the corner of her mouth. She winces, her entire body trembling in fear. Removing my glove, I do it again, this time feeling her cold, clammy skin beneath the pad of my thumb.

She's real. She's fucking real.

"Baby," I choke out, my throat clogged with emotions I've never been able to process. "You're ..."

She nods frantically, one bloodshot, hazel eye filled with water and staring back at me. The other is swollen and surrounded by a black and blue bulbous globe of broken blood vessels.

Removing my other glove, I cup her jaw in my hands, just to be sure it's really her. Her eye squeezes shut as tears streak down her beat-up face and turn a pinkish brown as they mix with the blood and filth on her cheeks.

Planting a gentle kiss on her forehead, I let out a sound that could only come from a wild, pained animal. When I'm certain she's real, that she's still alive, I kiss every inch of her face, not caring that she's covered in blood and dirt and whatever the fuck else.

"I'm so sorry, Stella. God, I'm so fucking sorry," I cry.

Then I shift to her side and inspect her arms bound behind her, scowling when I spot a deep gash across her palm. But then that gold bracelet winks at me, and I say a silent prayer in thanks to Giulia. I use the knife to carefully cut the plastic ties, freeing Stella from her binds, and drag her into my lap. My fingers fly over her body, beneath my T-shirt, over every fucking inch of her, checking for any further injuries.

"I'm okay," she rasps, cupping my face in her tiny hands. "You found me."

I bury my face into her hair and sob against the crown of her head. "I'm so sorry, baby."

She fists my jacket and cries into my chest. Lifting her battered face back up to mine, I place a gentle kiss on her lips. She grimaces, and my lips curl into a vicious snarl. That motherfucker hurt my girl.

I unzip my jacket and wrap it around her so she's cocooned in my warmth. Cradling her in my lap, I hold on tighter than I've ever held onto anything. I'm never letting her go. She's mine, and I'll spend the rest of my miserable existence making my failure up to her.

Stella turns her face and watches as Liam secures the sick fuck I'm itching to get my hands on.

"I need to get you out of here, baby. You need a hospital."

She peeks up at me and shakes her head. "No. I'm okay. I promise. It's just bruises."

That gash on her hand is deep and prone to a nasty infection if it's not treated and stitched up soon.

"I can't take any chances. Not when it comes to you." I slide one arm behind her knees, ensuring my T-shirt covers her bottom, and scoop her up.

Stella peers down at an unconscious Danvers and asks quietly, "Wha-what are you going to do to him?"

Vibrating with a renewed desire to seek revenge, I respond honestly, "Make him pay, slowly and painfully. Then kill him."

Stella shivers. She's ice cold and riddled with bumps and bruises. I carry her up the stairs and set her carefully down on a wooden chair in the corner where the next room is out of her sight, and drop to my haunches in front of her. She closes my jacket around her chest and hides her face behind the collar and inhales deeply.

Placing my hands on her bare thighs, I say, "I need you to stay here for just a second. Don't move."

"Where are you going?" she asks, panic sharpening the edges of her tone.

"Nowhere, baby. I just need to help Liam. Promise me you won't move."

She nods and I head back into the basement to check on Liam. He's got Danvers by the back of the collar and is dragging him across the floor to the stairs. The piece of shit's out cold, but Liam left no possibility of him breaking free. The rope is wound so tight around his body that he looks like an overstuffed sausage busting from its casing.

Liam hauls the limp body up the stairs, not bothering to make the trip more comfortable for Danvers, past Stella and into the room with the mutilated body of Danvers's last victim. We make quick work of securing him to a steel support beam that was likely installed for this exact purpose—to restrain and torture.

I return to Stella not a minute later.

"How did you find me?" She asks from her chair, her knees now tucked up to her chest and her body completely shielded within the warmth of my jacket.

I tip my head at the dainty gold chain around her bruised wrist. "Your bracelet has a tracker. Giulia had Mac install it before she died."

Her lips part, shock registering on her face.

I promise to fill her in on the rest later, but right now, I need to help Liam with one more thing. She agrees to remain seated where she is, and I move into the next room and stand shoulder to shoulder with Liam, who's staring grimly at the head hanging in the window. My stomach contents sour. She's a spitting image of Stella.

Poor fucking woman. There's a special place in hell for men like Danvers, and I'm eager to send him there sooner rather than later.

Liam mutters something I can't make out, then unhooks the woman's head and returns it to her body. I stand stalk still and watch as he sweeps her gummed-up hair away from her face and stares down at her like she might open her eyes and speak. Then he lifts her mutilated body into his arms.

I pull the tattered old cloth off the kitchen table and help Liam wrap her up, careful to conceal every part of her and tuck all of her exposed organs back into her body. Liam disappears out the door without another word. I turn around to head back into the other room but stop dead in my tracks when I see Stella standing in the doorway, a mortified look on her face.

Thirty-Three

Stella

I STAND IN THE doorway, my knees buckling and tears streaming down my face. I can taste them—the salty sadness—but I can't feel them right now. I can't feel anything, really.

All the pain was wiped away within a heartbeat, and all I can think about is the last breath that woman took.

She looks like me. Dark hair, a similar complexion. I can't see her eyes, but I'm willing to wager a few dollars that they're a shade of hazel.

Did Wyatt kidnap her, mistaking her for me? Or is his obsession so deeply rooted that he felt the need to sate his urges with a woman who resembled the one he desired to snuff the life out of? Was she just a temporary fix for him?

Oh god. What horrific pain she must have endured, all at the hands of a fucking psychopath that's been stalking me for fifteen years. I should have known. I should have caught on that I was being followed and put an end to it. It's my fault she's dead, and I'm not sure I can live with that guilt.

I try to hold it back, but a whimper escapes, and just as Liam disappears out of the cabin with the woman swaddled in a table cloth, Joel spins and our eyes lock.

My legs give out, but before I hit the floor, my body is lifted and I'm screaming into his chest. Everything inside me breaks, and I don't think I can be fixed this time.

"Shh. I know, baby. I know," he coos as he strokes the back of my head and carries me into the other room.

A second later, he's sitting on the wooden chair he made me promise to remain seated in, and I'm being rocked like a sobbing child while this giant, angry Navy SEAL soothes every ounce of my pain.

I think he can feel it—my pain—because there's a stiffness to him that wasn't there before, like my hurt is palpable and his heart is cracking beneath the pressure of it.

"I'm so sorry, Stella," he tells me over and over. And I know he is, but he shouldn't be.

None of this was his fault, and I tell him so, but his voice is plagued with guilt, and there's nothing I can do to fix that right now.

When the screaming in my head fades to hushed sobs and hic-cups, I peek up at Joel through blurry vision.

God, if you can hear me, please forgive me for what I'm about to do.

"Where'd Liam take her?" I rasp, my voice hoarse and barely audible from all the screaming I've done the last few hours.

"To the truck. He'll stay with her," he tells me softly, as if reassuring me that she's in good hands with him.

"We're alone?" I ask next.

Joel's brows pinch tight, and I can tell he's trying to piece my train of thoughts together. "We are."

Swallowing around the lump in my throat, I say, "I want to be a part of it."

Shaking his head, Joel responds, "Absolutely not. Mac and Sloane are on their way, and once they're here, you're going to the truck to wait with Sloane and I'm finishing this. You're not going to witness a fucking thing, princess. I won't let you carry that weight."

Disappointment thickens in my blood, and I refuse to let Joel take this from me. I've killed a man before. I know what it feels like to steal someone's last breath, and I know how to process that guilt, but what I don't know how to handle is having the man I love withhold what I need.

"Yes you will, Joel. Because you know I'll never be able to let this go unless ..."

"Unless you see it with your own eyes," he finishes for me, and I nod. Sweeping my hair behind my ear, Joel warns me, "This won't be the same, Stella. This won't be like Roger where the body goes missing. Because when I'm done with him, there will be no body to be found."

Such sweet promises.

"I know that. But please, I need to do this."

Concern flashes in Joel's eyes, and I know he's worried this will only cause me more trauma, but truth be told, I crave this revenge. I crave it on a level I've never felt before.

Caressing my swollen cheek with his thumb, Joel stares deep into my eyes in search of any signs of uncertainty. He won't find any, because I know without a shadow of a doubt that this is what will fix me. This is what will save me. And he has the opportunity to give that to me.

Before he has a chance to deny me, I crawl out of his lap and stand before him with trembling hands and adrenaline coursing through my body. The stale air of the cabin comes to life and a sense of urgency finds purchase in the tattered remains of my heart.

Joel slips his hand into mine, our fingers intertwining perfectly the way they do, and he stands to his full height. It's then that I drink him in.

His long legs are clad in camo fatigues, his thick thighs strapped with holsters of guns and knives. An army green T-shirt stretches over his muscular chest and shoulders, black ink pouring from the sleeves and slinking down his strong forearms. His right hand is bloodied, and his knuckles are busted and swollen.

Tracing my thumb across his battered hand, I peek up at his face. Hard lines, dark shadows, scruff that tickles the insides of my thighs when he's going down on me. And those icy blue eyes that make me shiver beneath their heated gaze.

"You're thinking too much again, baby," he says hotly, and I'm reminded of how he stole my thoughts from me in the shower a few days ago.

"What are you going to do about it?" I ask mischievously, dragging my finger down the planes of his hard torso, all the way to the waistband of his pants.

I know I'm fucked in the head for this, but quite frankly, I don't give a shit anymore. I need Joel to smear the horrors I was just forced to relive, and I want Wyatt to watch him do it. I know I won't truly be able to torture my stalker in all the ways Joel will, but I know one way that will hurt him more than any blade ever could.

Groaning, Joel steps forward and slips his hand around the nape of my neck, tilting my head back and bringing his lips to mine. "You want to fuck me while he watches, baby? Is that what you think you need?"

"Yes," I hiss out. "Then I want to kill him."

Joel's baby blues darken, and a sick thrill shoots through me, bringing parts of me to life that have no business being involved in this. Pressing my lips firmly to Joel's, I let out a soft moan and pray to God it's enough to light that fire inside him that I desperately need to burn beneath.

There's no blaze on earth as hot as the one this man can cultivate from merely the skim of a finger.

Breaking the kiss, I go to lead Joel into the next room, but he pulls me back into his arms.

"Not in there. In here," he says.

Then he disappears into the next room for all of thirty seconds. I hear some shuffling, some pained sounds that I know are coming from Wyatt, then he reappears with my stalker in tow, securing him to a pipe on the wall opposite from where I stand. Joel lowers to his haunches, smacks Wyatt's face a few times, waking him from his stupor, then beams brightly at him.

I stand awkwardly, watching as the man who saved my life threatens to take another. But Jesus, it's hot seeing Joel in his military attire and looking entirely too dangerous to be one of the good ones but knowing he is.

Once Wyatt's alert and squirming in his restraints and Joel seems satisfied with his state of distress, I find myself staring up into the eyes of the man I love. His thumb sweeps over my busted bottom lip, then he leans down and kisses me gently, and I know he's worried about hurting me.

Stepping out of Joel's magnetic force field, I stalk toward Wyatt and glower at him. He looks a little like his father, but not enough for me to have recognized him. And he's much thinner than Roger, so other than his eyes, they have very little in common.

Except for the evil they both wear like a second skin.

I have no words for him, other than, "I can't wait to hear you squeal like a pig."

Gripping the hem of Joel's T-shirt, I go to slip it off, but a set of familiar hands stop me, gently coaxing the shirt back down over my body as the solid heat I've come to crave presses into my back.

Joel's warm breath tickles my neck as he leans down and growls in my ear, "I'm letting you do this because I know you need it. But over my dead body will the last thing this motherfucker sees be an inch of your bare flesh. You're mine, Stella. Don't you ever forget that."

Grinning, I peel my gaze from Wyatt's desolate one and spin to face Joel, planting my palms on his chest to feel his strong, steady heartbeat.

Then I lead him backward to the chair, ignoring the aches and pains in my body, and spin it so it's sitting sideways to Wyatt, and shove Joel down into it and straddle him, the balls of my feet barely making contact with the floor beneath us. Planting my hands on his shoulders for balance, I press my chest into his and bring my lips to his ear.

"I'll never forget that, Joel. But maybe he ..." I tip my head toward Wyatt, "should be shown what it looks like, what it sounds like when you claim me as your own."

My words elicit a deep rumble from within Joel's chest, and his hips roll upward so the rough fabric of his fatigues gives me friction where I need it most. My breath hitches, and Joel grips my hips with both hands and drags me downward onto the bulge between my legs.

I match Joel's movements and peek over at Wyatt. He's awake, barely, but alert enough to know exactly what's happening. The curl of his lips tells me so.

"You wanted me for yourself," I tell Wyatt, moaning dramatically as Joel continues to guide my hips over him, my pussy weeping for him the way it does. "But you'll never have me." I let out another moan as Joel's fingers bite into my hips. "Do you know why, little piggy?"

Wyatt responds with a grunt, and that's when I see his erection lengthening in his jeans. Sick fuck.

"Because this man owns me in ways nobody else ever could. He fucks the sick memories of your father right out of my head. And pretty soon, he'll be fucking your memory out of me too. And you get to watch as you become nothing to me."

"Baby," Joel grates out, his gaze heated and fixated on my face. "You keep talking like that and I'm going to blow my load before I'm even inside you."

I must be mentally freaking unhinged, because that makes me smile.

Reaching between us, I unbuckle Joel's belt with trembling hands, and reach into his boxers to free his cock and wrap my hand around it. Joel snatches my wrist, his touch gentle but firm, and lifts my chin with his free fingers so I'm staring into his eyes. Something passes over his face, but I'm not sure what.

"I should have asked sooner," he grates out, his voice filled with anguish. He swallows, then continues. "Did he touch you, Stella?"

My head whips side to side. "No. He tried, but no."

Joel's lashes drift shut and he inhales deeply through his nose, then blows out a ragged breath. "Thank fuck," he rushes out, relieved that I still belong to him, and only him.

When his eyes meet mine again, they're filled with the desire to remind Wyatt of this simple fact.

Gripping my hips again, Joel begins guiding me over the length of his cock. When I'm bucking against him and my fingers are delving into his hair, he slips his hand between my thighs and pulls my panties to the side.

"Oh god," I cry out when his thumb finds my engorged clit and begins massaging it with perfectly timed circles.

"We're about to kill a man, princess, and here you are, soaking wet and desperate for my cock. What do you think that says about us, huh?"

"That we've stepped over that line, and we're walking in danger together," I repeat his words to me from in the shower when I confessed that I'm afraid of what was happening to me. That I'd crossed a line and wasn't sure if I'd ever find my way back over it.

Joel's lips lift into one of his earth shattering smiles, then he slips a finger inside me and curls it. My back arches and my head slams back because Jesus H. Christ, what this man does to me.

Peering over at Wyatt, I check in on his reaction. He's slipping in and out of consciousness, and although the whole point was to make him watch, right now, I don't care. I just need Joel. All of him.

As if he hears my thoughts, Joel fists the base of his cock, helps me lift onto my toes, then seats me slowly down onto him until I'm certain I can taste his cum from how deep he is.

A moan slips past my lips as I begin to ride him like this, with his T-shirt shielding my body from Wyatt's view and my panties still covering most of my bottom.

"Fucking perfect," Joel growls, his thumb working my clit and other hand fisting my loose strands and guiding me back and forth over his length.

My orgasm builds quicker than expected, and within a few short minutes I'm crying out, my pussy contracting around Joel's cock and my juices slicking the insides of my thighs and the front of his fatigues and boxers.

Joel meets me there a few seconds later, his thrusts rough and demanding but completely controlled. His cock pulses inside of me, then I feel the warmth of his cum filling me up as he grunts out, "Fuck, baby. Never enough. It's never fucking enough with you."

When our breathing returns to a somewhat normal rate, Joel slips out of me while kissing every inch of my face, then does something that leaves me completely shell-shocked and furious.

He lifts me into his arms, glares down at Wyatt one last time, then carries me kicking and screaming out of the cabin, stopping briefly only to slip on a pair of night vision goggles. I can't see a single thing outside except the faint outline of Joel's steely profile and the dimming light of the cabin as it disappears into the distance.

Thirty-Four

Joel

A BLACK TRUCK SKIDS to a stop behind mine, the headlights blaring through the back window, blinding me in the rearview mirror. Stella shifts in my lap and her good eye opens a crack, peeking up at me. She passed out on the walk back to my truck and has been sleeping for the last couple hours while we wait for Mac and Sloane to show up.

I have a plan that requires a little assistance. And the cops won't cut it because the law is black and white and we prefer to operate within the gray.

Liam hops out of the bed of my truck where he's been sitting with the woman's body. I know we should have left her where we found her, but I also know if I had told Liam to leave her, his response would have been a caveman grunt, then he would have done what he wanted anyway. I learned a long time ago to stop questioning why he is the way he is, why he does certain things, and just accept it for what it is.

"Hi, baby." I stare down at Stella and tuck a stray strand of hair behind her ear. She's so battered, she's barely recognizable, but she's alive. My little light lives on, and that's all that fucking matters.

"Who's here?" she asks, wincing as I help her sit upright.

Carefully sliding her into the seat beside me, I tell her, "Mac and Sloane. Sloane's going to take you to the hospital." Stella flattens her hands to my chest and shakes her head and I glare down at the blood-soaked bandage I wrapped around her palm while she was sleeping. "I cleaned that up when you were out but you need stitches."

She shakes her head again. "I'm not leaving you here. I want to be a part of this, Joel. I'll get stitches after. Please," she begs, and it nearly breaks my heart all over again.

I gave her a piece of what she wanted back in that cabin. I fucked her, or more so let her fuck me, while Wyatt watched. But I'll be damned if I allow her to taint her soul with the death of that sick fuck. He doesn't deserve to bleed beneath her touch. Nobody will ever be good enough to die at Stella's hands.

The last remnants of my willpower are left in the dust when I hear the pain behind her words. "Then you'll stay here with Sloane. And when I come back, we're heading straight to the hospital."

She rakes her teeth over her busted bottom lip and glowers at me. If looks could kill ...

"Fine. But, Joel," she hesitates. "Please hurry. I can't … I don't want to be alone."

Cupping her face in my hands, I kiss her forehead. "You won't be alone. Sloane will be here with you. She's one of us, and I trust her completely. The most harm she'll do is drive you nuts with her gum chewing. Here," I hand her my cell phone. "It's dialed into my comm. If you need anything, just call. I won't be long. Couple hours, tops. Then I'll be right back here with you, and I promise I'll never leave your side again." She blows out a shaky breath then nods. "Good girl."

I plant one more kiss on her forehead and hop out of the truck. I feel Stella's gaze on my back as I stalk toward my boss and Sloane. Both stare at me expectantly, their mouths pressed into firm lines. Liam slides up beside me a second later.

"Stay with her. Don't let her out of your sight," I lay my order out for Sloane. She nods once without question then goes to the driver's side of my truck and disappears into the cab with Stella.

"I'm not happy about this, Stone," Mac tells me, and I clench and unclench my fists. "But we're behind you. Whatever you need."

I rake a hand through my hair then begin to pace from one corner of my tailgate to the other.

"He's a serial killer. He has to be. What he did to that woman … Jesus Christ. There's no fucking way it was his first time."

"The graveyard," Liam says gruffly beside me, and I nod in agreement.

"What graveyard?" Mac snaps.

"On our way in, we found some sort of burial ground. Looked like some fucked up, ritualistic bullshit. Large circular clearing with stones lined up around the perimeter, dates hand carved into the faces. Not sure if they're birthdays or dates of death, but they're too old to be Wyatt Danvers's work."

"Roger's?" Mac asks, knowing damn well where we're headed with this.

I confirm his thoughts with a curt nod.

"So he buried his victims on his property, then left it to his son when he died?"

Liam grunts out, "Some of his victims, but not all."

All eyes slam to his. "What do you mean *some of them*? You think there were more?"

"Not a doubt in my mind. Roger likely groomed his son to take over the family business. So there will be more victims from both of them."

My chest tightens as I recall what Stella told me about the night Roger attacked her.

He dragged me out to this weird, open space in the middle of the forest. I hid my shredded undies under a rock around the outside of the clearing.

"Fuck." I bolt past Liam and Mac and head back into the burned down forest. I hear my teammates boots hot on my heels as we make our way toward the cabin where Danvers is tied up.

Kicking the door in, I burst into the room and glower at the degenerate hunched against the wall. A string of bloody drool hangs from his putrid mouth and pools on his chest. A chest that I will soon empty of its useless contents.

Stalking over to him, I slap him several times, waking him. Evil green eyes glare up at me. "You fucking …"

I slam my fist into his jaw before he has a chance to finish that sentence. His head whips sideways and he spits out a glob of saliva and a few rotten teeth.

"How many have there been?" I grate out. Danvers's eyes lazily track back to mine as his vision falters. Patience for sick fucks like him has never been something I've been able to muster.

Crouching in front of him, I pull a knife from my thigh holster and drag my finger over the cold metal blade. Danvers's eyes blow wide as he watches me toy with the shiny, sharp object that will ultimately end his life.

If I don't burn him alive instead. I haven't yet decided which I'd prefer.

"You're going to tell me how many, what their names were, and where you buried *every single fucking one of them*," I snarl, dragging the tip of the knife down his quivering cheek, a sick thrill moving through me as I watch blood bubble from the line I'm drawing from the outside corner of his eye, straight down to his mouth.

Disgusting gurgling noises erupt from within his heartless chest and I just know I'm going to enjoy this kill more than any of the others.

Glancing over my shoulder at Liam and Mac, I quip, "You boys ready to have some fun?"

Liam's lip twitches in amusement. *Demented bastard*. And Mac shifts his weight from one foot to the other, obviously feeling uneasy about what's to come.

Facing Danvers again, I smile grimly and sneer, "Let's get this party started."

Thirty-Five

Stella

I SIT BOLT UPRIGHT in the back seat of Joel's truck, my initial panic easing when I remember why I'm here. Relaxing back into the seat, I stuff my nose into Joel's jacket and let his scent calm me.

Sloane turns in the front seat and smiles sweetly at me, then blows a giant pink bubble and pops it. "Morning. sunshine," she chirps.

I groan, then clamber awkwardly into the front seat beside her. My entire body aches, but other than the cut on my hand and my swollen eye, I'm fine.

"What time is it?" I rasp, wincing when I realize my throat is just as sore as the rest of me.

"Too early to be doing this shit, that's for damn sure. But you know what?" Sloane's happy-go-lucky attitude is a little too much for me right now, but she's been nothing but nice. Besides her initial shock of my current state of being, she's made me feel, dare I say, normal.

"What?" I ask, struggling to open another bottle of water. Sloane gently takes the bottle from me, opens the cap, and hands it back to me with an empathetic look.

"I'm glad I'm here," she tells me.

My brows shoot to my hairline and I realize even that tiny movement hurts. When all the adrenaline and arousal from earlier wore off, the real pain settled in.

"I could think of better places," I mutter.

She swats a hand through the air like she's batting away a pesky fly and tsks. "You get used to it after a while, you know. These guys are always finding new ways to keep life interesting. If I'm not dragged along on one of their crazy adventures a couple times a month, I start to go a little ..." She points a finger at her ear and draws invisible circles.

I laugh softly, but it sounds more like I'm coughing up a fur ball.

Turning to face me, Sloane pins me with a serious look. The woman is fit and beautiful and totally scary in her camo fatigues and long, double Dutch braids. She exudes such a sure confidence and female power that I know I'm going to like her. Gum chewing aside.

"I know you just went through some serious fuckery. Trust me, if I could be down there with them right now and getting a few of my own hits in, I would be. It's been a hot minute since I've had some skin in the game. But truth is, I'm glad I got a chance to talk to you one-on-one."

"Why is that?" I ask over the top of my water bottle.

She shrugs one shoulder, then responds, "It'll be nice to have another girl around."

"Oh." I think about that for a second, swallowing the fit of jealousy rising in my throat. "You're the only woman on the team?"

Sloane nods and pops her gum again, then smiles. "Been trying to find ladies for these losers for years. But they're all too stubborn to settle down. The job, the odd hours, the major commitment to something other than their favorite weapons ... blah blah blah. It's all just a big, fat, stupid excuse to not catch feelings, as if they're contagious or some shit."

Disappointment niggles at my bruised-up insides. "The job ..."

"Mhm. Dangerous stuff sometimes, ya know. But hey, they're doing some amazing work that nobody else has the kahonas to do. And Stone, well ..." She whistles lowly. "That boy is so in love with you, it makes me want to ..." She sticks a finger down her throat and fake gags. "Anyway, he's solid. One of the best guys I know, in fact. And if you hurt him ..." Her brows lower over her eyes, but her twitching lips give her humor away.

Suddenly shy, I stare down at my fingers and begin picking at the bandage around my hand. But then a warm hand settles on top of mine and I look up to find Sloane staring at me with empathy, but not pity.

"Are you okay, babe?" she asks, genuine concern in her tone.

I nod and sigh. Fresh tears are brewing and I'm doing my best to enforce rule number two.

"Good. But hey, listen. As Joel's only female friend, I have to watch out for him. You know, like a sister would." She shrugs nonchalantly. "He may be a big, tough guy on the outside, but truth is, he's ooey gooey on the inside. All these guys are. Well, except Liam." She snorts. "That guy's got something else going on inside that big, sexy body of his. And it ain't ooey and gooey, that's for sure." A brief silence fills the air. I stuff my nose in Joel's jacket, filling myself with his masculine scent. Again. "Wait a second … you love Stone."

My face whips to hers and I'm sure I look completely stunned. I haven't said it out loud yet, but yes, I love the giant grump.

"I … I don't know what we are," I admit sheepishly.

"Girl, you're a smitten kitten, a drop-dead gorgeous one at that. But if you're not ready to admit it, that's fine. Just don't come crawling to me when you finally figure it out and have no idea how to handle it. Relationships aren't exactly my forte. Weapons though … if you ever want to carry a little somethin' somethin' in your purse, you let me know. I'll hook you up."

I smile, but my fat lip protests, and I quickly abort.

"Speak of the devil," Sloane chirps, then hops out of the truck. I stare out the passenger window and spot three large men all dressed in black approaching from the tree line. Then I see the orange hue rising over the treetops. I glance at the clock on the dash and know for a fact that it's not the sun coming up.

I whip the door open, practically falling face-first out of the truck, and run to Joel, not caring that sticks and stones are digging into my bare soles. He catches me and lifts me into his arms as I bury my nose in the crook of his neck and breathe him in. He smells like him, but there's a hint of smoke there too.

Liam strolls past, all broody and terrifying, then hops into the bed of Joel's truck and posts up with the body again. Mac stops at Joel's side and smiles politely at me.

"It's nice to finally meet you, Stella. Your mother spoke highly of you."

There's a crackling sensation in my chest. "You spoke to her?"

Mac nods, then drops a hand to Joel's shoulder and squeezes. "We'll catch up later," he says to me. "Think your man wants to get you checked out first."

Your man.

I peek up at Joel. He's all hard and sharp in this lighting, the orange glow behind him only intensifying his blue eyes.

"Don't," he growls, a playful smirk tugging at his lips. His mood has lifted, and I wonder what the hell he did to Wyatt that has him feeling so much better.

I feign innocence and bat my eyelashes at him. Er, one set of eyelashes. "Don't what?" I ask coyly.

"You know what, princess," he snarls, then carries me back to his truck and places me gently into the passenger seat again.

He buckles me in carefully, then grazes his lips softly over mine. A shiver rolls down my spine and a tingling sensation fizzes between my thighs.

Holy moly, I'm so horny for this dude, it's sickening.

"What did you do to him?" I ask, not sure if I really want to know the answer, despite my earlier urge to watch it firsthand. I'm grateful Joel didn't allow it though, because now that my adrenaline has metabolized, I'm not sure I could have stomached seeing that.

"Exactly what I promised I'd do." He shuts my door then climbs into the driver's seat.

A sick sense of relief washes over me. Lucas Donovan—Wyatt Danvers—is dead. Good. Him and his disgusting father can rot in hell together.

I angle my head and peek through the back window. "What about Liam?"

Joel shrugs. "This is what he does."

"I don't understand."

A pair of tired blue eyes meet mine. "Liam's somewhat of a protector." He pauses, then adds, "Of the dead. He won't leave a job without the victims' bodies. Brings them home to their families so they can provide a proper burial and get some closure."

Sloane's words spring to mind. Liam's definitely not ooey and gooey, but there's more than just darkness in that giant, scary man. There's something warm, I think. If there wasn't, he wouldn't be treating that dead woman with such tender care. Such respect.

I look back at Liam again. He's sitting, staring down at his lap. His profile is hard and expressionless. I imagine the woman's head is resting on his lap. I can tell he's haunted and my heart aches for him.

"And where do survivors go?" I ask, curious what happens when they rescue people from being trafficked.

"Depends. Most go home. Some end up in psychiatric care for a while. But many end up back on the streets, regardless of the resources we offer them."

"Oh." His response disappoints me for some reason, perhaps because I was so close to being a kid on the streets myself. I could have been picked up, trafficked. But Giulia, despite her many flaws as a mother, if that's what you could even call her, made sure that never happened.

Joel puts the truck in drive and navigates carefully as to not disturb Liam in the back. An eerie silence stretches on. Unspoken words hum in the back of my head. I have so many questions, but I'm too exhausted for the answers.

We pull up to a hospital. Liam lifts the cloth-covered woman out of the truck and stomps in through the main entrance, not caring that nearby people are watching him carry a dead, mutilated body through a crowded emergency room.

Joel lifts me into his arms and trails in behind him.

"I can walk, you know."

"Fully aware. But until a doctor clears you ..."

I sigh and roll my eyes. *Eye.* God, I hope I don't lose my sight in the other one. "I get it. You're macho. Are you sure your ego's going to fit through that hallway?"

Joel grunts, then struts straight past the nurse's station and into a private room and lays me down on the bed.

"Uh, Joel? I think we were supposed to check in first."

He pulls out his phone and types angrily, then tucks it back into his pocket. "There. We're checked in."

I angle my head in question. Joel sighs and explains, "We have people here on our payroll. We don't need to bother with proper hospital etiquette."

I accept that for what it is and rest my pounding head against the fluffy, white pillow and cross my ankles and stare down at my bare legs.

Sheesh. I'm a mess.

The tiny bed dips from Joel's weight when he sits down beside me, his giant, warm hand settling on my thigh.

A middle-aged doctor comes in a moment later, clipboard in hand. He introduces himself and looks me over. Then he calls in a nurse, who cleans up my arm and pokes me with an IV. Clear fluids drip steadily into the tiny hose inserted into my vein.

Joel sits by my side the entire time. It's not lost on me that the doctor didn't bother to ask him to leave the room. But I'm okay with it. I need him here with me.

"Well, Miss Clarke. Other than some pretty nasty bumps and bruises, an even nastier injury to your eye socket, and that gash on your hand, I'd say you'll be just fine. Whoever cleaned it up did a pretty good job." Doc side-eyes Joel then turns his attention back to me. Clearing his throat he asks cautiously, slowly, "Do I need to complete a rape kit?"

"No. That's not necessary." If they completed a rape kit, all they'd find is a swarming team of Joel's finest swimmers.

The doctor taps his pen on his clipboard. "Well then. Once we finish up with that bag of fluids and antibiotics and get you stitched up, I think you're safe to go home. But I want to see you back here in forty-eight hours to check in."

The doctor leaves and Joel's expression sobers. "You're coming home with me."

I chuckle and shake my head. "I know."

My compliant response seems to surprise Joel. "You're not going to put up a fight?"

"Maybe next time. Right now, I just need a hot shower and some sleep."

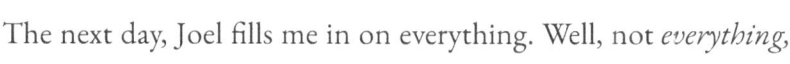

The next day, Joel fills me in on everything. Well, not *everything*, everything. But most of it.

Apparently, the PI had witnessed what Roger did to me and was the person who moved Roger's body before the police could find him. It was Giulia who instructed him to do so, oddly enough, to protect me. I'm still unpacking how I feel about that. I'm not entirely sure what compelled her to have the bracelet tracked, and I'll probably never have an answer since she's gone now, but nonetheless, I'm grateful she did. Because if not, then I might not be here today.

And it turns out that the boy in the police station in my flash-back was Lucas Donovan. He took that picture of me with his cell phone when he realized I was the girl with his father when he went missing. His obsession grew from there.

And now here I am, laying in Joel's bed, my entire body littered with bruises and scrapes, and all I can think about is how much I need Joel inside me right now, fucking me, telling me how beautiful I am. Loving me in his own unique way.

Tracing my fingers over the mountain peaks of his tattoo, I peer up at him. He hasn't left my side since we got home from the hospital, except to use the washroom or when he hears my stomach growl and races off to retrieve some food for me.

"Are you going to get another star?" I ask, curious if I'll be seeing a new inky dot on his bicep where all the other unsaved victims are remembered.

He stares down at me through hooded eyes, then he nods.

"Can I come with you?" I ask sweetly, praying he'll allow me into this part of his life. That woman died a horrifying death. She was tortured, raped, then ultimately mutilated and decapitated, all because she resembled me, and the baggage that comes with that type of guilt is some heavy shit.

Joel captures my hand in his and laces our fingers.

"If that's what you want," he responds sleepily.

Hope spreads through my chest. He's letting me in.

I wiggle closer to him, my cheek resting on his chest as he wraps an arm around me and gently skates his fingers up and down my back. His heart beat is slow and steady. Strong, just like him. Just like the man I know I love, but can't find the words to tell.

Because there are no words. There's nothing as big and insane and terrifying as the way I feel for him.

Thirty-Six

Stella

H OURS TURN INTO DAYS. Days turn into weeks. Nine
weeks to be exact.

I twist my fingers in my lap and chew on my lip as I stare at the
news anchor on Joel's television screen.

*Fourteen bodies have been discovered in a deeply wooded forest just
outside of Detroit. Including the gravesites located on the outskirts
of Clapton and Marland, this brings the total number of bodies up
to thirty-five. Detectives state that this is the third burial ground in
which an anonymous tipper has brought to their attention.*

Joel sits down beside me and hands me a cup of coffee. After he
filled me in on the graveyard him and Liam discovered, I couldn't
sleep. I couldn't eat. I couldn't think of anything other than those
poor souls. So many victims. So many innocent lives robbed far
too soon.

I won't rest until I know all of Roger's and Lucas's victims are found. Asking Joel to help me tip off authorities was just the beginning. I know there are more, and I'm going to make it my life's mission to bring each and every one of them home to their families.

Liam plops down in the chair on the other side of me. Glancing over at him, I give him a small smile. He nods once, but his expression remains indifferent. I've grown fond of the big grump over the last few weeks. Zak, too. Although Zak tends to keep a distance, mostly to avoid Harper, I think. They're like oil and water, those two. But I wouldn't be lying if I said every time they're in the same room together, the sexual tension's so thick, you could scoop it up and serve it with pie.

"You doing okay, baby?" Joel asks softly.

I force a smile. I don't have the heart to tell him I'm not at all okay. I don't think I'll ever truly be okay. But what I can be is strong. And determined. And I can stay hopeful.

But okay? No.

I circle back to the TV and stare at the screen. The news anchor has moved on to a different story. Something about a truckload of turnips on the highway.

And just like that, those victims are forgotten again.

But then my stomach turns and my mouth fills with saliva. I slap a hand over my mouth and bolt to the nearest bathroom, sliding in front of the toilet just in time before tossing my breakfast.

A familiar hand touches my back, soothing away the unease ripping at my insides. I can always sense Joel near before I see him, before he touches me. And it never takes him more than the blink of an eye to make some sort of contact.

"Shh," he coos, stroking my back and holding my hair away from my face as I empty myself until I'm dry heaving.

I hear heavy footfalls off in the distance, then the garage door slams, and I know Liam has left the building. He can handle dead bodies and psychopaths, but not a vomiting woman. How ironic.

"Ugh," I groan. Joel reaches over the sink, wets a clean cloth, then hands it to me. I wipe my mouth and drop back onto my bottom on the tile floor. I'm not sure if I'm going to be sick again, so I'll just sit here until the feeling passes.

"That's the third time in two weeks, baby."

"I know." I drop my head to my knees and take a few deep breaths. Joel's shoulder brushes with mine as he sits down next to me, his arms propped on his knees.

"I'm going to call a doctor to come check you out."

I lift my head and stare at him. No point in arguing with him about this. I never win. "Fine."

Joel scoops me up and takes me to bed. He tucks me under the covers, flips the lights off, and leaves the room.

I don't hear the door click shut before I fall into a deep sleep.

"Ouch," I whine when the nurse pokes my arm with a needle.

Joel's sitting at my side on the bed, his thumb gently rubbing back and forth over the top of my hand. We haven't had sex since the cabin, and every little touch is turning me on. I'm one sweaty ball of pent-up sexual frustration. I glare at his giant hand, willing it to roam further south to a spot a little more ... interesting.

"All done," the nurse chirps, then unwraps the giant rubber band from my arm and starts mixing up special potions of whatever right in front of me. I'm not normally squeamish around blood, but for some reason, those vials are making me woozy.

"Thanks, Joanie," Joel says politely, flashing the nurse a thousand-watt smile.

My clit throbs. Him and his stupid perfect smile and stupid perfect face and stupid perfect everything. How dare he refuse to fuck me for nine whole weeks?! Who does he think he is?

He's all ... *You're still recovering, baby. Your bruises still haven't healed, baby.*

Baby. Baby. Baby.

I prop my back against the headboard and wait patiently for the nurse to complete her little science experiment. Dipping a small paper swatch into a plastic cup of urine, she glances at me with a pink blush creeping into her ruddy cheeks.

Moments later, she's holding the little pee-soaked paper thing in front of her face as she hems and haws and grates on my very last nerve.

Then the nurse beams and says, "Congratulations!"

Joel and I both stare at her unblinking.

"What?" I ask, coming across a little harsher than I intended. She's been nothing but nice and courteous. I almost feel bad for the old prude. Mentally smacking myself for being such a bitch, I rephrase. "I mean ... come again?"

She angles her head at me, the shy smile that spreads across her face causing my heart to take off into a full-blown sprint.

Slapping my hand over my mouth, I shake my head in disbelief. "Noooo," I say in complete denial. "Nope. I'm on the pill. Run it again. It's not possible."

"I'm afraid these tests are highly accurate, dear." She pats my leg, shoots Joel an empathetic look, then packs all her tiny medical utensils into her giant black duffel bag and waddles out the bedroom door.

Joel's silent tension swallows me whole.

"Did she ... Are you ..." He stammers, a petrified look on his face.

I roll my eyes and sigh dramatically. "Afraid so."

His reaction catches me off guard. I've gotten pretty good at reading my stone man. But right now, I have no freaking clue what's going through his mind. Probably something along the lines of *run*.

Joel stands abruptly and leaves the room without so much as a peep. I sink down into the comfort of the bed and close my eyes, willing away the tears that threaten to fall. Maybe this is all a dream. Maybe I'll wake up and I'll be magically cured and none of this will be real.

Nope. No such luck. Because even though I'm utterly exhausted, sleep doesn't find me. Instead, I lay awake, my mind reeling and heart aching.

I'm pregnant with Joel's baby and he just took off.

But what plagues me the most is the thought of giving the child up like Giulia did.

Never. Not in a million years. Touching my hand to my belly, I whisper to the little cluster of cells taking up residence in my uterus, "You're already so loved."

Thirty-Seven

Joel

MY HEART HAMMERS AGAINST my ribs as I pace the living room.

Stella's pregnant. *I'm going to be a father.* I skid to a stop, my socks sliding across the polished hardwood.

Did she have unprotected sex with anyone before me? Could this be someone else's kid?

No. She said she'd always used protection and was on the pill. And she freaked the fuck out when I blew my load inside her the first time. And what did I tell her when she said she was on the pill? I had said, "For now."

But she's still on it, and I'm feeling a little twitchy.

Heading down the hall to my office, I rummage through the bottom drawer in my desk.

"Where the fuck is it?" I grumble to myself, panicking when I can't find what I'm looking for. Finally, my fingers make contact. "Gotcha."

Without another thought, I book it straight back to my bedroom and throw the door open wide, the knob no doubt making an indent in the wall behind it. My eyes dart to the empty bed, the sheets rumpled and messy.

I call out for Stella, but there's no response. A familiar unease coils in my gut. She better not have taken off again without telling me. I will hunt her down and spank that perfect ass until she can't sit right for a week.

The sound of water running in the bathroom chases away that unease, but it's quickly replaced by another feeling.

Nervousness? Anxiety?

Padding over to the bathroom door, I knock gently, then slowly swing it open. Stella's leaning over the counter, her palms flat on either side of the sink. My eyes meet hers in the mirror.

If looks could kill.

"You did this to me," she says bitterly.

I chuckle. "Glad you're confident it was me."

Her scowl only deepens. "Did you think it wasn't?"

My mouth opens, but then I think better of it and snap my jaw shut. If there's anything I've learned in my life, it's not to fuck with a pregnant woman. They spew flames hotter than any dragon.

"Not for a second," I lie, sidestepping that sneaky trap. Closing the space between us, I stop behind her and rest my chin on the top of her head. Staring into her tired eyes, I whisper, "You're beautiful."

She sighs and drops her shoulders an inch. "And you're full of shit."

"No, baby. You're gorgeous." Kissing the top of her head, I reach into my back pocket and pull out a tiny velvet box. Setting it on the counter beside Stella's hand, I watch in the mirror as her eyes track the movement, then fixate on the box.

She slaps a hand over her mouth and stares back at me in shock.

Grabbing her by the waist, I spin her around and lift her onto the counter, then push myself between her thighs. *Where I fucking belong.* Then I cup her jaw in my hands and lower my forehead to hers.

"Joel," she breathes out, then her jaw clicks shut and she shoots me an apologetic look. Every time she gets sick, she gets this silly idea that I'm repulsed by her mouth or something.

I trace my thumb over her bottom lip, then kiss her.

"You could puke directly into my mouth, princess, and I wouldn't bat a fucking eyelash. Your vomit is all rainbows and unicorns as far as I'm concerned. I love every bit of you. Even the annoying parts." She winces and closes her eyes. "Look at me, baby," I instruct softly, and she pops an eyelid. Gently stroking her cheeks, I whisper against her mouth, "I love you, Stella Clarke slash Emma Romano." I feel her lips smirk against mine. "The second I laid eyes on you I knew I was fucked. You bring the best out in me, even when you're being a giant pain in my ass. If I could take every ounce of pain you've ever felt and somehow absorb it, make it disappear for you, I would. A million times over."

Her eyes begin welling with tears and I know she's going to be an emotional wreck for the next eighteen years.

I drop to my knees in front of her. Not just one knee, but two. Because I'm fully prepared to beg her for this. She stares down at me, her lips parted, the pulse in her throat ticking fast and hard. I clasp her tiny, trembling hands in mine.

"You're having my baby, Stella. You're making me the luckiest man to walk this godforsaken earth. I'd be stupid to ever let you think I don't want to give you the world. So, you're going to be my wife. The mother of my children. You're the only fiber holding my being together." I swallow the lump in my throat. "I thought I lost you nine weeks ago and my entire world crumbled to ash at my feet. I refuse to go on without you being fully tethered to me. In every possible way. Forever, baby. You're my forever."

Seconds tick on. Minutes, maybe. I'm not sure. But with every beat of my heart, the feeling of complete doom feeds off itself inside of me. Disappointment tags closely behind.

But then Stella smiles and everything in my world rights itself. "Yes," she whispers, then says more clearly, "yes."

"Oh, thank fuck," I breathe out, then stand and grab the box, popping it open and sliding the custom-made, teardrop diamond on her finger.

Stella's arms fly around my neck, and I wrap mine around her waist, pulling her tight to me. Our mouths meet in a clash of teeth and tongues. It's sloppy and wet and full of the love I don't deserve.

She breaks the kiss and I groan out loud. It's been too long since I've been inside of her and she's hitting the fucking pause button.

"On one condition," she remarks with a pointed finger.

"Anything," I grumble, needing to get this conversation over and her naked beneath me.

"You get sidesteps for that ridiculous truck of yours. No way am I climbing my fat, preggers ass up into that thing without some assistance."

I chuckle. "Once a princess, always a princess." She swats my chest. "I'll buy you whatever the fuck you need, baby. Anything you want, it's yours."

She quirks a brow, taps her lips with a finger, and looks up and to the corner. "Hmm," she hums, probably making a mental list.

I snatch her hand away from her mouth and seal my lips over hers. Fuck, she's so sweet and soft.

She whimpers and I pull back, concerned I'm being too rough with her.

"Oh my god," she pants. "Don't go soft on me now, Stone."

I'm mildly offended that she thinks I'm soft, but then I realize the true meaning behind her accusation. I'm being too gentle. Too considerate.

"You haven't had sex with me in over two months."

"Because you've been—"

"Yeah, yeah, yeah. I get it. But I want you. All of you. If you want me to keep this ring on my finger then you better straighten up your act, soldier. Mama needs to be properly fucked."

"Mm," I growl. "Mama, huh?"

"Well, that's what I'm going to be soon. So ... might as well get used to it, *daddy*." There's a mischievous glint in her eyes.

Growling into her neck, I scoop her off the counter and carry her into the bedroom. Setting her carefully on the bed, but not so careful she gets worked up about it again, I crawl between her thighs and lower my face to hers. She wiggles beneath me, a playful giggle escaping her. Wrapping both of her wrists in one hand, I lift them over her head and pin them to the bed.

"Call me that again," I growl, then nibble on her earlobe.

She lets out a soft moan, then whispers, "Daddy."

Releasing her wrists, I peel off her sweater, then her bra. Placing a palm to her chest, I shove her back down onto the bed and bring my mouth down to her nipple. Rolling the other between my fingers, I swirl my tongue around her hardened peak, relishing in the way she writhes beneath me.

Then I switch sides and repeat the same process until her hands are driving into my hair and her hips are bucking up to meet mine.

"Joel," she pants, clawing at my shoulders and arms.

I sit back on my knees, peel her leggings and panties down her legs, flip her over on her stomach and hoist her ass into the air. Her hands ball into fists in the comforter as she lays her cheek down on the bed and stares over her shoulder at me.

"Are you going to be a good girl and take this cock? Or am I going to need to punish you?"

"I ... I'll be good. I promise," she assures, but there's a spark of something wild in her eyes.

"Mm," I hum, licking my lips as I palm the soft curve of her ass. "This ass." I give her cheek a light swat, eliciting a tiny yelp from her. Her hips rock from side to side. Her teeth graze over her bottom lip. I've already claimed her in more ways than I ever thought possible. I've taken the only orgasms she's ever had with a man. It's my ring that's weighing down her left hand now. And it's my baby in her womb.

She's mine.

I unbuckle my belt and drop my jeans and boxers just enough to free my cock. Gripping the base, I slide the fat, red tip from the front of her folds up to her soaking pussy, lining it up with her tight hole.

"Please, Joel." Her ass rocks toward my cock. "I need you. God, it's been too long."

Gripping her hip with one hand, I ease into her, hissing when I sink my cock all the way inside her pussy. She clenches around me, greedily sucking me in further until my balls are pressed against her swollen pussy lips.

"Jesus, baby. You feel so good." Fisting her hair with one hand, I reach around and slip a finger through her wetness, smearing her slick juices around, then circle her clit. "You're running hot these days, princess."

Stella moans and rocks back into me to meet my thrusts. "Core temperature rises when you're pregnant."

Something about knowing she's going to be this hot and ready for me the next few months while she grows our baby pushes me nearer the edge. It's fucked up, I know, but I don't really give a shit.

Knowing we'll be forever tethered not only legally, but by a bond that can never be compromised does something to my insides.

"Ah," she cries out and bucks against my hand and cock.

"Not yet," I snarl, pulling back on her hair so her back is arched. The curve of her body allows me to get that much deeper.

But I can feel her coming undone around me. I can feel her walls tightening, threatening her release. As a reminder of the power I hold, I pull my hand away from her pussy and come down with a warning smack on her clit. But that only drives her further toward climax.

Before I have a chance to stop her, she comes hard, my name spilling from her lips like thick, sweet syrup.

I deliver a few more hard thrusts then seat myself deep inside of her and let it all go. Nine fucking weeks of holding back. It's been painfully difficult to resist the urge to stick my dick in every one of her holes every time she so much as breathes in my general direction.

Panting, I collapse on top of her, but quickly retreat when I realize I'm crushing her and the little sprout inside of her. Slowly easing out of her, I roll us to our sides and pull her back against my chest, pinning her down with my leg over hers.

Burying my face in her hair, I tell her, "I've missed you."

I don't need to see her face to know she's smiling. I can feel the satisfaction radiating off her in waves.

"Missed you too." She lifts her left hand in front of her face and stares at the ring. "Hmm," she hums with mild curiosity. "How'd you get the size just right?"

"You sleep like the dead, princess. Wasn't difficult to slip a ring sizer around your finger while you were snoring and drooling all over my pillow."

"I do not snore. Or drool," she shrieks.

"Whatever you say, baby."

"So, is this how it's going to be from now on? You're just going to buy me whatever I want and agree with everything I say?"

I slip my hand around her throat and tilt her head back. "I'll give you the world, Stella. But don't push your luck. You're still a pain in the ass." She stares up at me with giant doe eyes. I drop my hand and slide out of bed, pulling her with me to the bathroom.

We shower together. I wash us both while she stands under the hot spray of water and watches me. Then I help her blow-dry her hair, get dressed, and into my truck. I make a mental note to get those sidesteps she mentioned, even though she won't be getting in or out from now on without my help.

I spend the drive listening to Stella as she outlines her project plans to eventually bring all of Danvers's and Donovan's victims home to their families. To say she's obsessed with the case would be putting it mildly. She's practically the female version of Liam, just without the tattoos and doom and gloom attitude all cloaked by a veil of disturbing darkness.

She fills me in on her intentions to oversee Riva Jewellers as the majority share owner, but that she trusts the people Giulia employed to take the reins on operations while she figures her next moves out. And that she's not really sure what she wants to do with the rest of her life, but that she's certain it's not finance.

We pull up to Casa del Sol. The gates part in front of us as Stella grips the seat belt at her chest and gnaws on her bottom lip in agonizing silence. She hasn't been here since before Giulia's funeral. Anytime I brought it up, she'd make an excuse not to go. But there's a whole guesthouse being built, and she promised to honor Giulia's wishes to design it once the walls were constructed.

"Why are we here?" she asks me hesitantly.

"You've been avoiding this place like the plague, Stella."

"Yes, I have. Because it feels ... weird to be here."

I park the truck at the front of the main house, lift Stella out of the passenger seat, then grab her by the hand and lead her through the garden and down the path to the guesthouse. She stops at the front entrance and stares up at the stone building. The masons have been hard at work, and the outside is coming together nicely.

Squeezing her hand, I pull her up the stairs and inside. Her expression sobers as she takes in her surroundings.

"What ... what is all this?" She lets go of my hand and pads through the foyer to the main living area stacked with boxes and files.

Standing beside her, I pull her under my arm and kiss the top of her head. "You have a passion, baby. I already know you'll correct me if I'm wrong, but this is the first time in your life you've really felt that kind of fire inside you. I had some help, of course, but these are all cold cases of missing people. Mostly women and children. They've been dropped. *Forgotten*. Unless someone miraculously comes forward with new evidence, nobody will ever give these cases another thought."

Swiping a tear from her cheek, I tell her, "We have more resources than you can shake a stick at. Mac's already granted you access to all of it. Thought maybe you'd like to join the team and focus on finding some of these people."

Her lip trembles and her eyes dart from stack to stack of files. Some date back over fifty years, others were dropped cold only months ago.

A warmth spreads in my chest as I watch her roam about, her finger trailing lightly over the tops of the dusty cardboard boxes. She stops in front of me and stares up at me through wet lashes.

"You have no idea what this means to me," she rasps.

I coil an arm around her waist and drag her against me. I drop my forehead to hers and whisper, "I love you, Stella. I want you to be happy. I think this is something you need to pursue."

She nods, that cute bottom lip shaking. "I don't know where to start with all of this."

"Well, first thing's first. We need to get you set up with a proper workspace."

She glances around the unfinished living area, her mind reeling and eyes darting from one corner to the next. Looking back at me, she says, "I think I know the perfect place."

Epilogue

Stella

"Eek!" Harper's shrill squeal echoes through the trees. Next thing I know, I'm being body slammed by a leggy blonde dressed head to toe in hot pink. "I'm on team girl," she chirps.

I groan out loud. "I'm on team *get this thing out of me.*"

"Jeez, Stell. You're grumpy when you're preggers."

I swat her away from me and begin whining. "It's hot, Harper. My feet are swollen. I feel like I'm carrying a hundred-pound beach ball around under my shirt. And yesterday, the doctor described the state of my mucus plug. Like I needed to know that."

Harper frowns and I want to smack that look right off her pretty face. "You have a little way to go yet, sweetie. But once it's all over, you'll have a whole human baby in your arms. A family."

A family. I sigh and awkwardly sink down into a nearby patio chair. Harper sets a pillow on the coffee table in front of me and I drop my puffy cankles onto it.

"I'm sorry. I'm just miserable. Who knew pregnancy would suck so bad."

Harper shoots me an empathetic smile. "You look incredible though. I don't think you gained an ounce of weight anywhere but your belly and boobs. And judging by the way Joel keeps staring at you ..."

I glance over at my fiancé. His heated gaze does nothing to cool the raging inferno inside of me.

"I think maybe he likes you like this. All grumpy and miserable and growing his baby."

I peel my eyes off him, his intensity entirely too much for me to handle right now. "I think he has a pregnancy fetish or something," I mutter to Harper, careful that nobody else overhears that my fiancé might have a kink I'm only learning about recently.

She giggles, then disregards my statement. "Nah. That's not it. All these guys are the same. Alpha, possessive, dominant jerkholes. He's just thrilled that it's his baby that'll be responsible for destroying your vagina. But don't worry. I hear doctors these days can stitch things up all nice and tidy again and it's like nothing ever happened."

"Thanks for that visual, Harper."

She angles her head. "Really, though. I think he's just ... *happy*. It's kind of gross, actually."

I put a hand in the air. "I'm going to stop you there. Can you please just admit that you're putting on this tough-girl act because you're secretly attracted to one of those alpha, possessive, dominant jerkholes and don't want to admit it?"

Harper's eye roll makes me want to stab her with a rusty fork. "I am not attracted to that man. He's the most irritating, annoying, overbearing asshole I've ever met."

"And you fucking love it."

She shakes her head. "Nope. I prefer nice guys. The kind who show up with flowers on the first date and don't lock me away in my bedroom like I'm some sort of fairy tale princess being guarded by a fire-breathing Navy SEAL."

I shrug my shoulders and set my hand over my bump, then peek back over at my very own fire-breathing Navy SEAL. "Well, you're missing out. It's kind of the best thing ever."

Harper sucks back half a glass of whatever fruity cocktail she's working on, then sets the glass down on the table with a thud and turns to face me. "Can I?" She points her gaze at my stomach and wiggles her fingers as if to say *gimme, gimme, gimme.*

I giggle and smile at my best friend, warmth blooming in my chest. "Of course. It's been moving around a lot lately."

Harper sets both palms on my bump and begins feeling around, then frowns when nothing happens. "Doesn't like me much, huh?"

"Oh, stop it. Baby is going to love its Auntie Harper. You get to teach him or her all the things I can't. Like fashion coordination and foreign languages."

"And how to mix a mean margarita," she adds with a not-so-subtle wink.

"You ladies okay over here?" Joel's growly voice cuts in, sending a shiver rolling right down my spine. I glance over my shoulder to find him standing directly behind me.

"Oh my god! She kicked!" Harper squawks, feeling around my belly like she's navigating a foreign place in the dark.

"She does that when she hears her *daddy's* voice," Joel says, then moves around to my side. He takes a long pull of his beer and all the blood in my body rushes to my clit. These pregnancy hormones are no joke. I don't know how I haven't worn that man out yet, but I have every intention of trying again later. He flashes Harper a smile. "When you're done groping my fiancé, I'd like to steal her for a moment."

And just like that, the moment is gone.

Harper glowers at Joel but doesn't remove her hands. "I'll grope her all I want. I saw her first."

"Okay, you two. That's enough." I point a finger at my fiancé. "Especially from you." Joel scowls and opens his mouth to speak, but I shoot him a warning look. His mouth snaps shut. "I'm the one that has to push a turkey out of a hole the size of a golf ball. Don't test me." I look over at Harper. "And you ..."

Recoiling, she blurts, "What the hell did I do?"

"You need to figure your shit out and stop pretending you don't have the hots for Zak." Joel snorts and I whip my face to his and throw invisible daggers. He makes a zipper motion with his fingers over his lips and tosses the invisible key. I turn my attention back to Harper, who's now slouched down in her seat, pouting like a child. "I'm getting tired of you two avoiding each other like you're old high school enemies. For the love of god, the sexual tension between you guys is off the freaking charts."

I almost feel bad for calling Harper out on her bullshit, but damn that girl is stubborn and she needs to hear it.

"I don't have the hots for Zak," she snips.

I hold out an expectant hand. Joel takes it and helps me practically roll to a standing position.

"Whatever you say, Harper. Now if you'll excuse me, I need to pee for the thousandth time today. Apparently, this baby thinks my bladder is a trampoline."

Leaving my friend to sulk, I head to the nearest washroom. Joel stands outside the bathroom door and waits for me while I relieve myself. After I had a little spill in the bathtub a few weeks ago, he's refused to let me do anything alone. I don't argue, because I know the safety of me and this baby is his top priority.

"Feel better?" he asks when I exit the washroom. I groan out loud. "There's someone here who'd like to see you," he informs me immediately after.

I swallow hard, my heart dropping into my uterus alongside my baby. Everyone important to us is here already, showering Joel and I with gender-neutral baby gifts. Nobody else was invited.

"Who?" I drop my hands to my belly and scare away the butter-flies.

"If it's too much, you say so and that will be the end of it."

My scalp tingles, just like it always does when something, or someone, from my past decides to pay me a visit.

Joel reaches for my hand and brings it to his mouth, skimming his lips over my knuckles.

"Come on." He drags me across the house. We pass Zak and Liam on the way through. I stop to let Zak know Harper's outside, you know, just in case he wants to say hello. Or whisk her off to one of the spare bedrooms and fuck her brains out. He responds with a scowl and a grunt, then busies himself at the snack table.

Joel leads me outside the back door to the private little patio he built for me to read on and I come to a sudden halt. My stomach does a weird flip-flop thing but it's not the baby this time.

I stare at the back of a plump, older woman facing out into the wooded area. Her grey hair is piled up into a tidy bun on the crown of her head. Her knee-length floral dress floats in the breeze. Her pale legs and arms are weathered from age.

Joel clears his throat, and the woman turns around.

Warm brown eyes meet mine, and a rush of memories flood my system.

"Hi, sweetheart." The wind snatches her voice and carries it away, but it doubles back and slams into me.

I drop Joel's hand and take a cautious step toward her. "Harriet?"

The smile lines around her eyes deepen. "Joel reached out." She glances over my shoulder then back to me. "He told me you were going to have a baby, and, well ..." She swipes away a tear. "I just had to see for myself."

Hot tears prick behind my eyes, and my heart slowly works its way back into my chest and begins beating again. I lunge toward her and she captures me in a hug, smothering me in her breasts just like she always used to when I needed someone to cry on. She was always a safe place for me. The only stability I had in my childhood.

"I'm sorry," I blubber. "I'm so sorry." The floodgates open and the tears begin to fall.

"Don't you be sorry for a darn thing. You did what you had to do. But I'd be lying if I said I wasn't heartbroken when you disappeared on me."

"I shouldn't have done that to you," I mumble into her chest, squeezing her so tight I think her head might pop off.

"No, you shouldn't have. But there's no sense in dwelling on that. What matters is that you're safe." Her voice cracks. She's crying. I've always hated when Harriet cries.

I pull back and lick the salty tears from my lips.

"I'm so proud of you, sweetheart. What you're doing for those families ..."

"So, you've seen the news," I say gently.

She nods. "Yes. And Joel has filled me in on everything. No need to explain. I'm here, and I hope that maybe this time you won't run away from me." She forces a small smile and dries her tears with the back of her hands. A simple gold wedding band winks at me. I hope whoever she married has made her happy. She deserves that.

I glance over my shoulder at my fiancé. He's incredibly handsome in a pink T-shirt and faded blue jeans. I tried to convince him pink was the wrong color to wear to our baby shower, but he's determined that it's a girl. His confidence is unwavering, and I'm beginning to think the blue dress I'm wearing is entirely wrong.

"I'm done running." *In more ways than one.*

She pats my arms and steps back, taking a moment to inspect me. "You look beautiful. Like a woman in love," she coos.

I bite down on my bottom lip and nod.

"I've never been happier." Her eyes soften, as if my response gives her some sort of peace.

"I'm so glad." She peeks over at Joel again. "Well, sweetheart. I'd love to catch up some more, but I know you're busy with your shower today. How about a cup of tea tomorrow?"

"Stay." I snatch her hand. "I mean, I'd love if you could stick around for a while. Come meet our friends, have a piece of cake with us."

I feel Joel behind me, smell his masculine scent, feel the warmth of him at my back. Harriet blinks up at him looming behind me.

"Would that be alright with you, Joel?" she asks hopefully.

Strong, familiar hands settle on my shoulders. "I'd be honored if you'd join us, Harriet."

Harriet accepts the invitation and settles into a seat between Harper and Sloane, who both instantly take a liking to the only true mother figure I had in my childhood. Something about having her here fills a void I didn't know existed until now.

I glance around the room and something in my chest clicks into place, like a key sliding seamlessly into a lock. I'm surrounded by everyone I've ever loved. Harriet, the group of SEALs that have imbedded themselves in my life, Sloane, who's quickly becoming a good friend of mine, Harper, who I couldn't survive without. Even Martina and Mr. Marchetti are here.

And of course, Joel.

My man of stone.

Hot breath tickles the sensitive spot behind my ear. "When the party's over, I'm ripping that silly little dress off with my teeth."

I grin and wet heat pools in my panties. "Fine. But you should know … I have four more of them in different colors."

"Mm," Joel hums into my neck. His fingers drift down my arms, eliciting a shiver from me. I peek around to make sure nobody's watching me squirm beneath his touch.

Harper's blabbering on to Harriet and Sloane about one of her recent trips to some touristy destination. Martina's chirping at Liam about his manners while he silently broods in the corner and glares at a smudge on the window. Mac is scaring the crap out of Carlo and his wife, droning on about some fancy, new rifle someone just invented. Zak's at the appetizer table filling his plate for the third time. His eyes keep sliding to Harper, but he catches himself and mutters something under his breath.

Joel's deep timber snaps me back to reality. "Guess I have my work cut out for me."

"Yes," I whisper, pinching my knees together to dull the growing ache.

"I'm feeling generous today, so when everyone leaves, I'll give you a ten-second head start to get your sweet ass to the bedroom. But if I catch you before then, I'm going to fuck you where you stand."

"That's not fair. I'm pregnant and gigantic and can't run," I whine.

"Hmm." His lips brush my neck and my head lolls to the side. "Then I'll give you twenty seconds."

Smiling, I turn to him and throw my arms around his shoulders. He kisses me softly, but I can feel the desire behind his tenderness. The raw intensity of his love for me is something I don't think I'll ever grow tired of.

Brushing my lips over his, I say, "I'm done running. Forever and ever."

THE END

Acknowledgements

FIRST, I WOULD LIKE to thank my wonderful editor, Kylie Abel. The tolerance you have for me and my terrible time management skills, procrastination, and disappearing acts is what sets you aside from every other editor. I appreciate you more than you know. And to my developmental editor, Kim, thank you for being so thorough and an absolute delight to work with. I'd also like to thank my traumas for providing me with just the right amount of creative juice to feed the insanity in which we call storytelling.

But most of all, I'd like to thank my readers for your love and support. This journey would be entirely pointless without you.

If you enjoyed Written in Stone, I'd be honored if you dive into Written in Blood, Zak and Harper's story. Because who doesn't love a smutty enemies to lovers tale?!

About the Author

A.D. WILDE IS A Canadian author, born and raised in rural Ontario. When she's not reading or writing, she can be found hiking, road tripping to random North American destinations, or stuffing her face with carbs and wine.

Her favorite color is morally gray, her favorite MMCs are, at the very least, mildly psychotic and possessive, and her favorite FMCs are strong, stubborn and independent with a take-no-shit attitude.

A.D. is a mental health advocate, and encourages readers to always check the trigger/content warnings before diving in to any dark romance story.